Awaken Fro

by
Kevin Harker

Dedicated in loving memory of Harry Harker

1

"Come on, Charlie! You can do it!" Mitch yelled back to his best friend as he ran down the railroad tracks. He looked up at the setting sun and knew the party at the Benches was just getting into full swing. He let the warm, breezy air of early September whip across his face while he ramped up his stride from a brisk jog to a full sprint.

"Slow down," was all Charlie managed between breaths as he stumbled down the tracks, making a valiant effort to keep up with Mitch.

Mitch and Charlie had been going to the Benches since freshman year, when the unwritten laws of high school permitted their presence. It was nothing more than a few logs in the woods, strategically placed around a massive fire pit. But for the kids who went there, it was nothing less than a sanctuary—a place to escape the rules and constraints constantly placed upon them by adults.

Mitch looked back and saw the sizable lead he had gained over Charlie. He pulled up and sat on a granite boulder adjacent to the tracks. "Let's go, Charlie!" he yelled with a big grin on his face.

Charlie caught up to Mitch, but said nothing as he sucked in mouthfuls of air. He reached into his pocket and extracted his inhaler. He fumbled with the top for a second and then raised the inhaler to his lips and took two long, hard drags off it.

"We're not gonna take the railroad tracks the whole way in, are we Mitch?" Charlie asked between breaths.

"Hell yeah, we are. It's the quickest way there," Mitch replied. "You're not afraid are you?"

"No. Well, kinda…you know—"

Mitch cut him off. "Charlie, would I ever lead you down the wrong path?"

"No," Charlie replied. He had always trusted Mitch. They'd met in elementary school when Mitch was playing football with his buddies and noticed a group of guys bullying a smaller kid. Mitch immediately raced over to the mob and said, "If you want to fight someone, you can start with me. Who's first?" All declined Mitch's invitation, and the unlikely friendship that developed that day had endured. Now they were beginning their senior year of high school.

"Let's go," Mitch said as he popped himself off the rock and continued to jog down the tracks.

"Mitch," Charlie protested, doing his best to keep up.

The two continued down the tracks, pushing each other and throwing rocks into the woods. Darkness had begun to obscure their surroundings when Mitch stopped abruptly. "What's that, Charlie?"

"What, Mitch? What is it?" Charlie said, nervously scanning the area around him. "Did you hear something?"

Mitch raised his finger to his mouth, prompting Charlie to remain silent.

Charlie complied, nervously looking at Mitch. "What is it?" he asked again in a nervous whisper.

Mitch paused, allowing the silence of the night to fill the air. "Shit!" Mitch blurted, exploding down the tracks. "Run, Charlie!"

"Mitch!" Charlie pleaded, "Mitch!"

Mitch ran until he heard the sounds of music and laughter. He reached the opening of the path to the Benches, and he stopped and positioned himself behind a giant oak tree. Down below, he could see the partygoers laughing and talking. He breathed in heavily, inhaling the distinct smell of a campfire mixed with the sweet, smoky aroma of marijuana. He waited.

"Mitch," Charlie said, still stumbling down the tracks. He reached the familiar opening and quickly stepped off the tracks. His heart raced as he navigated the narrow path. "Mitch where are you?" he called.

Mitch waited patiently, listening for his friend's footsteps. He closed his eyes to heighten his sense of hearing. The crunching of gravel became more distinct, and Mitch sensed that Charlie was on the opposite side of the massive oak. Covertly, Mitch moved around the tree as Charlie passed by, and then without warning, he casually walked up behind Charlie and put his hand on his friend's shoulder.

Terrified, Charlie yelped and jolted forward, tripping over a dead log on the ground. He spun around and landed on his backside. Immediately, he scrambled backward on the ground in an effort to escape his unknown assailant. He jumped to his feet, about to sprint away, when Mitch's familiar laughter filled the air.

"That was great," Mitch said in between the bouts of laughter, "you should have seen your face, Charlie."

"Screw you, Mitch. You scared the shit out of me," Charlie said as he wiped the leaves and dirt off his pants. "Why do you do shit like that?"

"Because it's funny," Mitch said, still laughing.

"No. No it's not funny," Charlie said.

"Oh, lighten up," Mitch said as he began wiping leaves from Charlie's shirt. "Here, let me get that for you, Charlie."

"Get off me, Mitch," Charlie said swatting at Mitch's arm.

Mitch laughed and turned in the direction of the party. "Come on, buddy, let's go have some fun."

The roaring fire stretched ten feet up into the night sky, creating an orange hue against the trees. Logs hissed and crackled, launching random glowing embers upward. Mitch circled the fire pit watching kids drink and kiss.

"Mitch Blais, you want a beer?" a voice yelled out.

"No thanks, Jack," Mitch said. Mitch had never been much into drinking. He remembered the problems it had caused at home for his father when he returned from Afghanistan.

"How about you, Charlie?" Jack asked. "Want a cold one?"

"No thanks," Charlie said.

"Suit yourselves, gentlemen," Jack said as he took a long sip from his can of beer. "More for me, I guess."

"What's the word around town, Jack?" Mitch said.

"Not much," Jack replied, "except rumors are that Grabowski is dating your ex."

"Angela?"

"That's right, buddy."

"Grabowski and Angela together," Mitch said with some disbelief. "Shit, they'll make a good couple—they're both idiots."

Mitch had broken up with Angela during the summer when she'd started complaining about Charlie tagging along with them on some of their escapades. "Why do you hang out with that kid, Mitch, honey?" she asked one night. "You know you're better than that." That was all Mitch had needed to hear. He'd never told Charlie the real reason he dumped Angela. He'd simply said, "She's a bitch, Charlie, and I don't have time for a bitch in my life."

"Speak of the devil," Jack said, gesturing with his head toward the woods, "here comes the happy couple now."

Sure enough, Grabowski and Angela emerged from the woods arm in arm and strolled toward the fire. Grabowski immediately made eye contact with Mitch and began walking over to him hastily, pulling Angela along. Grabowski stood about three inches shorter than Mitch's six foot two, and he was far more rotund. He didn't have the slender, muscular build of Mitch, but he carried a natural, hulking strength that made most kids in school respect him out of fear. Grabowski had a reputation as a bully, and he enjoyed this notoriety.

"Oh, look who we have here," Grabowski said as he approached the group. "If it ain't Mitchell Blais and his boyfriend, Charlie. How you sweethearts doing this evening?"

"Why don't you go away, Grabowski, before I teach you a lesson," Mitch said, looking Grabowski up and down. Then he turned his attention to Angela. "And take your little play thing with you."

Grabowski turned red and the smile disappeared from his face. "You teach me a lesson, you little punk," he barked. He took a step in Mitch's direction, but Angela grabbed his arm. The two boys had fought before in what most would have called an evenly matched scrap until Mitch had thrown a straight right into Grabowski's nose, shattering the bone. To this day, Grabowski wore a souvenir of that fight on his face in the form of a crooked nose. His pride had never fully healed, either.

"Come on, Steve, baby. He's not worth it," Angela said, pulling Grabowski's arm in the opposite direction.

"Yeah, Steve, baby, why don't you go home now," Mitch mimicked Angela.

"Screw you, Blais," Grabowski said, "and that goes for you too, Charlie. When I'm done kicking your boyfriend's ass, I'm coming after you."

Charlie felt a lump develop in his throat, and butterflies filled his stomach. *What the hell did I do?*

"That's right, Charlie. I'm gonna snap your neck like I was killing a chicken and there's nothing you or Mitchy-boy can do about it," Grabowski said as he hurled his half-full can of beer at Charlie's head.

Charlie ducked, but the can caught him just above his eye, knocking his glasses off and hurling him backward onto the ground. Charlie looked up and wiped his hand across the top of his eyebrow. "Shit," he said, looking at his palm, now red with blood.

Before even realizing what was going on, the adrenaline pulsed through Mitch's veins. He leaped forward and caught Grabowski on the side of the head with a roundhouse right, knocking him to the ground. Grabowski jumped to his feet and ran erratically, his head down, slamming his shoulder into Mitch's stomach. Mitch gulped as the air left his body. The two crashed onto the ground with a violent thud. With a bolt of energy, Mitch rolled Grabowski over, gaining a slight advantage. The adrenaline consumed Mitch. He felt excited and intoxicated by it. Adrenaline was truly Mitch Blais's drug of choice.

The two rolled around, digging their fingers into one another's flesh and tearing at their clothes. People gathered around and began cheering and yelling while the two fought for an advantage. Mitch could feel himself being pushed closer to the fire as they wrestled. Grabowski kept grunting and turning Mitch over and over until Mitch felt the heat from the fire on his neck and face. With a pulse of adrenaline fueled by survival instinct, Mitch mustered all the energy he could and heaved Grabowski off, hurling him face-first into the fire.

Grabowski let out a primal scream as his face made contact with a smoldering log. He instantly grabbed the left side of his face; the smell of burning flesh filled the night air.

"Cops!" someone from the crowd screamed. Mitch and Grabowski instantly jumped to their feet and squared off, each thinking the other might ignore the warning and pounce.

"This ain't over, you pussy," Grabowski yelled, his face clearly roasted by the fire. He turned and grabbed Angela, dragging her into the woods.

Mitch debated whether to give chase. Then he saw flashlights heading in his direction. "Let's go, Charlie," he said, helping his friend up. The two ran for the woods with the police right on their trail.

2

Intoxicated with adrenaline, Mitch bolted through the woods, hearing Charlie's constant pleas to wait for him. A slight burn on the side of his arm continuously shot pain from his elbow to his wrist. Cautiously, while waiting for Charlie to catch up, he touched the damaged area, only to feel an increased burning sensation. Mitch looked around and everything in his vision appeared red due to the pain. He didn't see flashlights anymore and concluded that he and Charlie had given the cops the slip. His pulse pounded as the excitement and intensity continued to build inside of him.

"Holy shit! We have to get out of here, Mitch," Charlie pleaded as he staggered up to where Mitch stood waiting.

"Follow me," Mitch said, "we can follow the stream up to old man Smith's Country Store and try to find a ride back home."

Mitch and Charlie kept a steady pace while they followed the water downstream and then ran up a steep incline adjacent to the country store. At the top, Mitch quietly surveyed the situation, studying the parking lot as he contemplated their next move.

"What do we do, Mitch? The cops are going to be everywhere," Charlie said.

"Shhh. Let me think."

"Hurry up, Mitch."

"We'll wait here until we see someone we know pull in."

"Wait here?"

"Yeah. Wait here until we can catch a ride home."

"I don't know. We're sitting ducks here, Mitch."

Charlie was right. Mitch knew that they couldn't just sit in one place and wait. They had to take action and keep moving if they wanted to avoid the cops. "You wait here. I'm going around the back of the building to see if anyone is on the other side."

"Hurry, Mitch," Charlie said.

Mitch made his way to the parking lot, looking in all directions to make sure there were no cops in sight. He knew that any kid in the area would be picked up, and he wasn't taking any chances with six months left on his probation. His probation officer had warned him that if he got into any trouble, it could mean jail time. More importantly, it would also mean no marines. Mitch was not willing to let that happen.

Mitch crept to the back of the store and ducked behind the dumpster. He peered around the corner, looking for any familiar cars.

Nothing.

Charlie waited in the shadows, biting his nails while watching the dumpster behind which his friend had disappeared. He just wanted to go home and start fresh tomorrow.

He scanned the parking lot, looking for anyone they knew. The headlights of a car became visible down the road. Approaching the store, it slowed down and pulled into the parking lot. Charlie examined it. Then fear shot through him as he realized that it was an unmarked police car. Charlie froze. The car was heading for the side of the building closest to the dumpster. Charlie knew he had to do something. In an effort to notify his friend, he said as loud as he could without the driver hearing him, "Mitch!"

No response.

The driver opened the door and stepped out of the vehicle. Charlie watched as the female police officer talked into her radio. "Yeah, no sight of any kids yet. I'm going to grab a coffee."

"Mitch," Charlie hissed, trying to warn his friend again.

At that moment, Mitch looked down at the ground and froze. Fear engulfed him. Crawling at his feet from under the dumpster, Mitch saw a big, filthy dumpster rat. He involuntarily flung himself backward, knocking a mountain of boxes over. A metal grate crashed against the cement. He couldn't move. He hated rats. Paralyzed with fear, Mitch sat motionless, waiting for the rat to move on to better things.

The crash caught the attention of the officer. She stopped in her tracks and decided the noise warranted further investigation. Walking back to her car, she removed a flashlight from the front seat and began shining it in all directions.

Charlie ducked just in time. The light passed quickly over his head and it continued toward the dumpster, illuminating everything in its path. He thought about warning Mitch but knew that would give them both away. He covered his head and didn't move.

The officer worked her way to the back of the store, continuing to seek out the source of the noise. Deliberately making her way to the dumpster, she saw the metal grate on the ground. Still unsure, she placed her back against the dumpster and prepared to swing around the back of it to catch anyone lurking there off guard. "All right, it's the police," she called. "If there's anyone behind there, come out now."

No response.

"Police, get out here," she repeated in a sharp tone that demanded compliance.

Again, no response.

The cop swiftly swung herself around the side of the dumpster, shining her light at the ground and finding nothing but a large rat scurrying away. She jumped back in surprise. "Jesus," she said, turning her flashlight off. She put the flashlight into her coat pocket and retrieved some napkins from lunch to throw out.

Charlie peeked above the mound of dirt, sure that he would see Mitch in cuffs, but to his surprise, he only saw the cop standing alone on the side of the dumpster. She was pulling something out of her pocket. "Where are you Mitch?" Charlie said in a soft whisper.

At that moment, she lifted the lid on the dumpster to throw out her trash. She was immediately thrown backward when the lid flew open as Mitch popped up and hurled himself out. He sprinted past the cop and ran over to the incline that concealed Charlie. "Hide," he yelled as he ran by.

Stunned, Charlie looked at his friend running by him at full speed and then he quickly ducked his head below the ridge. He heard the female cop yell, "Stop! Police!"

She too ran right past Charlie without ever seeing him.

Mitch ran down the street to the bridge that crossed the stream. In one motion, he jumped down the hill leading to the water, losing his balance and rolling over several times. He popped up quickly and looked back to see the cop working her way down the hill. He took off, running downstream on the bank until the path became overgrown with brush, forcing him to jump in and thrash his way through the water. Eyeing a slight ledge that was visible in the light of the full moon, Mitch decided that it would be his escape route.

"Stop! Police!" the cop yelled again, continuing her pursuit. "Stop!"

Mitch kept running at full throttle. His pulse quickened as he made his way to the ledge, and without breaking his stride, catapulted himself upward just far enough to grab the root of a tree.

"Stop!"

Mitch gripped the root and with all the strength he had, he pulled himself upward toward the top of the ledge. "Shit, yeah," he said, hoping that the cop wouldn't be able to pull herself up to the top. He reached up and with one hand, grabbed a well-secured rock. With one last burst of energy, Mitch went to hoist himself upward. But something was stopping him. His leg wasn't coming. It felt burdened with weight. He looked down, and in the moonlight, he could make out the face of the female police officer. She had a firm grip on Mitch's pant leg and was pulling him downward.

"You're under arrest, kid. Let's go," she said.

"Bullshit," Mitch said as he began flailing his legs, trying to break free. He could feel her grip loosening, and he continued kicking. Then with one final thrust downward, Mitch kicked her in the chest, freeing his leg.

A groan left her mouth and she dropped on her back into the water. Mitch pulled himself up to the top and stood up, turning back toward the stream. The cop slowly made her way to one knee, gasping for air. Then she looked up at him. Their eyes met briefly before Mitch dashed into the woods and disappeared into the night.

3

No one could deny that there was a buzz in the air at the start of the new school year. The news of the fight at the Benches was the talk of the town, and appreciative nods and looks of gratitude came Mitch's way. Not many kids in the school liked Steve Grabowski—mostly because he picked on people—and many lacked the courage to stand up to him. The fact that Mitch had thrown him into a fire was a victory for many kids who sought retribution against the class bully.

Mitch scanned the cafeteria, searching for Charlie's trademark glasses and red hair, which usually stood out in a crowd. Seeing him sitting at a back table, Mitch casually strolled over and greeted Charlie and the other students who were sitting there consuming their breakfasts.

"Holy shit, Mitch, we thought you got locked up. What happened to your arm?" Charlie asked.

Mitch's arm bore a noticeable burn mark that Charlie hadn't seen when they were running into the woods after the fight. "They can't catch me, Charlie. You should know that."

"What? That woman cop was running right behind you. She didn't get you?"

"Let's just say that almost catching me doesn't count," Mitch said with a slight smile on his face. He always lived on the edge and enjoyed the rush he got from doing crazy things.

"Well, you're lucky, Mitch," Charlie said, shaking his head in disbelief. "If you had been busted, you'd be in big trouble with Mr. Rooney."

Charlie was right, as he was in many instances. Mitch's probation officer, Mr. Rooney, didn't particularly like Mitch and wouldn't need much of a reason to get him in deeper trouble. Mitch forgot about those things when he was in the moment, but not Charlie. That was one of the things Mitch appreciated about Charlie. He was smart and could think things through. Mitch often acted first and thought second.

Mitch liked the action; Charlie liked to think. Maybe that's what made them a good pair.

"Charlie, you gonna eat the rest of that toast?" Mitch asked as he picked it up and put it in his mouth.

"I guess not," Charlie replied sarcastically.

A sudden silence fell upon the cafeteria, and heads swiveled to Mitch. Then chatter began to fill the air and a voice rang out from an adjacent table, "Hey Mitch, your buddy is here."

Mitch turned toward the entrance of the cafeteria to see Grabowski and Angela enter together; both were looking around for Mitch. Angela looked great, as usual, with her hair and makeup perfect. Never did she leave the house without getting her look just right. Mitch knew that beneath all that artificial perfection lay a superficial girl who thought about no one but herself. He was glad he had dumped her.

Grabowski, on the other hand, didn't look so good. A fresh gauze pad was taped over the left side of his face, concealing the burn he'd suffered in the fight.

"Mitch, take a look," Charlie said, gesturing in the direction of Grabowski and Angela. "They're headed this way."

"Yeah. I see."

"Mitch Blais, we still have some unfinished business to attend to," Grabowski barked as he surveyed the table. "And don't forget, Charlie. You ain't off the hook either, you little shit."

Charlie looked timidly at Grabowski, not offering any reply.

Mitch let a slight grin come to his face as he looked at Angela and Grabowski. He offered nothing in reply either, but his non-answer was a calculated effort to piss off Grabowski. Mitch could feel his muscles tense. He stared directly into Grabowski's eyes, ready for anything.

"What's it gonna be, Mitchy? Let's do this right now," Grabowski said, looking at Angela, seeking validation for his toughness.

Mitch said nothing but felt his pulse quicken in preparation for an attack.

"See baby? You're with a real man now," Grabowski said, turning to Angela.

Mitch felt the adrenaline build inside him. He looked over at Angela and remembered why he hated her. He looked back at Grabowski and rose to his feet. "You know, Grabowski, it can't be any worse than it was."

"What's that, Mitchy?"

"Your face. It can't be any uglier than it was before the plastic surgery I did on it."

"You son of a—"

"No, don't thank me now. Wait till the job's done," Mitch said, taking a step in Grabowski's direction.

"Screw you, Blais."

"Grabowski, Blais, knock it off," the voice of Assistant Principal Grant echoed throughout the cafeteria. "Grabowski, get to class. Blais, go to my office. Now. Your probation officer is waiting for you."

"You're screwed now, Blais," Grabowski said as he motioned to Angela to follow him. "And Blais, if I were you, I'd thank Rooney for saving your ass from being kicked."

"Hey Grabowski," Mitch said, holding his middle finger up in the air, "you look really pretty with your new face."

Known for being fair, but unleashing swift punishment when needed, Probation Officer Danny Rooney made his way around the southern part of Maine, meeting with kids who had difficulty meeting the expectations of the law. He sat in a chair in front of Assistant Principal Grant's desk, ready to dish out some discipline to Mitch Blais. Waiting impatiently, he looked down at his cell phone while nervously wiping perspiration from his balding head. He adjusted his belt around his bulging stomach and wondered when this kid would show up.

The door swung open, and Grant entered in front of Mitch. He motioned for Mitch to take a seat in the smaller, plastic chair reserved for students. Grant rounded his massive oak desk and perched himself high upon his leather chair. Looking down at Mitch, he asked, "Do you know why we're meeting today, Mitch?"

"No idea," Mitch replied, feigning ignorance.

"Well, let me tell you, Mr. Blais, why I'm here today," Rooney intervened, still eyeing the clock and looking in the direction of the window. "You had six months left on your probation and you were all set. Your record would have been cleared and you could have moved on with your plans."

My plans, Mitch thought. *Graduate high school and join the marines*. Mitch's dad had been a marine, and it was the only thing he wanted to do. He wanted to make his dad proud by avenging his death. He wanted to go straight into the infantry in Afghanistan and seek revenge against the Muslims who had hurt his father.

"Now Mr. Blais, it appears we have an issue on our hands that we must address," Rooney continued. "Can you tell me what you were doing Saturday evening?"

Mitch hesitated, realizing where this was going. He searched for an excuse but came up with nothing. He looked at Grant, then back at Rooney, and decided that honesty might be his only salvation. "I was at a party at the Benches."

"Anything happen there that may have brought me here today?" Rooney asked, again shooting a deliberate look at the clock and then at his cell phone.

"Come on, Rooney," Mitch said, becoming annoyed with the questioning. "Why don't you tell me what's up?"

"I will, Mr. Blais," Rooney said. "We have an Officer Clarkson down at the station that identified you as the kid that she chased Saturday night and, as she put it, was assaulted by. Says she knew your father and recognized you."

"Oh her," Mitch said, quickly changing his mind about honesty. It might not be the best policy after all. "She was a cop? I just thought she was some crazy lady chasing me down the stream."

"Yeah, she's a cop," Rooney said.

"Well, I'm glad we cleared this up," Mitch said, clapping his hands together. "Please explain to her that it was a terrible misunderstanding and I am truly sorry about the confusion." Mitch stood up to exit the room.

"Sit down, Mitchell," Grant ordered.

Mitch complied.

"You see, Mr. Blais, this isn't good," Rooney continued. "You resisted arrest and assaulted a police officer. You leave me no choice but to report you to the courts."

"Come on, Rooney."

"No, I'm sorry, Mr. Blais. You leave me no choice," Rooney said. He began to fill out a form, documenting Mitch's violation of the terms of his probation. "You have a court appointment on the twenty-fourth and the judge will decide what to do with you. But I can guarantee you this will affect your plans of going into the military."

"What?" was all that came out of Mitch's mouth. Anger instantly overtook him. Joining the military and avenging his father's death was the thing that motivated him. He dreamed of getting into combat in Afghanistan and getting those responsible for what happened to his dad. He felt as much anger for Rooney now as he felt for the Taliban and al-Qaeda. "You can't do this!"

"It's done and…" Rooney stopped in midsentence in response to a beep that sounded from his cell phone, indicating that he had a text message. "Excuse me," he said, anxiously reading the text.

Mitch sat in furious disbelief at what he'd just heard. He tried to think of something to say to plead his case, but only angry, insulting comments came to mind.

"Shit!" Rooney suddenly blurted. He jumped from his seat and made his way across the room to the window, opening the blinds slightly so he could peer out.

"Are you OK?" Grant asked with genuine concern.

Rooney continued to look out the window and then hastily pushed the blinds back to their original position. "I have to go," he said curtly.

"Go?" Mitch said. "We need to talk about this. You can't just leave."

Rooney quickly gathered up his papers and shoved them into his briefcase, dropping several on the ground. Jamming the briefcase under his arm, he headed for the door.

Again, Grant displayed genuine concern. "Mr. Rooney, are you OK?"

"Yeah, Rooney, where the hell are you going?" Mitch asked. "You can't just come in here, drop this shit on me, and run off."

"Court on the twenty-fourth," was all Rooney replied. He flung the door open and exited through the Guidance Office.

Mitch and Mr. Grant sat in confusion for a moment, and then Mitch sprang from his chair to give chase.

"Good-bye, Mr. Rooney," the secretary offered to Rooney, who ignored the formalities and flashed passed her desk without comment.

"Hey, Rooney," Mitch yelled across the office as Rooney frantically made it to the door, only to drop his briefcase on the floor. Papers scattered everywhere, and Rooney hurriedly crammed as many back into his briefcase as possible. "Rooney you can't just do this."

No reply.

"Rooney, get back here," Mitch said as the man bulled his way through the exit. "You're gonna *pay* for this, Rooney!" Mitch yelled.

Probation Officer Danny Rooney disappeared into the parking lot.

Mitch headed after him, only to be stopped by Mr. Grant at the exit.

"Let's go, Mitch. Back to class. I'll write you a pass."

"What the hell was that, Mr. Grant?" Mitch asked.

"I'm not sure, Mitch, but you need to worry about yourself right now," Mr. Grant said.

Mitch looked up at Grant. "OK," he said, turning. As he walked away, he noticed a paper on the floor that Rooney had neglected to retrieve. Hoping that it was his probation violation paper work, Mitch reached down and picked it up. To his disappointment, Mitch noticed that the names of three girls were written on one side. He quickly crumpled the paper in his hand and stashed it in the pocket of his jeans.

5

Probation Officer Danny Rooney waited until dusk to go back to his apartment. He knew he had to get the research he'd gathered to the newspapers before it was too late. He didn't know whom to trust, and he wasn't taking any chances. Going to the police was not an option. They may be in on it. He circled his apartment complex three times before determining that it was safe. He found a parking spot down the street and headed into the woods that bordered the complex.

The walk was mostly uphill and Danny Rooney struggled to navigate the terrain. He worked his way up a long, narrow path that local kids used as a bike trail. His breath was labored and his hands bled slightly from grabbing branches to pull himself up the incline. It didn't matter. He needed the rest of his papers if he was going to keep himself safe. He hadn't asked for this, but he came across the information and knew he had to do something about it. He reached the top of the path and sat behind a tree that overlooked the sliding-glass door at the rear of his one-bedroom apartment. He waited and watched.

Time crept by slowly for Danny Rooney while he watched the inactivity around his place. *Maybe they're looking somewhere else for me*, he thought. They probably didn't realize that he'd left more incriminating material in his apartment. They probably figured he would never be stupid enough to come back here. But he had to get the information he had collected. It was the only thing that would keep him safe. It was time.

Rooney slowly emerged from the woods, crouching and trotting to his back door. He gingerly stepped onto his back deck and stopped to listen for anything out of the ordinary.

Nothing.

He slowly placed his key into the door and turned it, thinking that the click of the lock had never seemed so loud. He slid the door open and slivered his way into his living room. The shades were drawn; the apartment was dark. Danny Rooney had no intention of turning on a light.

He stood motionless for several seconds, listening to the quiet. It was eerily quiet. More quiet than his apartment had ever been with him in it. He listened.

Still nothing.

Slowly he inched his way down the hallway to his bedroom. He placed one hand on the half-closed door and pushed it open. A creaking sound that Rooney had never noticed before filled the air. With the door ajar, his small desk in the corner was visible. He worked his way quickly across the room, opened his bottom drawer, and extracted a file folder full of papers. *My salvation,* he thought. He grabbed an empty bag next to his desk and shoved the papers into it. These, along with the other papers he had, could bring down some very powerful people or keep him alive, if need be. Right now, he was more concerned with staying alive.

Rooney headed back out to the living room. He moved a little more freely now that he'd secured what he came for and his apartment was clear. A hunger pang shot through his stomach, and he realized he hadn't eaten since the morning. He went to the refrigerator, opened the door, and gathered a leftover ham sandwich and a beer. Standing up, he popped the cap off the bottle of beer and took a long, generous sip. Knowing it could be a long night, Rooney continued to search for things he could take to eat later. He opened the freezer door, finding only a box of frozen pizza and ice trays. He took another long sip from his beer.

Rooney closed the refrigerator and freezer doors and was immediately propelled backward as the figure behind the door came into focus. The black ski mask emphasized the anger in the intruder's eyes. Rooney dropped his beer and turned to make a run for the door.

But time had run out. Something smashed against Rooney's head with a vicious force. Dropping to one knee, Rooney tried to regain some focus. He didn't understand what was happening until he felt a wire around his neck. The intruder violently slammed him to the floor facedown, put a knee squarely on his back, and applied force to the wire. Rooney attempted to break free, only to find that he was immobilized by the weight of the intruder. Gasping for air, he tried to scream, but no sounds would cooperate. Light-headedness set in, and Rooney's eyes felt as if they would pop out of his head with each unsuccessful attempt to acquire air. Blood began to dribble down his neck, and he felt faint. Then, with a sudden flash, everything went black.

Danny Rooney lay dead in his kitchen, a piano wire wrapped around his neck and a half-finished bottle of beer on the floor by his face.

6

"Be a sweetheart, Mitchell, and get down here and grab me some of these bags of soil, honey," Mitch heard his grandmother yell from the garden below his bedroom window.

"Yes, Grandma," he responded. He picked up the old blue jeans he wore to help with the chores around the house. Stepping out his school pants, he rolled them up and threw them into his closet, adding to the mountain of laundry that needed washing. He headed out his door and down the stairs, not noticing that the paper he took from Rooney peeked out of his pants pocket in the laundry pile.

Mitch threw the fifty-pound bag of soil over his shoulder and made his way toward his grandmother's makeshift greenhouse at the far corner of the garden. The late-season offerings still flourished, and Mitch carefully walked down the path between rows of red tomato plants.

"Place it right here, Mitchell, honey, over by my workbench here, and cut that bag open for me," Mitch's grandma said. She watched her grandson handle the weight of the bag with ease. "Thank you, Mitchell, honey. I couldn't do any of this without you. You're sure a lifesaver."

Mitch gave his grandmother a genuine smile as he took a pocketknife from the small, garden toolbox and cut the bag open. He closed the knife and put it in his pocket. Grandma Jackie, as he called her, was an active woman who constantly had projects going around the house. Mitch, by default, had been her helper on the vast majority of her endeavors since he was just a small boy. As time passed, he began inheriting the majority of the workload. Grandma Jackie, who could conceivably do anything in the eyes of that little boy, was now appearing more mortal. She was more dependent on him than he cared to realize. He watched her move about the garden and knew she could no longer do any of this on her own. At seventeen, he knew that without him, the garden would no longer exist, and Grandma Jackie would lose something very important to her. Mitch didn't want to see that happen.

"Grandma, when do you think we will finish up for the day?" Mitch asked, looking up to the sky. Day had begun its descent into night. He wiped the perspiration from his forehead and waited for a quick and decisive reply.

"Oh, just a couple more hours and we should be done, Mitchell," Grandma Jackie said. She gingerly moved about in her sundress and wide-brimmed hat, cleaning up hand tools and placing them in an oversized bucket.

"A couple more hours, Gram?"

"That's right, honey. A couple more hours and we should be done," she said, turning her back to Mitchell to conceal her smile. She always enjoyed teasing Mitchell, even now that he was no longer a little boy. She had raised him since he was nine and the two had always shared a loving relationship. Mitch respected her, not because she demanded respect and made it a prerequisite to staying in her home, but because she was Grandma Jackie. Naturally, with adolescence came some trouble, given his impulsive nature. But throughout all of the trials and tribulations of growing up, Grandma Jackie had stayed by his side.

"OK, Grandma. A couple more hours it is."

"Mitchell, honey, should I even ask what happened to your arm?" Grandma Jackie said, looking at the burn.

"It's nothing," Mitch said.

"Well, it sure don't look like nothing, Mitchell."

"I had a little accident with a campfire."

"Accident?"

"Yeah, Grandma, don't worry. It's OK."

Grandma Jackie was no stranger to the trouble Mitch had gotten himself into in the past. She had attended every court hearing and took an active interest in his education. Love and discipline had been intertwined, but now, as they were both getting older, she found herself stepping back a little.

"Everything going OK, Mitchell, honey?"

"Yeah…everything's OK, Gram. No need to worry yourself."

"Mitchell?" Grandma Jackie said in a tone that indicated he was not going to get off that easily.

"Well, I have a probation hearing on the twenty-fourth, but it's routine," Mitch said, bending the truth in an effort to alleviate any worries from Grandma Jackie's mind. He knew it was anything but routine.

"Routine, huh," Grandma Jackie replied with some skepticism. "Remember what the marine recruiter said, Mitchell, honey—no trouble."

"I know, Gram."

"Well, we need to box up all those veggies for the VFW, and Mrs. Simmons needs her delivery also," Grandma Jackie said in an effort to change the subject.

"OK."

"You know, Mitchell, you should keep your old Grammy company tonight. We could watch a movie and eat popcorn like the old days," she said with an obvious smirk on her face.

Mitch, accustomed to the banter the two shared, played right along. "You know, Gram, you could come out with me and Charlie tonight. You could dance the night away and maybe meet a nice fella."

"Well, Mitchell," she chuckled, "it sure would be nice to dance with a nice fella, but I don't have to go anywhere for that. I got you," she said, extending her hand to Mitch. "Can I have this dance?"

"Grandma," Mitch replied, "I don't dance."

"Well, how about a hug then?" She pulled Mitchell close and gave him a loving embrace. "You be careful tonight, Mitchell, honey, and be home at a decent hour. But most importantly, honey," she said as she pulled her grandson even closer, "listen closely, because this is very important. Are you listening?"

"Yes," Mitch replied.

"Most importantly, bring the boxes of vegetables to the VFW and to Mrs. Simmons before you go out. Got it?"

"I sure do," Mitch said, taking a half step away from Grandma Jackie and planting a kiss on her cheek. "Consider it done, Gram."

"It better be done—or else," Grandma Jackie said. She flashed a warm smile in Mitch's direction. He picked up the boxes and headed down the street toward Mrs. Simmons's house.

7

The hand reached for the buzzing cell phone. With the push of a button, the message appeared on the screen:

Did you take care of the package?

The hand hit "reply" and began pressing buttons.

The package has been delivered and it won't be coming back this way again.

There was a slight pause, and then a buzz.

Before sending the package, were all the necessary papers collected and destroyed?

The hand trembled.

Not sure.

A brief moment passed.

Not sure? Not good news.

The hand waited, and then typed:

We're looking for some lost information now that may reveal some identities. We will get them.

There was nothing for several minutes, and then the distinct buzz of the cell broke the silence.

You better or you may be the next package sent out without a return address.

8

Mitch banged loudly on the screen door with his free hand, a box of vegetables occupying the other. "Mrs. Simmons, are you home?"

"Come in, Mitchell," a fragile voice said from inside the house.

Mitch made his way into the house, taking the vegetables directly into the kitchen, as he had done countless times before. As always, he found Mrs. Simmons sitting at her kitchen table, a crossword puzzle and cup of tea in front of her. "Mitchell, can you put those veggies right on the counter, honey?"

"Sure, Mrs. Simmons," Mitch replied as he dodged an oversized black cat that lounged on the kitchen floor.

"How's your grandmother, Mitchell?"

"She's fine, Mrs. Simmons."

"Here honey, let me give you some money," Mrs. Simmons said, knowing that Mitch would refuse the offer as he had every time in the past.

"Put your money away, Mrs. Simmons," Mitch said with no further explanation.

"Oh, OK, Mitchell. How's school?"

"Good. I'm graduating this year."

"Oh geez, you boys grow up so fast," Mrs. Simmons said, gingerly bringing her teacup to her lips. "What are you doing after graduation, honey?"

"The marines," Mitch said, puffing his chest out with a slight show of pride.

A flash of concern crossed Mrs. Simmons's face. "Oh geez, you be careful, Mitchell."

"I will, Mrs. Simmons," Mitch said. He headed toward the kitchen door. "I have to get over the VFW with their veggies now. Grandma Jackie's orders."

"Well, you take care, Mitchell."

"I will, Mrs. Simmons."

"And please be careful," Mrs. Simmons said almost to herself as she heard the screen door close.

Mitch jogged the mile from Mrs. Simmons's house to the VFW. He arrived and ran up the steps two at a time. Slinging the door open, he headed to the bar area. Normally, anyone under twenty-one was prohibited from going into the bar unless he was working, but since Mitch's dad had been an active member of the VFW, he was allowed. Mitch made his way down the hall, stopping to read the plaques and dedications on the wall. He stopped in front of the one that he always read.

Dedicated to the Memory of
David M. Blais
United States Marine Corps
1975-2006
Veteran of the Wars in Iraq and Afghanistan

Mitch ran his finger down the plaque and took enough time to remember his dad without the sadness taking over. Without further hesitation, he turned and proceeded into the bar.

"Mitch Blais," a hoarse, gravelly voice hacked from the bar, "come and sit over here, son."

Mitch complied, placing the box of vegetables on the bar. "Hey, Mr. Johnson," he said.

Old Man Johnson, as the kids in town referred to him, sat at the bar, twirling a rocks glass full of bourbon, clinking the ice off the sides, and chain-smoking cigarettes. He proudly wore the same Khe Sanh Vietnam 1968 hat that always adorned his head. The overgrown, white beard on his wrinkled and hardened face had the remnants of peanut shells in it, and the smoke from his cigarette streamed upward. He looked at home.

"Mitch, rumor is you're headed to the marines next summer; good for you, son."

"Yeah, Mr. Johnson. That's right," Mitch replied with pride. "Paris Island for boot camp next July."

"*Semper Fi,*" Old Man Johnson said with a hard cackle. He raised his bourbon glass to his lips. "I'll drink to that. And what's this Mr. Johnson bullshit, Mitch? Call me Bob."

"OK, Mr. John...I mean Bob."

"Hell, Mitch, you're old enough. Soon you'll be over in the desert killing terrorists just like your old man did. He was a hard-ass son of a bitch that didn't take shit," Johnson continued in between drags on his cigarette. "You know, fourteen confirmed dead al-Qaeda because of your daddy. You should be proud of him."

"I am," Mitch said.

"Shit, your old man and me sat here talking old times many a night," Old Man Johnson continued, the smile fading from his face. "Talked about killing terrorists and little North Vietnamese Communists.

You know, I was there for two years, Vietnam," Johnson explained pointing to his hat.

Mitch looked around the room at all the war veterans sitting around drinking and sharing stories. He missed his dad and wished that he were here with him now. He started thinking back to when his father returned home from combat, when all the changes started. He wondered if his father would have been sitting here right now beside Old Man Johnson sharing stories, reliving the past. *The marines,* he thought. *I'm going to be a marine and I'll get those bastards for what they did to my dad. Then I can come in here with my own stories—stories about killing the terrorists that took my dad away.* Mitch felt himself getting mad. He was ready and wanted to leave right now for Paris Island.

Suddenly Old Man Johnson grabbed Mitch's arm. Squeezing it tightly, he stared straight into Mitch's eyes. His face was fiery red against his white beard. Mitch noticed a twitch in his left eye. "You listen to me, son. You get those terrorists for what they did to your father, and you make them pay. You hear me, son? You make them pay. Then you come back here, and we can drink together just like me and your daddy did." Old Man Johnson stared through Mitch's eyes into his soul. "You hear me, boy? Semper Fi!" Johnson yelled into the air, and then he began howling like a coyote.

Calls of "Semper Fi!" echoed through the crowd, as a handful of retired marines were more than happy to sound off with pride.

"Thanks Mr..." Mitch stopped himself in response to the glare from Johnson. "Thanks, Bob."

"Shit, go kick some ass, kid," Johnson said, downing his drink.

Mitch grabbed the box of vegetables and headed toward the kitchen. As he walked away, he heard Johnson say, "I used to kick some ass. Vietnam. Perimeters overrun, Johnson. Secure that flank, Johnson. Yes sir," Johnson barked out raising a hand to his hat and saluting his reflection in the mirror.

Mitch pushed his way through the swinging doors to find the kitchen empty. The nightly news was on the small, portable television that the cooks watched. He placed the box on the table and filled a glass with water from the sink. Pausing, he listened to the news broadcast.

"And from the coastal newsroom, an inmate at Sherman Point Rehabilitation Center has escaped. Seventeen-year-old Christie Lambert was reported missing yesterday," the newscaster said as a picture of a beautiful, blonde-haired, blue-eyed girl filled the top left corner of the screen. "An extensive search of the grounds and surrounding area was conducted, but the girl did not turn up. The police ask that if you see Ms. Lambert, you immediately call the number at the bottom of the screen."

Mitch half listened and turned his back to fill his glass with more water. "And in breaking news," the newscaster continued, "the search is on for seventeen-year-old Mitchell Blais, who is wanted for questioning in the murder of Danny Rooney."

Mitch dropped his water glass into the sink, not noticing that it shattered into pieces. Spinning around, he saw his senior picture filling the television screen. "Holy shit!" Mitch said. His heart started pumping. *What the hell is going on?*

"Rooney was a probation officer for the court system," the newscaster continued, "and his death is believed to be related to his work. The police have not released details of the murder, saying only that Rooney's body was found hours ago in his apartment. They ask that the public contact the police with any information, and they advise people not to approach Mr. Blais, as he is being considered dangerous. This is Sarah Thomas reporting."

Numbness settled over Mitch's body. Had he just seen his picture on TV? A murder? Rooney dead? How? *Think, Mitch, think!* Nothing came to mind. Mitch stood motionless in the kitchen of the VFW.

Nothing.

"I've got to move," Mitch said aloud to himself. He headed back toward the swinging doors to the bar. At the door, he looked through the round window to see Mr. Johnson talking to a woman. It wasn't just any woman; it was one who had a badge and a gun on her belt. Immediately, Mitch recognized her as the police officer who had chased him down the stream on Saturday night.

Old Man Johnson was bouncing out of his seat as he talked to the woman, who held a picture in her hand. Johnson alternated between howling in the air and saluting the woman, the bartender, and his reflection in the mirror. The woman kept holding the picture up to Johnson's face, but the old man kept swatting it away and continuing with his war stories. She began looking around the bar in frustration, trying to pinpoint another person to question.

Mitch froze momentarily, taking in the scene. That was a mistake. The woman's gaze reached the window of the kitchen door, and she locked eyes with Mitch. Sensing her prey was within her grasp, the officer jolted forward without hesitation. Mitch turned and bolted for the back door, hearing her yell, "Stop! Police!"

9

Sprinting through the kitchen, Mitch knocked over several trash barrels and metal tables. He heard the distinctive sound of the kitchen door swinging open and footsteps in pursuit. "Freeze! Police!" the cop insisted. He did not stop or look back.

Mitch made his way through the parking lot of the VFW, ducking between cars. He stopped and peered over the hood of a Cadillac de Ville. The officer stood at the top of the stairs, her gun drawn. Deliberately making her way down the stairs, she looked left and right, heightening her senses in search of her fugitive. Reaching the bottom of the stairs, she turned away from the Cadillac, slowly working her way around the parking lot.

Mitch crouched near the open window of the Cadillac. Determining that the cop was far enough away, he lifted himself through the open window into the driver's seat. His heart continued to race, and nervous excitement resonated through his body. He didn't know why people were saying he killed Rooney, but he knew it was trouble, no matter what. He was scared, but the adrenaline created an exhilaration that was difficult to live without. Excitement and impulsivity brought something alive in him and made him feel strong. He knew this would be an advantage for him in the military. A single bead of sweat dripped down the side of his cheek. Mitch did not bother to wipe it off.

Time came almost to a standstill. *I've got to get out of here and think.* He thought back to when his dad use to let him sit on the cars and watch him work under the hood. Mitch thought then that his dad was the smartest man in the world, fixing cars and building things around the house. Mitch remembered one car, an old clunker, that his dad let him play with in the driveway. It was cool because it had no key, and Mitch used to start it by touching two wires together. He looked down to the ignition of the Cadillac and an idea came to him. He reached into his pocket, pulled out the pocketknife he'd taken from the garden box, and went to work jimmying the ignition plate off the steering column.

The plate popped off with little difficulty. Mitch stopped again to listen. The sounds of police sirens filled the air and it was clear that they were getting closer. He pushed the knife into the newly formed hole. Several wires popped out.

The sirens were blasting now, and they were accompanied by the squeal of tires turning into the parking lot. His heart pounded. Car doors slammed, and a woman shouted, "Look on the west side! You come with me!"

Mitch took a deep breath, knowing he had one chance to get away. He pulled the two ignition wires from the column. As he prepared to touch them together, he heard two voices, one female and one male, speaking softly just in front of the Cadillac.

"You circle this way and I'll go over here," the woman ordered.

Mitch heard footsteps approaching the side window of the car. They would be sure to look into the car and find him slinking down under the steering wheel, and it would be over. *Murder,* Mitch thought. *I'm not going away for murder.* In one smooth motion, Mitch touched the ignition wires together, and the Cadillac roared to life. He snapped his head up above the dashboard and glanced to his left, through the driver's side window, only to meet the eyes of the woman cop, who was three feet away, staring in utter disbelief.

"Stop!" she ordered, pointing her gun at Mitch.

Mitch slammed the car into reverse and pushed down on the accelerator, squealing the tires and violently smashing the car into the front of a car parked in the next row. He jammed the car into drive and fishtailed out of the parking lot, smoke billowing into the air as the rubber gained traction on the pavement. Mitch didn't look back when he heard the sounds of two gunshots and the clinking of bullets hitting the car. "Holy shit, they're shooting at me," he said as he raced down the street.

10

Accelerating to top speed, the car sped around the corner sideways—almost out of control—as several police cars took chase, blue and red lights flashing and sirens blaring. Mitch was sure he could outrun the cops.

"Come on!" he shouted at the top of his lungs. "You'll never catch me!" Stealing a car was one thing, but murder? *Why are they saying I killed Rooney?*

A sharp left sent a hubcap spiraling down the street. The stolen Cadillac sideswiped a mailbox, the scrape of metal against metal sending sparks spiraling into the night.

Mitch's heart was racing. He punched the gas, speeding the car down the center of Main Street. As he passed stores and curious onlookers, his excitement was building into a frenzied high. Mitch fled from town at speeds approaching one hundred miles per hour.

The dirt roads around the lake, Mitch thought, *I could lose them there*. He pushed the gas pedal to the floor. Houses and trees sped by, his adrenaline pumping at a dizzying pace. *It's well worth the risk*, Mitch thought. *There's no way I'm going to jail for murder.*

As the Cadillac approached the railroad crossing at the edge of town, Mitch could see warning lights indicating that a train was approaching. With a deep breath and a quick check of his nerves, he made an impulsive decision to go for it.

"Come on, let's do this!" Mitch yelled, checking the mirror to make sure he was still being pursued. "Let's see what kind of balls you have back there!"

Out of the corner of his left eye, Mitch could see the oncoming train. *I can make it,* he thought as he sped toward the crossing. The Cadillac barreled down the straightaway while the train proceeded toward the intersection. Mitch's heart was pounding, sending nervous energy through his veins.

I can make it!

The train got bigger in his peripheral vision, closer.

I can make it!

The wooden guardrail began to go down in front of the track. A warning siren wailed from the train. Blue and red lights of the police cars danced in the rearview mirror. Mitch felt like his heart was beating out of his chest. It was a high like nothing else.

I can make it!

The train continued coming, the engineer unable to adjust its speed. The Cadillac reached the perilous intersection and smashed through the wooden warning rail, snapping it in half. Mitch looked to his left. The train appeared almost on top of him.

"Oh shit!" Mitch screamed. He closed his eyes and braced for impact.

The car almost cleared the track. The rear quarter of the Cadillac remained exposed, taking the full brunt of the collision with the train. Mitch suddenly realized he was spinning in chaotic rotations on the other side of the tracks. The back end of the car disintegrated while the remainder of it rolled over several times. The Earth spun around incoherently, and pavement rushed toward Mitch's face. Rotating violently several more times, the car finally came to a stop.

Mitch sat motionless and stunned. Through the smoke, he could see the vague image of the train speeding off into the distance. Across the tracks, he saw the blue and red swirling lights of the police cars.

A voice yelled, "Put your hands in the air! Put them up where I can see them!"

Mitch sat dazed.

The outline of an officer approached through the smoke, gun fixed on Mitch.

"Put them up, I said!" ordered the police officer.

The world was becoming more defined, and Mitch's head began to clear along with the smoke. He looked up, realizing that a dozen or so police officers surrounded him, guns drawn, shouting, authority evident in every movement. Mitch surveyed the situation and realized he was beaten—this time. With one last display of rebellion, Mitch looked up and smiled. Peering directly into the gaze of a police officer whose gun was fixed on him, Mitch said, "You again?" He looked at the badge attached to her jacket. It read Clarkson.

11

"Trouble son, that's what you're in right now," Assistant District Attorney Jack Hamilton said authoritatively, looking across the table at Mitch.

Mitch offered no reply. He sat in the cinder block interrogation room of the county jail, scrapes on his face and a burn mark on his arm. His public defender, Rachel Phelps, rifled through papers, organizing them into various piles. Across the table, Officer Robin Clarkson eyed Mitch.

"A heap of trouble," Hamilton continued. "Murder, resisting arrest, grand theft auto, and assaulting a police officer."

"Murder? I didn't kill anyone," Mitch protested.

Rachel Phelps placed a hand up in front of Mitch. "Don't say anything," she instructed.

"Well, Mitch that's great," Hamilton continued, looking up from the paper in front of him, "but we have several witnesses at your school that say they heard you threaten Mr. Rooney just hours before his death."

"I didn't say I'd kill him."

"My client," Rachel Phelps said, putting a hand on Mitchell's wrist, "is adamantly denying the charges of murder."

Hamilton shuffled through his papers, pulling one out and peering down at it. "You're gonna *pay* for this, Rooney," he said, reading from the paper. "Isn't that what you said to Mr. Rooney?"

"That's hardly a threat to kill someone, Mr. Hamilton," Rachel Phelps said, sitting back in her chair.

"Usually one wouldn't think so," Hamilton said, "but in this case, we have ourselves a dead body at the end of a threat. That's a game-changer in my book."

"This look familiar to you, Mr. Blais?" Clarkson joined the conversation, placing a plastic bag on the table that contained a wire with dry blood on it.

"No."

"This was the piano wire used to strangle Mr. Rooney," Clarkson said, pushing the wire in Mitch's direction, "and I know you're the one that wrapped it around his neck."

"Bullshit," Mitch said. "I didn't kill anyone."

"Oh bullshit, you didn't," Clarkson said, her tone sharpening. "You knew Rooney was reporting you to the courts, so you killed him. You knew if you violated the terms of your probation you would probably do jail time, and you could kiss the marines good-bye. So you did what any good soldier would do—you tracked the enemy down and eliminated him. Let me tell you something, kid. I knew your father. I served with him, and he was a good man. But don't think for a second that I won't put your ass in a sling because of that."

Mitch felt the anger build inside him. There was no reason for his father to be brought into this. "I didn't kill Rooney!"

"My client is done answering your questions," Rachel Phelps said, gathering her papers up and placing them in her briefcase. "Are you charging him with murder?"

"No, at this time the state doesn't have enough evidence to officially charge your client with murder," Hamilton said, disappointment coloring his words. "However, we are holding him for assaulting a police officer, resisting arrest, grand theft auto, and, oh yeah, I almost forgot, violating the terms of his probation."

"And believe me, Mr. Blais," Clarkson said as she rose to her feet, "I will find the evidence I need and I will put you away myself." She turned and stormed out of the room.

12

Judge Jeremiah Butler was a cantankerous old man who hated most everyone, especially troublemaking teenagers who put the public at risk. His high blood pressure was evident in the red hue of his face, and oftentimes he was heard mumbling obscenities at teenagers who stood before him. Known for making examples of kids, he was equally infamous for the bottle of bourbon he was rumored to keep in his desk drawer. Mitchell Blais's public defender, Rachel Phelps, was not optimistic about the upcoming appearance and feared that her client would be going to the state penitentiary for a long time.

"Mr. Blais, you stand before the court today on charges of grand theft auto, assaulting a police officer, and resisting arrest," Judge Butler said. "How do you plead?"

Mitch visually scanned the room until he could see Grandma Jackie. She sat in the back corner wearing a scarf around her neck and a look of sadness on her face. Grandma Jackie was the only one who had ever been there for Mitch since his parents died, and true to form, she was here again for him. She never looked up as she listened intently to the proceedings.

"Son, I asked you how you plead," barked Judge Butler from the bench.

"Yeah, I heard you," snapped Mitch. "Not guilty."

"Son, in this court you will address me by sir or your honor," the judge said angrily, spit flying out of his mouth. "Do you understand?"

"Your honor, if I could intervene," Rachel Phelps said, rising to her feet. "My client has been presented with many obstacles in the not-so-distant past that create a unique situa—"

"Ms. Phelps, save your breath. I've read your client's file and I'm well aware of his past," Judge Butler said, looking down at Mitch over the rims of his glasses. "I am aware that your mother was killed in a car accident when you were very young. I also understand, son, that your father was a decorated war hero, serving in both Iraq and Afghanistan. Unfortunately, I understand that he is also no longer with us." Judge Butler continued to read casually from his court documents. "After his death, you were sent to live with your grandmother."

Mitch felt the blood rise inside him as the judge casually recapped the most devastating events in his life as if he were reading a grocery list.

"I am also aware that this is not your first time in front of this court. Your rap sheet includes assault, disorderly conduct—two counts—and disruption of a school assembly, at which you were responsible for initiating a food fight that escalated into a brawl requiring police intervention," Butler said, shaking his head in disapproval. "Several years ago, a court psychologist diagnosed you with attention deficit hyperactivity disorder, and clearly you have issues with impulse control. You have been receiving counseling services for this ailment, or, should I say, you were *offered* counseling services that you have not taken advantage of to date."

Mitch felt the courtroom close in on him. His secrets were now out, and everyone stood staring at him in judgment. Paralyzed with intense embarrassment, he felt the anger rise in him.

"The court recognizes these issues. However, I must also tell you that society cannot have this. In addition to your current charges, we are dealing with the possibility that you murdered your probation officer," Judge Butler continued in a condescending tone. "Frankly, many people in the world have overcome similar hardships and don't ask anyone to cry for them."

Cry for me? I never asked anyone to cry for me, Mitch thought. A red flash of irate energy shot through him. He stared defiantly into Judge Butler's puffy, red face. "I didn't do it."

"Well, Mr. Blais, can you imagine if the court took the word of every defendant who stood before it? No one would be guilty," he said, chuckling. "The only reason you're not dead after that stunt you pulled is pure luck. I have, however, taken into consideration some information your grandmother supplied to the court."

My grandmother, thought Mitch. *Don't you dare bring my grandmother into this.*

"Your grandmother has informed the court that she has been responsible for you taking your medication for ADHD over the last several years, and that she has been supervising you. Well, it's evident that she has not been up to the challenge and has failed at this task." Judge Butler stared in the direction of a subdued Grandma Jackie.

Mitch's anger came to a boiling crescendo as he heard Butler insult his grandmother. Without a glimmer of hesitation, Mitch yelled, "Go to hell, you fat son of a bitch!"

"How dare you—"

"Oh, I'm sorry. Go to hell, Your Honor!" Mitch yelled as he hopped over the table and rushed at the judge.

The court officers converged on Mitch, grabbing him and slamming him to the floor before he could reach the bench. Mitch felt the oppressive weight of the officers restricting his movement. The carpet scraped Mitch's face while the raw burn on his arm ignited with pain. He felt himself having trouble breathing while the guards manipulated his joints in order to put handcuffs on him. Mitch could hear Judge Butler pounding the gavel.

"Although we don't have enough evidence to hold you on a murder charge at this time, we sure have enough to hold you while the investigation proceeds," he said, looking down at the chaos below him. "You're hereby remanded to the Sherman Point Rehabilitation Center while you await trial," barked Judge Butler.

A cry resonated through the courtroom from Grandma Jackie's mouth.

"And believe me, Mr. Blais, if the evidence comes back pointing to you as the murderer of Mr. Rooney, I will be glad to put you away for life."

13

The teenage girl ran through the woods faster than she'd ever run before. Terror engulfed her while the rain pelted her face. She could see the lights of their flashlights and hear them yelling.

"Christie, come back here, honey! We are not going to hurt you!" a voice called out through the darkness.

She knew this wasn't true. They had already hurt her. Only a brief lapse in their concentration had given her the opportunity to escape, and now she was going to get away at any cost. Her white hospital gown was covered in mud, and she slipped on the wet ground. Her breath filled the air. She couldn't remember ever breathing so hard, being so scared. She kept running. Tree branches slapped her in the face and raked against her arms.

"Christie," the voices continued.

She ignored them and continued sprinting frantically until, without notice, her shins slammed into a fallen pine tree branch, tripping her. Her skull took the full impact of the fall, smashing into the ground. Pain reverberated through her body, and dizziness overtook her head. She felt like she would be sick. Blood rapidly covered her eyes and entered her mouth, dripping from her forehead. *Got to keep moving,* she thought as she stumbled to her feet. *They're getting closer*. She continued racing through the woods, accepting the pain that branches inflicted. She kept moving, even though blood now covered her face and gown.

Suddenly, she exploded from the woods and found herself on a dark road. The rain continued to wash over her, causing the blood to drip more quickly. She ran forward, toward a bend in the road.

"There she is," a voice yelled, "on the street!"

Christie's heart sank. "No!" she cried. "No!"

Suddenly, she could see lights coming from the direction of the bend. *A car,* Christie thought. "Help!" she screamed straining her vocal cords.

Her pursuers, seeing the headlights, stopped in their tracks and slithered back into the woods, fearing they might be seen.

"Help!"

The young couple in the car laughed and sang aloud to their favorite song as they drove along, unaware of the impending danger. The man behind the wheel followed the road and negotiated the bend, continuing to sing and enjoy the company of his girlfriend. Suddenly, in a flash of visual awareness, he saw the girl, dirty and covered in blood, running toward the car.

"Look out!" his girlfriend yelled.

He instinctively pushed down on the brakes. The car skidded uncontrollably on the wet pavement, and despite the driver's best effort, slammed head on into the girl, sending her smashing into the windshield and hurtling over the roof of the car. She landed behind the car with a horrific thud.

The world went black and ended instantly for Christie Lambert as the young couple frantically called 911.

14

Mitch Blais sat in the back of the blue van that transported him to Sherman Point Rehabilitation Center. Shackled at the hands and feet, wearing the standard-issue orange jumpsuit reserved for those prepared by the state for transport, Mitch had nothing but his thoughts. *Murder*, he thought while he watched the road through the back window. *They can't possibly think that I killed someone.* This was craziness and Mitch was determined to prove that he was innocent.

The blue van turned sharply into Sherman Point Rehabilitation Center, sending Mitch off balance to his right. He repositioned himself and saw the approaching security gate.

A security guard who was clearly losing the battle against weight bounced to life upon seeing the van. He jumped up, adjusting his belt, and jockeyed his pants up to a more acceptable level. A tag on his shirt indicated that his name was Felix. Grabbing a clipboard and pen, he put a serious look on his face to show that he was ready for duty.

"How we doing today?" Felix asked as he approached the van with two Doberman Pinschers obediently following at his feet. The dogs barked loudly in the direction of Mitch. "Shut up and sit," Felix commanded as he reached down and gave both dogs a solid backhand across the snouts. Submissively, they sat, without taking their eyes off the van.

"Not bad, Felix. I've got another one for the docs up here to have fun with," the driver said, looking back through the security cage that separated himself and his inmate. The two dogs resumed barking in the direction of Mitch.

Mitch made brief eye contact with Felix through the security gate. He could see the dogs staring into the van, their teeth exposed and saliva dripping from their mouths. They continued to growl, no doubt intending to intimidate him.

"I said, shut up!" Felix shouted at the dogs, this time only needing to raise his hand before the growls subsided in volume.

Looking at his rotund figure, Mitch concluded that there probably wasn't much of a fitness requirement for working here. He watched as Felix waddled back into the security booth, slapping one of the dogs on the head. Returning with the appropriate paper work, Felix handed the clipboard to the driver and retrieved it once he'd signed it. "Thanks, chief," Felix said as he pushed a button to open the gate.

The van pulled away and Mitch watched the security shack fade into the distance.

Felix walked back into the booth, plopping down into his chair and placing his feet up on the window ledge. The dogs followed and took their places below Felix's feet.

The road continued for some time, ascending and taking a serpentine route through the woods. The forest ran deep on each side, and Mitch could see nothing but isolation as far as he looked.

Sherman Point sat on a peninsula that overlooked the Atlantic Ocean. It would have been categorized as an island if it were not for the one, thin piece of land that extended out to the cliffs. It was the only roadway in and out of the facility. The main building sat high up on the rocky cliffs, surrounded by the ocean on every side.

Mitch looked forward, peering through the cage that separated the driver and himself. Moving past a basketball court, he noticed several kids shooting hoops while others sat around a picnic table, playing cards. All activities were being conducted under the ever-watchful eyes of Sherman Point security guards.

Looking to the other side of the drive, Mitch became angry at what he saw. What appeared to be a Muslim family was spread out on the lawn. Mitch had never seen Muslims in person before, and the sight was bizarre to him. They were all kneeling and bending downward at the waist on what looked like small, individual rugs. After several seconds, they sat upright and then bowed down again. Mitch saw a younger guy wearing blue pants and a white T-shirt—the uniform of Sherman Point. The kid had jet-black hair and dark, Middle Eastern features. Mitch figured the kid was about his age. Two women wore flowing scarves wrapped around their heads that draped down over their shoulders. An older man with a long, gray beard knelt on a rug next to the kid's. The older man was wearing clothes that looked like pajamas to Mitch.

Anxiety raced through Mitch as he watched the family scene. He remembered what his dad had told him about terrorists and how they wanted to kill Americans. He wondered how many more terrorists were being held at Sherman Point. Was it like Guantanamo Bay, Cuba, where they held members of al-Qaeda for interrogation? All Mitch knew was that they had better not mess with him.

The van continued forward, rolling over an old bridge with rusty guardrails and boards that moaned with concern. The main building was old and sat high up on a rocky cliff. The jagged cliff descended about one hundred feet down to the ocean. Stones stuck out at various angles and with various degrees of sharpness. At the bottom, the Atlantic slammed into the cliff, wearing permanent patterns in the stone. Sherman Point was a fortress unto itself.

Mitch felt the van come to an abrupt halt in front of the main building. The driver jumped out of the van and made his way behind it. The back door snapped open. "Let's go," he ordered.

The two walked slowly up stone stairs that were cracked and scarred with age. The shackles around his ankles obstructed Mitch's stride, causing him to settle for taking half, stutter steps. Mitch looked at the building. *It's old*, he thought, *old and huge*. The building stretched its granite neck fifty feet upward, meeting a large, circular dome at the top. The circular dome seemed to offer a view in all directions. Mitch imagined it as an eye, watching everything in its view. During the nineteenth century, the tower doubled as a lighthouse, guiding ships around the point. The façade of the building was redbrick with granite trim running along it, framing the windows in its path. A small guard post stood next to the massive oak doors. As they approached, Mitch noticed a large plaque that had faded and deteriorated with age. The lettering began to reveal itself as they got closer, allowing Mitch to decipher it:

Sherman Point
Founded 1850

The formalities at the guard station were expedited, and at a push of a button, the massive doors opened, welcoming Mitch into his new home. Greeted by several staff members, Mitch waited as keys released him from his restraints. He was led down a wide hall. The hallways were old and spoke to the age of the building. Each step caused the wooden floors to creak like an old man's bones. Mitch swore he heard a faint moan emanating from an unseen region of the building.

Nostalgic black-and-white pictures of the Sherman Point of the past lined the walls, creating a museum like photo history of the facility. Mitch looked deep into the grainy pictures from back when cameras were first invented. The structure of the building looked the same, but it was less worn and weathered. The occupants of the facility were documented each year in a group picture. It was strange, Mitch thought, to photograph those committed to the facility, but when cameras were a cutting-edge technology, people documented everything they could.

"Hold up here," the guard escorting Mitch said. He clicked his two-way radio and contacted another party to announce their upcoming arrival in another section of the building.

Mitch stopped and fixed his gaze on one photo in particular, labeled "Sherman Point Insane Asylum, 1868." The offenders from the past seemed to stare into Mitch's eyes. They were faces devoid of smiles and seemed to be hardened with despair and misery. In the center, Mitch noticed a blonde-haired girl who looked slightly younger than he was. He stared deep into her eyes, as if they were two strangers on the street making initial eye contact. It seemed to Mitch that the girl's eyes were seeking help and freedom from her captivity.

"OK, keep moving," the guard ordered.

Mitch kept looking at the girl, entranced by her image. Proceeding forward as directed, Mitch kept eye contact with the girl. It appeared to Mitch that her eyes were following him as he walked away. An uncomfortable and eerie feeling began to consume Mitch during the trip down the corridor. He couldn't quite put his finger on it, but he swore that the walls were watching his every move.

15

Mitchell Blais sat in the office of Dr. Wes Brady in a state of uncertainty. He surveyed the office and decided that the man had too many awards and certificates in his possession. The oak bookshelves housed a plethora of books and journals, and Mitch wondered how one man could have read all of them. The frayed spines seemed to be old and from another time.

Dr. Brady sat in a high-backed, red-leather chair behind an enormous, mahogany desk. His face was old and wrinkled, and his completely bald head glistened under the overhead lights. A graying beard stretched down to his chest and harkened back to another time. Mitch thought he must be very old; he reminded him of the Civil War generals he had seen pictures of in school.

"Mr. Blais," Dr. Brady said as he examined the file in front of him, "you certainly have made some ill-advised decisions in your life, haven't you?"

"Sure, I guess," Mitch said.

"Well, here at Sherman Point, we will not tolerate such behaviors. You will abide by a strict code of conduct," Dr. Brady continued, watching Mitch slowly sinking in his chair in disinterest. "And if you are unable to conduct yourself according to the standards we have set, well, then the consequences will be swift and, of course, educational in their nature."

Mitch was only half listening, as he visually wandered around the room.

"Mr. Blais, Sherman Point has a long history dating back to 1850," Dr. Brady said, standing and walking toward a row of pictures. "Many great men have run Sherman Point," he continued, arriving at portrait of a distinguished and stuffy-looking man who also sported a long beard. "Dr. Timothy Sherman started the hospital for the less fortunate of his time. He was a pioneer in the field, and we are proud to keep his legacy of innovative, cutting-edge treatment alive."

Mitch found himself examining the row of historical pictures that showed, in chronological order, the past leaders of Sherman Point, with the last picture being that of Dr. Brady. He began wondering how long he would need to stay here. His examination of the room continued, and he noticed a row of wooden file cabinets along the back wall. They ended at an old, scratched and pitted cabinet secured with a padlock.

Dr. Brady watched intently as Mitch scrutinized the room. "As an inmate here, you will be assigned to the adolescent facility as long as your behavior warrants such a placement. At this time, you're being held for violating your probation and various other charges, but you and I know it will just be a matter of time before they find evidence that you killed your probation officer. And then, Mr. Blais," Brady said, pausing and giving Mitch a stern look for several seconds, "then, Mr. Blais, once those facts come to light, you will be sent to the federal state prison, and you will no longer be my concern."

"I didn't kill anyone."

"Yes, Mr. Blais," Dr. Brady retorted, "of course you didn't. But that, Mr. Blais, is a matter for the authorities. You are now an inmate of Sherman Point and you will have the opportunity to become a better person—under my direction, of course."

"Or become the person you want me to be."

"Become the person, Mr. Blais, that you must become to get along in society, and, yes, that happens to be the person I would like you to become. According to your file here," Brady said as he inspected the file in his hands, "you have been diagnosed with ADHD and you clearly have an impulse-control issue. In other words, you don't know how to control your behavior. But here, Mr. Blais, you will control yourself and take responsibility for your actions."

Mitch wondered what else his file revealed about him. "Well, I can't make any promises."

"Mr. Blais, I don't think you fully understand the predicament that you find yourself in at this point in your life," Dr. Brady explained, circling Mitch's chair. "Judge Butler could have easily sent you to federal prison. After all, you are seventeen and therefore an adult in the eyes of the court system. You are suspected of murder and therefore are a danger to society. He did you a favor by sending you here to me. You may want to consider taking advantage of it."

"If you call being locked up in this joint a favor, then don't do me any favors."

"Yes, of course," Brady said with a crooked smile on his face. "Here at Sherman Point, we are innovators in treatment. You will not be in a locked cell, but rather, live in a secure dormitory setting. We will treat you with the same amount of respect that you show for others. You will go to group therapy daily with both young men and women and will be an active part of our community. After all, Mr. Blais, if you cannot function as a contributing member of our small community, how do you think you will ever survive in the larger community that society offers?"

Nothing from Mitch.

"Also, you will not have access to any electronic devices here, except while in school for your education. This way you can focus on obtaining the appropriate interpersonal skills your generation seems to be lacking," Brady continued, looking down at the papers in front of him. "Oh yes, and much to my disapproval, you will share your dorm room with a roommate."

"Roommate?"

"Yes, Mr. Blais, because we have so many young adults in need of our guidance, we haven't any single rooms for you. So you will be assigned a roommate. His name is Turtle and you will treat him with respect."

"Turtle?" Mitch asked, unsure if he was rooming with a person or a reptile.

"Yes, Turtle. Everyone refers to him as Turtle—even his mother," Brady explained, circling Mitch's chair again. "He is a young man with autism and he is very, very quiet. He shouldn't…how should I say this…create any excitement for you which might cause you to act on your impulses. It should be a very therapeutic match."

"Sounds like a hoot, Doc."

"Well then, Mr. Blais," Dr. Brady said as he stood behind Mitch's chair and put his hands on Mitch's shoulders, "let me remind you that every move you make here will be monitored by our staff, and you will be held accountable for any transgressions. Hopefully, you'll meet our expectations or your stay here will become, let's say, a very painful life lesson."

Mitch felt Brady's fingers dig into his shoulders. He suddenly realized that his stay at Sherman Point might be extremely unpleasant.

16

Group therapy was a large part of treatment for all the inmates at Sherman Point, and Mitch Blais was no exception. After dropping his bag off in his new home, a twelve-foot-by-twelve-foot room he was to share with some guy named Turtle, Mitch was led down to a lounge, where a group of kids sat in a circle. The walls were adorned with posters and pictures of pleasant country settings and sayings like, "Hope is the Future Meeting Your Dreams" and "Inspiration: Reach for the Stars." The only thing Mitch could think about was getting out of this place and proving his innocence.

A nonthreatening-looking guy in his thirties led the group. He dressed casually, wearing blue jeans that were far from faded and a neatly pressed polo shirt. His hair was tied in a ponytail, and a neatly trimmed, black beard covered his face. He looked empathetically at Mitch through round, wire-rimmed glasses. Mitch thought he was making too much of an effort at trying to look young.

"Ah, Mitchell. Thanks for joining us today. I'm Dr. Paul Cavanaugh, a therapist here at Sherman Point," he said, extending his hand to Mitch. "You can call me Dr. Cav, if you like. All the kids do."

Mitch reached out and tentatively shook his hand.

"I'd like you to meet everyone in the group," Dr. Cav said, smiling at Mitch.

Mitch looked around the room and instantly deduced that he did not belong in this place. No one in the group moved, and a strange and uncomfortable silence engulfed the room. Three of the teens looked up at Mitch and stared at the scrapes on his face and the burn on his arm. A smaller kid with a shaved head sat in the corner, staring at the floor.

Noticing the uneasiness, Dr. Cav intervened to begin the introductions. "That's Turtle," Dr. Cav said, gesturing at the kid in the corner with the shaved head.

No reply.

"Hello," Mitch said in a friendly tone, "I guess we're rooming together."

Turtle never lifted his head.

The next young lady stared at Mitch. She was the only person in the group wearing a white hospital gown instead of the standard blue pants and white T-shirt. Her eyes were heavy, with dark circles under them. She looked at Mitch half smiling and wiggling in her seat.

"Tina, would you like to say hi to Mitchell?" Dr. Cav asked.

"What the hell happen to you?" Tina asked as she continued to survey Mitch's wounds, her half smile morphing into a full one. "You look like you were in a fight. Is that it? You were in a fight? Can you tell me about it? Did you kick some ass?"

"That's enough out of you, Tina," Dr. Cav said.

"All right, all right, all right," Tina said, her eyes fixed on Mitch. "I just thought maybe Mitch here had some stories to liven this place up."

"Tina, remember how we talked about making good first impressions."

"Ah, shit, Doc. Come on."

"Don't bother with Tina," the kid sitting next to her said.

Mitch immediately recognized him as the dark-haired kid with the Middle Eastern features he saw sitting outside on his way into Sherman Point. He was about Mitch's size and age, and he had an equally athletic build.

"Tina, she's just crazy. You know, always looking to rile people up and get things cranking. My name's Sameer," he said smiling.

Mitch flashed a confrontational glare in his direction without saying a word. The smile instantly left Sameer's face.

"Hi, my name's Cassandra," said a Cape Verdean girl sitting beside Sameer. "Welcome to our group."

"Hello," Mitch said, taking a second look at her. Cassandra had long, black hair, light-brown skin, and beautiful, almond-shaped eyes. She spoke quietly in a soft, non-threatening tone. Mitch instantly found her attractive.

"Well, then why don't you take that open seat next to Cassandra," Dr. Cav said, pointing toward a vacant chair.

Cassandra moved several items she had on the chair, freeing up the seat for Mitch. Mitch walked over and plopped himself down in the chair.

"All right then," Dr. Cav said, clapping his hands together. "Sameer, let's pick up where we left off. You just had a visit with your parents who are leaving on a trip to the Middle East. How did it go?"

"Well, you know, it was good. It was nice to see them."

"Did they tell you about their trip?" Dr. Cav asked, pressing for information.

"They're going to visit my cousins in Pakistan and make their religious pilgrimage to Mecca."

"That's bullshit," Mitch said under his breath.

"Excuse me?" Sameer said, caught off guard.

"Is that what they call it—a religious pilgrimage?" Mitch said.

Cassandra looked over at Mitch, her welcoming look now replaced with one of guarded confusion.

Turtle kept looking at the floor.

Tina's smile came back instantly at the thought of a possible confrontation.

Dr. Cav looked in Mitch's direction, surprised at his early contribution to the group discussion. "Did you want to say something, Mitch?"

"Yeah. What do they teach at these 'religious pilgrimages,' how to make pressure-cooker bombs? Or maybe how to fly planes into buildings?"

All eyes, except Turtle's, darted in Mitch's direction. Tension instantly filled the room.

Cassandra found herself edging away from Mitch, concerned about this stranger's unprovoked animosity.

Sameer sat up with a complete understanding of what Mitch was implying. "Who the hell are you, asshole, to be accusing my parents of such things?"

"I saw you and your parents on the lawn."

"So what."

"So, what are you, a junior terrorist-in-training?"

"Slow down, everyone," Dr. Cav instructed.

"Yeah, slow down, kid," Sameer repeated in a harsh tone. "My parents are taking a religious pilgrimage to Mecca—the holy land for Muslims. It's one of the Five Pillars of Islam to visit the holy land once in your lifetime."

"Holy land, terrorist camp. What's the difference?"

"The difference, asshole, is that I'm not a terrorist and my family aren't terrorists," Sameer said, rising to his feet. "We're American citizens just like you."

"Not like me," Mitch said, also rising to his feet. Mitch felt his heart race as he remembered his father's words after his last deployment. *Never trust a Muslim, son. Never turn your back on one of them. They'll stick a knife in your back when all you're doing is trying to help them.*

"What is your problem?" Cassandra asked, an uncomfortable irritation evident in her voice. "Sameer isn't a terrorist. Why would you say that?"

Nothing from Turtle.

"Dr. Cav," Sameer questioned, "do I need to take this shit?"

"Please, Sameer," Dr. Cav said calmly, standing between the two in an effort to dissipate the tension. "Mitchell is new to our group and hasn't developed trust with us. Let's give him some time. He'll come around."

"Trust," Mitch said. "I don't trust people that fly planes into buildings killing innocent Americans. I don't trust people that kill innocent kids minding their own business, and I sure as hell don't trust people that kill American soldiers when they're just trying to help them have a better life."

Sameer looked in disbelief at Mitch. "What planes? Soldiers? What the hell are you talking about, man? I'm as American as you are."

"Bullshit. I bet you have cousins over there shooting up Americans. Shit, I bet you have family in America waiting for their chance to bomb us," Mitch said, his blood beginning to boil. "How do we know that you're not in a sleeper cell? Anyone check this guy out?"

"Dr. Cav, this is bullshit. Do I have to take this from this guy?"

Turtle kept looking down, terrified by the chaos going on around him.

Cassandra sat in stunned confusion. She flashed Mitch a look of contempt.

"Oh, we're gonna have a fight," Tina said with excitement in her voice as she sat up tall in her seat. "My money is on you, Sameer! Kick his ass!"

Cassandra glared at Tina. "Why don't you calm down over there? This isn't positive for the group, right Dr. Cav? Didn't you say we needed to keep things positive to build trust?"

"That's right, Cassandra," Dr. Cav said, maintaining his place between Mitch and Sameer. "We obviously have a lot of work to do here."

"Yeah, we've got a lot of work to do," Sameer said, staring at Mitch.

"Piss off, towel head."

"Towel head?"

The two gestured toward one another, and then everyone's head snapped toward the hallway as a blood-curdling scream filled the air.

17

Everyone jumped to their feet and headed for the double doors between the lounge and the hall. The scene in the hallway was chaotic. Staff members rushed to a screaming girl while others attempted to organize the concerned inmates.

"She's dead!" screamed the girl, as she thrashed and hit the wall with her fist. "She's dead…no…no…no!"

The staff ran to her in show of solidarity, grabbing for her flailing limbs.

"She's dead! Christie's dead!" The screams continued to flow out of her in an uncontrolled chorus of anguish.

The scene escalated as people began to comprehend what the girl was saying. Christie Lambert, the girl who had disappeared a week earlier, was dead. As others began processing the news, the cries and comments of disbelief increased.

"Everyone to your rooms! Sound the code blue!" Felix demanded as he scrambled about, organizing makeshift lines in an attempt to regain a semblance of order. Lines of inmates began filing into the corridor that housed their rooms.

"There will be no talking," Felix barked. "We are in code blue status."

"What's code blue?" Mitch asked Cassandra as they exited the lounge.

"Be quiet," Cassandra said in a sharp tone. "Trust me; you don't want to end up in the Chamber."

Mitch filed into what was now his room with Turtle following the orders of Felix, who was directly behind them. "Turtle, you and your new boyfriend get into your room now, if you know what's good for you!" Felix said, giving Turtle a shove in the back, knocking him off balance. Turtle did not react.

Mitch went to his bed and sat on the edge. He tried to understand what had just happened in the hallway. Cries continued to bellow from various rooms, and a low, constant buzz of conversation filled the air.

"Hey, Turtle, what the hell is going on?" Mitch asked, looking at Turtle, who was sitting at his desk. Turtle was only five foot two and his small, frail frame made him look far younger than his sixteen years. His shaved head and pale skin made him look sickly. Mitch looked over Turtle's shoulder to the wall behind his desk. Strangely, there was nothing on the wall except drawings of the same building. After further examination, Mitch concluded that all the drawings on the wall were of Sherman Point itself. No pictures of family, friends, or anything else decorated Turtle's portion of the room. Instead, only hand-drawn pictures of the very facility that suppressed his freedom filled his space. Mitch found it to be a strange hobby.

Turtle looked up without saying a word. He was frightened by his new roommate and by the chaos in the hallway. He just looked down again, not daring to make eye contact with Mitch.

"Turtle, what's the story? Who's Christie?"

"Don't hurt me."

"What?"

"Don't hurt me," Turtle said, keeping his gaze fixed on the floor.

"What are you talking about? I'm not gonna hurt you. Why would you say that?"

Turtle was relieved somewhat to hear that his life was not in immediate danger. "Murder?" Turtle said, surprised by the words that had left his mouth.

Mitch sat looking at Turtle, understanding what he was getting at. Obviously, the word had gotten out that Mitch was being investigated for murder. He was now being viewed as a killer. Mitch looked at Turtle, knowing that the kid was probably scared out his mind. Turtle probably thought that Mitch would kill him in his sleep or something. A sudden sense of empathy filled Mitch. "I didn't murder anyone, and I'm not gonna hurt you."

No reply.

"Look, they say I killed my PO, but I didn't."

Nothing.

Mitch put his head down. How was he going to prove to everyone that he wasn't a murderer? More importantly, how was he going to keep himself out of jail for life? "Do you believe me?"

"Sameer?" Turtle said.

"What about him."

"He didn't do anything," Turtle said in a voice that quivered with fear.

"Well, that's a different story. I have issues with people like Sameer."

"I'm safe?" asked Turtle.

Mitch looked at Turtle and felt a degree of sadness for the kid. He honestly thought Mitch was going to hurt him, and judging from his size and frail-looking body, Mitch realized that Turtle probably couldn't fight off anyone. The poor kid must live in a constant state of fear.

"No man, I'm not going to touch you. I promise," Mitch said, flashing a genuine smile at Turtle.

"Good."

"Christie, is that the girl that escaped?" asked Mitch.

"Weird," said Turtle.

"Why's that?"

Turtle looked around and went to the door, concerned that someone might be listening. "She left Sunday but was found yesterday, one mile from here."

Mitch quickly realized that it was now Saturday. Where had she been for a week? How had she eaten? Why did she only get a mile away from Sherman Point in a week?

"Not all," Turtle continued, as his eyes shifted down the hall. "Two others."

"Two others what? Dead?"

"Don't know," Turtle said, beginning to fidget.

Mitch could see that Turtle was genuinely terrified as he told the story, and he could not deny that a creepy feeling had engulfed him. He was now a patient at Sherman Point, and apparently, at Sherman Point, kids could disappear and wind up dead! "Hey Turtle," Mitch said.

No reply.

"It's OK, I'll make sure no one hurts us," Mitch assured Turtle.

"Thanks," Turtle said, as a small smile briefly filled his face.

18

The group reconvened the next day, but Dr. Brady sat in this time to help the inmates process the events that abruptly ended the session the day before. All immediately sensed his self-importance and the condescending attitude that helped him validate his own intelligence.

"Obviously, the events of yesterday are not common here at Sherman Point. A great tragedy has befallen us, and I'm sure everyone has a plethora of questions," Dr. Brady said, stroking his beard and looking at everyone over the rims of his glasses.

"What happened to Christie, Dr. Brady?" Cassandra asked in a soft monotone voice. "Did she really get hit by a car?"

"Christie ran from the program, as she made the unilateral decision that she no longer needed help," Dr. Brady explained, his visual scrutiny of the kids in the group continuing. "Subsequently, she was hit by a car and died."

Everyone sat in utter disbelief at the information now being shared. Turtle was emotionless, afraid to say a word. Tina listened, vigorously chomping away at a piece of gum. She wrapped her arms around her hospital gown.

Tears streamed down Cassandra's face. She wiped them away.

Sameer looked toward Dr. Brady and respectfully raised his hand. Dr. Cav quickly intervened and said, "Sameer, we are all adults here, we can just speak up as long as we respect the other members of the group."

Sameer shot a thankful smile at Dr. Cav and said, "Dr. Brady, where was Christie before she was killed?"

"Killed?" Dr. Brady retorted. "I think the word 'killed' is inappropriate in this particular instance. Christie died due to a terrible accident that was brought about by her own overt behavior."

"My bad, Dr. Brady," Sameer said. "Where was Christie before she was hit by the car?"

"We are not sure," Dr. Brady said. "She was probably hiding in the woods, foraging for food, and surviving on scraps she probably hoarded and took with her."

"Why would she have done that, Dr. Brady?" Cassandra asked, as tears continued to well up in her eyes. "I knew her. She was happy and in love. She had a boyfriend waiting for her. Why?"

"Dr. Brady, may I please?" Dr. Cav asked, looking toward Cassandra. "Cassandra, sometimes people may seem happy on the outside, but deep down they are troubled. It appears that Christie had many of us fooled."

"What about the others?" Mitch said suddenly from the far side of the room.

The rest of the group looked puzzled, wondering what he was talking about.

"What others?" Dr. Brady inquired.

"Come on, Doc, you know, the two other girls that disappeared from here that have never been heard from again. What about them?" Mitch asked, hoping to elicit a response.

"Mitch, what are you talking about? Where did you hear such a thing?" asked Dr. Cav.

Turtle was overcome by the feeling of his heart dropping. Would Mitch reveal the secret he told him last night? Turtle was surprised by the sweat forming in the palms of his hands.

Dr. Brady intervened. "In the past, we have had people run from the facility, and later they were denied the opportunity of rejoining us. Again, Mr. Blais, that was their choice and the consequences are theirs to own."

"I'm talking about two girls that disappeared in the last year that never came back and no one ever heard from them again. What about them?" Mitch said in a confrontational tone, challenging the leader of Sherman Point.

Cassandra looked around the room, waiting for a response. She was close to one of the girls, Kathy, who used to run from the facility to see her boyfriend. One time she told Cassandra she would be back, but she never returned. Cassandra always assumed she'd just run away. Now she began to wonder.

Dr. Brady looked toward Mitch. His eyes were full of anger. "Excuse me, Mr. Blais. You obviously have not learned that disrespect and insubordination will not be tolerated here at Sherman Point. If you have something to say, you are expected to do so in a manner that is befitting a young, respectful adult."

"OK, Dr. Brady," Mitch said, "but your story ain't adding up. How does a young girl like this Christie survive in the woods alone in the fall, when the temperatures get cold enough at night that you could freeze your ass off? Rumor is she was wearing nothing but a hospital gown when the car hit her. Is that true?"

Dr. Brady looked at Mitch as if answering a troublemaker like him was beneath him. But he sighed and responded, "Mr. Blais, are you aware of the tremendous feats a person can perform when put under stress?" Dr. Brady peered over his glasses. "There are stories about mothers lifting cars to free their trapped babies during natural disasters. Does this sound normal to you? You see, Mr. Blais, Christie had many issues that she was working on. Her anger at the world because her parents abandoned her had a profound, and shall I say, a negative effect on her. Of all people, Mr. Blais, you should relate to this. After all, you haven't any parents either, Mr. Blais. Isn't that correct?"

Mitch felt all eyes in the group fixed on him. He felt as if they could see right inside him, see all there was to know about him. A furious resentment toward Dr. Brady was ignited inside Mitch. He visually panned the room to look for reassurance from the others in the group.

He received none. The looks reserved for him were those of anger and distrust after the events of the day before. Mitch suddenly felt very alone.

Turtle was overcome by shaking when he saw Mitch's face turn red. He looked down at the floor. Cassandra stared directly at Mitch, indifference on her face. Mitch looked to his left at Sameer, who was staring straight ahead, wearing a slight smirk on his face, happy to see the new guy getting it from the docs. Anger raged inside of Mitch and the need to defend himself quickly surfaced.

"What the hell is your problem, Saddam, or whatever your name is?"

Sameer instantly felt a defensive anger overwhelm him. "Again, man? What are you sweating me for? I didn't do anything to you, asshole."

"Asshole? Who are you calling asshole? I'll teach you a lesson, you homegrown terrorist." On an impulse, Mitch lunged toward Sameer. Before he could get across the room the security guards ran in and intervened, slamming him to the floor and placing him into a well-executed restraint with both arms pinned to the ground and his feet crossed behind him and folded upward. With all his might and effort, Mitch struggled to break free, but the pain of the rug scraping across his face and the weight of the three guards on top of him were too much.

Dr. Brady made his way over to Mitch, who was still attempting to wiggle his arms and legs free.

"Get off me!" he yelled.

Removing a leather case from his pocket, Dr. Brady took out a syringe already filled with a liquid. He knelt down and jabbed it into Mitch's shoulder. A brief, yet sharp pain ensued. "You see, Mr. Blais, like

I told you before, you may have to learn some very, very painful life lessons during your stay here at Sherman Point. Take him to the Chamber," Dr. Brady ordered. "Maybe there, Mr. Blais will have time to think about proper decorum and respect."

Before he could protest, Mitch felt any desire to continue fighting leave his body. A black void filled his head. He slipped into unconsciousness.

19

The Chamber was nothing more than a windowless room with nothing in it. In every direction, the stone walls spoke of their age: they were covered with engravings and markings made by others who had suffered there. The Chamber gave off a cold, damp feeling of loneliness and seclusion. The only contact with others was afforded by one small, vertical security window on the door that was screwed in tightly and protected with safety glass. Mitch paced on the cracked concrete that the Chamber offered as a place to walk, sit, and sleep. The Chamber held secrets that it had suppressed for years.

Time crept slower than Mitch had ever experienced in his life. He tried to talk with the guards stationed at his door, but they were under strict orders not to engage in conversation with him. He didn't have access to a phone, video games, television, or anything else to occupy his time. He slowly paced the room while time lagged behind. Twice a day, he ate a peanut butter sandwich and drank water. This became the highlight of his stay in the Chamber. He was hungry, tired, and cold.

His thoughts turned to his mother, who had always been there for him when he was young and vulnerable. She had died when he was just a little boy of four, but Mitch had vague memories of her that were warm and filled with love and compassion. Most of his memories were filled with her absence, though. As a young boy, he couldn't understand what had happened. There was a funeral, and she existed no more. She was gone, and for a young Mitch, the security and reassurance of his mother's embrace would never be there again. His grandmother immediately stepped in as a proxy for his departed mother, and Mitch never went without the love and tenderness of a maternal relative. He loved his Grandma Jackie and missed his mom.

Isolation can wreak havoc on the mind quickly, and this was true for Mitchell Blais. The silence tortured him.

Silence.

After day one, the quietness and lack of human contact weighed on his mind. He continued to think. The Chamber did not offer views of the outside world. It was an entity unto itself, and Mitch slowly learned the shape, color, and characteristics of every stone and its etchings. Each huge, granite block of the chamber had a purpose in relation to the other ones. Mitch studied them. He felt the contour of every rock in the Chamber. How old, Mitch wondered? How many years and how many kids had suffered down here in the belly of Sherman Point? Did they all survive? Mitch counted seconds and minutes again and again.

He began to notice older, more weathered etchings in the stones. He looked closely into the bottom left corner of the Chamber and noticed a partially exposed carving on a big, gray stone used as a base to support the others. Mitch noticed the first two numbers, a one and an eight.

Quickly, Mitch started clearing away the years of dirt. He mustered as much saliva as possible and spit on the stone, rubbing it clear and revealing the rest of its secret. It read, *1868 Therese Harriet Coleman...help me.*

Mitch jumped back and studied the writing. *Eighteen sixty-eight. A different world,* he thought. What had happened to her? How long did she spend in the Chamber? Was he ever going to get out?

By day three, Mitch's thoughts wandered further and became incoherent. He hadn't thought much about Charlie since arriving at Sherman Point, and he wondered how he was faring without him. Images of Mitch's father entered his thoughts. He was deployed in other parts of the world as a marine; absent most of the time when Grandma Jackie was raising Mitch. Mitch recalled his excitement when his dad would show up at his school to pick him up unannounced, wearing his uniform. The surprise and happiness that filled Mitch was only second to his showing off such a great dad. It wasn't until later that the changes occurred.

Mitch waited for nothing. He was hungrier than he could ever remember being. His stomach growled and his head hurt. How long had he been down here? Would he ever get out? He could hear thunder and lightning, rain pelting the building. He listened until the rain became a constant rhythm in his head. He stared at the walls and a sense of doom overwhelmed him.

His eyes could barely focus as the walls of the Chamber began discharging moisture. Slowly, drips started coming out of every crack and crevice of the Chamber. In some spots, the drips became constant, and Mitch stared at them in an almost hypnotic state. He knew the Chamber held him and he would be part of its secrets forever. Mitch thought he would die in here, and the Chamber was crying for him. The tears kept rolling down the face of the Chamber, and Mitch realized he was fighting back his own tears. He felt sick and alone and wanted to talk to someone. Anyone.

Time slowed, and Mitch began questioning what day it was and what time it was. He could only gauge night because they shut his light off. Or did they shut it off in the morning to play tricks with his mind? The guards outside would know, but they weren't telling. They weren't speaking, and they certainly didn't give a shit about Mitch. Maybe they were special guards, Mitch thought. Maybe they killed that girl, Christie. Maybe they killed the other two kids who "ran away." Suddenly, fear swept over Mitch, and he realized that he was in trouble. He started pounding the cement with his fists until blood streamed from his hands.

"No…no…no."

Mitch curled into a ball on the floor and closed his eyes. He began shaking. "No," he murmured under his breath until the mental exhaustion took his thoughts away, and he slipped involuntarily into sleep.

20

Mitch jolted awake to find the Chamber dark except for the dim light of the tiny window in the door. Mitch went to the door and peeked out. "Hello…Hello. Is anyone out there? This is bullshit," he said.

Mitch paced the room as an enormous uneasiness consumed him. He hurried back to the door.

"Is anyone out there? How long have I been here?" he shouted. From behind him, Mitch felt a rush of cold air surround him and he heard a soft voice.

"You've been here for five days, but others have suffered more."

Fear threw Mitch backward, and he spun around in one startled motion. He looked over to the corner of the room where a girl, about fifteen years old, looked nervously at him. "Who are you?" Mitch said. He felt his heart pumping in his chest.

"My name is Therese."

Mitch continued to scrutinize the young girl, not sure how to react. She looked harmless enough, if not frail. Her long hair was a light blonde, and Mitch noticed that she was wearing a hospital gown that was torn and yellowed with age. A baffled fear filled Mitch as he suddenly realized that he was staring at the girl from the old, grainy photo that he'd seen in the hallway on his first day at Sherman Point.

"What? How did you get in here?" Mitch asked, still confused.

"Oh, I've been here for a long time," the girl said. "I know how to get all around here. I know all the secrets that Sherman Point won't reveal to others."

"What do you want?"

"I want to help you, of course, and for you to help me," the girl said, motioning for Mitch to sit down.

"OK," Mitch said, as he sat, unsure of what else to do.

"You mustn't trust them here," she said. "They try to exorcise your demons, but they will cage you for eternity if you let them."

Mitch did not take his eyes off the girl. *I must be nuts,* he thought. Nevertheless, loneliness had become his only companion, and crazy or not, he welcomed any interaction—no matter how unbelievable it might be.

"What can I do? How can I get out of here?" Mitch asked, peering over his shoulder to make sure the guards hadn't returned.

"There are ways. But first you must be aware. They will poison your mind. Don't let them poison your mind. They will use you to feed their own demons. It's been going on for years."

Mitch sat confused, staring at the figure of the young girl. Was she real? What was she talking about? "What's been going on for years?"

"This place is evil, pure evil," the girl said, appearing to hover over the cement.

"Why are you telling me this? What are they going to do?" Mitch asked, uncertainty evident in his voice.

"I have been waiting a very long time for someone to end the cycle of abuse and set me free. Others have tried, but none has been worthy," the girl said pointing directly at Mitch. "But you are different. I saw it in your eyes the other day. You remember, in the hallway. You are the one."

"The one for what?" Mitch asked.

"Time will reveal the secrets, Mitchell; and as it does, you will learn more about yourself," the girl said. "You must open your heart, Mitchell, and let the goodness within be seen by all."

With that, the sound of a key turning in the lock filled the air. Mitch sat up, rubbing his eyes, coming to the realization that he had been asleep. *A dream*, he thought. *It was all a dream.* "I have to get out of this place," Mitch said to himself.

Mitch repositioned himself on the floor, gladly accepting food from the guard. He ate and searched the Chamber for anything to occupy his mind. He scanned the stones until he reached the etching on the large rock in the corner: *1868 Therese Harriet Coleman...help me.* A lump formed in Mitch's throat as he suddenly realized who occupied his dreams: Therese Harriet Coleman.

21

Removal from the Chamber involved a stern lecture from Dr. Brady, a shower, and a visit to the nurse. The last two days in isolation for Mitch were filled with self-doubt. He questioned his own sanity. The doctors at Sherman Point had told him that there was something wrong with his mind, an impulsivity-control issue, they called it. He knew this didn't mean he saw people who didn't exist, and he refused to believe that he was starting to do so. He reassured himself that he was fine; he certainly didn't trust anyone at Sherman Point enough to talk about his dream.

"Mitch, OK?" Turtle asked, filled with surprise as Mitch entered the room they shared.

"I'm fine," Mitch assured him. "Turtle, can I ask you a question?"

"Sure."

"Do you know a girl here named Therese? She's about fifteen years old and has blonde hair."

"No. Why?"

"No reason. I just thought I saw someone I knew."

Felix turned the corner into Mitch and Turtle's room, clipboard in hand, authority in his voice. "Line up, shithead," he said to Turtle. "You too, Blais. Let's go. It's med time."

"I don't take meds," Mitch said in protest.

"You do now, shithead. After the little stunt you pulled last week, the docs decided you could—how did they put it?—*benefit* from the positive effects of a pharmaceutical intervention," Felix said as he laughed in Mitch's direction. "Now, don't make me tell you again."

There was no talking in the med line; doing so resulted in swift discipline. Mitch thought everyone looked kind of like robots standing on an assembly line, waiting their turn to be tuned up just the way the doctors liked. Nobody liked a robot that was too slow and couldn't work, and at the same time, no one wanted a rebellious robot that would be overly difficult to handle. Just right. That's the way they liked them. A twist here, some oil there, and a magic drug in the form of a pill to keep them all in line. All of the robots took their turns, one at a time, and got *just right*. Mitch began saying over and over in his mind the words that Therese Harriet Coleman had said in his dream: *They will poison your mind. Don't let them poison your mind. They will use you to feed their own demons.*

Mitch waited impatiently in the hallway for his turn to see the nurse. "Mitchell Blais," a woman's voice called from inside the office. He turned and entered the nurse's office.

"Hello, Mitchell Blais," said a stout woman with graying hair. "We missed you when you first arrived. Seems you spent a little time in isolation," she added with a scornful look on her face. It reminded Mitch of how his elementary school teachers had looked at him when he misbehaved at recess.

"Yeah, they're pretty strict around here," Mitch said. He looked down at her nametag. It read Anne.

"Well, I'm sure it was for your own good. Besides, now you're out and you can get on with your treatment," she said, holding a small, oval, red pill and a small cup of water out to Mitch.

Mitch looked uncertainly at the pill. "What's that?"

"Something, Mitchell, to help you control your impulsivity," Anne answered, holding her hand in the same position.

"I'm all set," Mitch said.

"Mitchell," Anne said, sporting the same scornful look, "if you don't take this pill, I will have to notify Dr. Brady, and as you just learned, he doesn't take too much BS from anyone. So please, Mitchell, if you don't want to be in isolation again, please take your medicine."

Mitch stood motionless for a second, thinking about the Chamber. He knew he didn't want to go back there. With some hesitation, Mitch took the pill, put it in his mouth, and followed it with a quick gulp of water. He turned to walk out the door but was stopped by Anne.

"Hold on, Mitchell. I need to check," she said. "Open your mouth and stick out your tongue."

Mitch opened his mouth and stuck out his tongue, as ordered, to show that he had swallowed his pill.

"Thank you, honey."

"You're welcome," Mitch replied as he walked out the door and took his place in line, waiting to return to his room.

The routine after seeing the nurse was the same as waiting to see her. Everyone faced forward and did not look to the left or to the right. They marched quietly and without confrontation in fear of being disciplined. Mitch played the game and headed back to his room silently.

He found his way to the chair in the corner of the room, while Turtle sought the comfort and security of his bed, the top bunk. Mitch listened intently until he determined that Felix wasn't directly outside his door.

Mitch sat in the chair, waiting until the time was right. Quietly, he stuck his finger down his throat and gagged, underneath a towel so no one could hear. Again, he gagged, and finally, after the third time, he stopped.

He reached into his mouth and removed the red pill the nurse, Anne, had given him. He remembered the words in his dream: *They will poison your mind. Don't let them poison your mind. They will use you to feed their own demons.*

Mitch Blais did not intend to have his mind poisoned.

22

The recreation room at Sherman Point was one of the few places that inmates could feel even the slightest sense of freedom. Many kids wasted days away playing video games, Ping-Pong, or pool, and sitting around talking under the ever-watchful eyes of the Sherman Point guards. Boys and girls were in class and in group therapy together, but the rec room was one of the few places they could freely interact. According to Dr. Brady, this was an important part of their reintegration into society. Some of the more adventurous souls even attempted contact with the opposite sex in hopes of a mutual attraction.

"Four o'clock!" a girl yelled from the television area. Four o'clock in the rec room at Sherman Point was nothing less than a ritual. At four o'clock, the television was turned to the *Dr. Bob Show*. The show featured the most terribly troubled people in the country in a one-hour spectacle that highlighted their downfalls into misery and despair. The show had taken on a life on of its own. Without planning, everyone except the most depressively isolated stopped to watch the show and engage in the controlled chanting of "Dr. Bob, Dr. Bob!" that mimicked the live student audience's response to the outrageous and sometimes vicious brawls that broke out on stage. Even the staff of Sherman Point came in and watched the humorous spectacle. Never was there an issue or a confrontation when the *Dr. Bob Show* was on. For an hour a day, the incarcerated youth of Sherman Point could look at others and actually feel sorry for them. It was quite empowering.

Mitch sat alone in the back, watching the chaos on the television set, and wondering why those people were willing to humiliate themselves on TV.

"Anyone sitting here?" Cassandra asked, motioning toward a vacant seat.

"No, help yourself," Mitch replied, looking Cassandra over. She was an extremely pretty girl, but not in a supermodel kind of way. There was an unspoken confidence in her movements that Mitch found appealing.

"Thanks."

Mitch continued to explore Cassandra's physique with his eyes. She was toned, and her body had the feminine muscularity of an athlete. She was different from the girls he was used to dating. She possessed a self-assurance that clearly indicated that she was comfortable with who she was. She didn't hide behind makeup, and Mitch thought she would be a knockout in just about anything she wore. Mitch suddenly realized that he was becoming aroused.

"Not getting a front-row seat for the show?" Mitch asked, while he covertly continued visually discovering Cassandra.

"I've seen this one before," Cassandra explained. "This is the episode where the guys explain to their fiancées that they still love them and want to marry them, but they have in fact been sleeping with the girls' mommas."

"No."

"That's right. Then the mommas come out…look," Cassandra said, pointing to the TV just as the moms came out of Dr. Bob's dressing room to tell their daughters about their taboo betrayals. A frenzy exploded in the rec room. The kids sprang to their feet and started chanting, "Dr. Bob, Dr. Bob!"

"This show is crazy. Do you think it's real?" Mitch said.

"Who knows? Life can sometimes get really crazy."

"You better believe it."

"Is it true?" Cassandra asked.

"Is what true?"

"They say you're in here because you killed your probation officer."

"No," Mitch said, somewhat aggravated, "and I'm gonna prove that I didn't do it."

"Well, I don't know. You look like you could've done it," Cassandra said, eyeing Mitch up and down. "Yeah, you look like you could've done it."

"What's that mean?"

"It means what it means."

"Really."

"Well, you seem to be nasty enough to do something like that."

"Nasty enough?" Mitch shifted in his chair, becoming increasingly annoyed. Now everyone thought he was a killer—even girls he didn't know.

"Yeah, nasty enough. You were a jerk to Sameer in group for no reason."

"I've got a reason."

"What's that?"

"He could be a terrorist."

"And you could be a murderer," Cassandra said with attitude in her tone.

Mitch thought about that for a minute, and then dismissed the comment.

"Well, I'll tell you what," Cassandra said, defiance continuing to grow in her voice, "I've known Sameer for over a year, and he's chill. I trust him, and I don't trust many people. He's got my back. He's got all our backs. You don't believe that bullshit you were throwing around in group the other day, do you?"

"What bullshit?"

"The bullshit about Sameer flying planes into buildings, pressure-cooker bombs, and all that sleeper-cell nonsense."

Mitch thought Cassandra had no idea what she was talking about. She was blind like the rest of them and didn't understand what was happening to this country. She didn't realize that there was a war playing itself out daily, and people like Sameer and his family were involved.

"You come in here like your shit doesn't stink, attacking my friend. You think you're special? You're an accused murderer, Mitch, but you want everyone to believe you're innocent because you say so."

"I am innocent."

"Says you."

"That's right."

"So we should all just believe you. Sameer said he wasn't a terrorist, so why don't you just believe him?"

"That's different."

"The only thing that's different, Mitch, is that Sameer isn't accused of killing someone. You are."

Cassandra and Mitch looked at each other for several seconds without speaking. Mitch felt himself getting angry being challenged by this girl who didn't even know him or know that his father died because of people like Sameer. The uneasiness was temporarily interrupted by the collective chant of "Dr. Bob, Dr. Bob!" as the inmates exploded into the ceremonial appreciation of the misfortunes of others.

"Sameer is no terrorist, Mitch."

"You don't know that."

"Yeah, I do. He was born and raised in America, just like us. He may be a Muslim, but he's no terrorist."

"How do you know that?"

"The same way that I know you're an asshole!" Cassandra said as she rose from her chair. She looked down at Mitch. "Like I said, Mitch, you're the only accused murderer in our group, so if anything, we should all be protecting ourselves from you."

Mitch watched as Cassandra stormed toward the rec room exit. He was annoyed with her, but at the same time, impressed. She had a confidence that Mitch found attractive. She was direct, and it didn't seem like she was hiding behind something or trying to be someone she wasn't. He didn't like her words, but Mitch heard them and appreciated that she had the courage to say them. He watched Cassandra stride out of the rec room, taking in every one of her movements. He found himself becoming further aroused by Cassandra.

23

With the slide of a thumb, the cell phone screen displayed the incoming text message:

There seems to be another package in need of delivering.

The hand quickly replied:

Thought all packages sent already?

The hand waited, knowing an explanation would be sent.

Seems some information leaked and the package must be delivered to keep the project alive. Understand?

The hand rapidly punched letters, knowing full well what needed to be done.

Understood...send mailing information as usual.

The hand closed the cell phone and sat idle for several moments. Suddenly, with clear decisiveness, the hand grabbed a red backpack and placed it on the glass coffee table. With a clean, crisp motion, the hand unzipped the bag, plunging itself deep inside. A brief search ensued, and within seconds, the hand pulled a black ski mask from the bag. The hand held the mask for several seconds and then folded it and returned it to the bag.

Cassandra looked around the room with great hesitation. She knew today was the day she would bring up her past in group therapy. It was inevitable. Both Dr. Brady and Dr. Cav had told her that this was a major part of her treatment and that trusting the group was the first step in trusting people, in general, again. Her stomach turned with anticipation. She felt slightly sick.

"Cassandra," Dr. Cav began in a reassuring and supportive voice, "we are all here for you, and you can trust us. We want to help you get healthier, and by talking about the past, we can help you with your future."

Cassandra continued to muster up the courage to speak. She trusted Dr. Cav and the group. She didn't trust Mitch.

"Go on, honey, we're here for you," Tina said.

Cassandra felt a lump form in her throat as the pain of her past resurfaced. Tears slowly filled her eyes.

"My mom used to disappear for days to do drugs," she began tentatively, as a daze came over her face. She seemed to be making herself numb to the pain. "And one day, she never came home. Some people came to my house and told me my mom had died of a drug overdose, and I'd be going to live with a new family. Just like that, my world was flipped upside down. I was only ten years old." Cassandra paused, looking ahead at nothing in particular, as if the past was coming alive again. "Ronnie and Nicole were my new foster parents. They had a nice home and a cat—Sebastian. They were really kind at first, and I trusted them. I really loved being with them, until things changed."

The others began to see a change in Cassandra's demeanor. She paused to wipe her tears away. An unfamiliar agitation surfaced in her voice.

Cassandra looked up from the ground to find a sympathetic and attentive audience. "Nicole was super nice and caring, and Ronnie, he put on a good show for her when she wasn't at work. He played daddy real nice until Nicole left," Cassandra said, her tone further changing from one of sadness to anger.

"Ronnie used to love bath time. He would say, 'It's time to wash away our sins.' I'll never forget those words—it's time to wash away our sins," Cassandra paused, the pain of the words stinging as though it happened yesterday. "The first time, I didn't know what was happening as he led me into the bathroom, but once we were in there, things were never the same again. He…he began touching me, and I was just young and didn't know what was happening. I wanted my mommy, but she wasn't there for me. Why wasn't she there? Your mom is supposed to protect you from evil, but when evil showed up, my mom wasn't there to keep me safe. She was dead because she chose drugs over me."

The room was silent. All eyes were on Cassandra. Mitch listened intently, feeling awkward but somewhat thankful that Cassandra would actually bring something like this up in front of him after the way he acted in group the other day.

Tears began to well up in her eyes again, and she stopped to wipe them away. Dr. Cav intervened, "You're doing a great job. Do you want to take a break to gather yourself?"

Without a response, Cassandra continued. "Why wasn't my mom there to help? Adults are supposed to protect little kids, but she was gone." A pause followed and Cassandra again collected her thoughts. "At first Ronnie just touched me in the bath. Then he made me touch him. Then, after he perfected his routine, he began raping me."

No one spoke. Everyone realized the severity of what Cassandra was saying. Mitch sat quietly. He began to feel a great sense of empathy for Cassandra. He felt like he could relate to her in different ways. He wanted to help her somehow.

"After a while, I would run when Ronnie told me it was bath time. I'd run all over the house, and he'd chase me. He seemed to like it, like it was getting him excited. He'd chase me around with a big smile on his face, saying those words over and over, 'It's time to wash away our sins.' Eventually, he'd catch me and bring me up to the bathtub. He hurt me so bad!"

Tears covered Cassandra's face now, and Dr. Cav handed her a box of tissues. "Here you go, Cassandra. Take your time. You're doing great. You're in a safe place, and you can trust us. We're here to help you."

Cassandra again wiped the tears away as she sat up in her chair in an effort to remain strong. "As I got older, I began to fight back and tried to fight him off, but this only made it worse. When I would fight him, he would hold me down under the water in the bathtub until I couldn't breathe. That sick bastard would bring me up just enough to allow me to get a slight breath, and then he'd push me under again. I remember…I remember thinking I'm gonna drown here, right now, and then everything would turn pitch black. The darkness came and I thought it was over. Then, when I came around, I knew I wasn't dead because he was raping me. That's when I realized I wanted to be dead. To this day, I still can't take a bath. I can't go swimming. I swear that he'll be waiting for me in the water, just waiting to hold me under again."

Cassandra stopped and stared straight ahead.

Tina sat sobbing, also wiping tears from her eyes.

Turtle didn't dare look at Cassandra, unsure how to react to the story.

Both Sameer and Mitch looked at Cassandra, trying to think of what to say to her.

Dr. Cav gave everyone a minute before he began talking. "Thank you, Cassandra, for trusting us, for letting us in so we can help you. I'm sorry for what happened to you, and you need to know that it is not your fault. People can be terrible, especially when they betray our trust. Trust is the most important thing in a relationship, and you have to believe that you can move forward with life and trust people again as long as you keep talking and getting healthier."

The group listened intently to Dr. Cav, everyone looking at Cassandra to make sure she was OK.

"Trust," Dr. Cav continued, "is a hard thing to build between two people, and once someone betrays your trust, it's hard to trust anyone again. But Cassandra, you can trust us, and I think you know that now. Look at me, Cassandra," Dr. Cav said in a nurturing and caring voice.

Cassandra lifted her eyes to meet the eyes of Dr. Cav. His green eyes seemed soft and genuine to Cassandra. They invited her to trust him and to let down the walls that protected her emotionally for so many years. They were the eyes of a protector, a paternal figure who ensured that she would be safe, even in the darkest of hours. Cassandra felt an unspoken security, like that of a vulnerable child in the protection of her family.

Dr. Cav continued, "You can trust me. You can trust us. We are here for you, and I promise we will never do anything to hurt you. You're safe with us, and I promise that I will do everything I can to help you. Does anyone have anything they would like to say to Cassandra?"

Turtle squirmed, intimidated by the thought of speaking up.

"Cassandra, girl," Tina said, breaking the silence, "if you want to talk, you know, woman to woman, I'm always here for you."

"Thank you, Tina."

"Yeah, Cassandra, we're all family here, and you can tell us anything," Sameer said. "We're not gonna let anyone hurt you anymore. One thing I've learned from treatment is that you have to leave the past behind and move forward. I hope you know I'll always be your friend, and you can always count on me."

"I know, Sameer. You've always been a good friend. Thank you."

"What about you, Mitch? Do you have anything to say to Cassandra?" Dr. Cav asked.

Sameer shot Mitch a scornful look, indicating that if he said something offensive to Cassandra, he would have to answer to him.

Cassandra sat in silence. She was uninterested in what Mitch had to say. She would be just as happy if Mitch said nothing at all, but she knew getting feedback from others in group was part of the process.

Mitch felt like an outsider. This strange collection of people had come together to form a community that reached out to one another, seeking and receiving support and reassurance in an otherwise cruel world. He sat in the middle of this community, but couldn't have been more of an outsider. He wanted them to understand who he was deep in his heart. They should know that he was a good and caring person who helped protect others. He hadn't killed anyone, but they didn't know that. They only knew what they were told. They didn't trust him, just as he didn't trust Sameer. But they were wrong about him. Mitch began to wonder if he was wrong about Sameer.

Mitch cleared his throat. "I thought a lot about what you said to me the other day, about me expecting people to believe that I didn't kill my probation officer just because I said so."

The others looked around, confused, unsure of what Mitch was talking about.

"You were right. You have no reason to trust me," Mitch said looking at each member of the group. "No one here has any reason to believe me, because I haven't earned anyone's trust."

Cassandra looked confused, wondering where Mitch was going with this.

"I'm sorry that you were hurt and I'm sorry that it's hard for you to trust people. Shit, it's hard for me to trust people too," Mitch said, looking directly at Sameer. "I had things that happened in my life too that changed me forever, so I can relate to that. I guess I just want you to know that the things you just said, well, you can trust that…I guess I'm saying that you can trust that I wouldn't say or do anything to hurt you."

The group paused, surprised by this unexpected but welcome side of Mitch.

Turtle looked up from the floor and focused directly on Mitch.

"I know I have some work to do myself and maybe I've been wrong about some stuff," Mitch continued, searching for the right words, "but if everyone just gives me a chance, you'll see that you can trust me too."

The room was silent.

Cassandra looked at Mitch and simply said, "Thank you."

25

Mitch casually walked through the door of Mr. Conklin's history class, looking in the direction of the students assembled in neatly arranged rows. He immediately noticed Sameer and Cassandra.

"All right, class, find your seats. Let's get going here," Mr. Conklin said.

Mitch walked down the aisle, and Sameer flashed him a confrontational look when he passed him. The words Mitch had said were still fresh in Sameer's mind, and he was seething with anger. The tension was evident. Sameer did not like Mitch.

Mitch had always done well in history class, especially when the discussion turned to American military campaigns. He looked around and met Cassandra's eyes. Her expressionless glance left Mitch wondering where he stood with her.

"Class, we're continuing our studies of World War II," Mr. Conklin said, "specifically, the mobilization of the home front during the war."

Mitch listened as Mr. Conklin continued his lecture that was supplemented with videos on the white board. Mitch found himself looking around the small, cinder-block classroom. It was much smaller than his classes at Central High were and it came with two guards outside the door. Mitch diverted his attention from the video of Japanese Americans being placed in internment camps during the war. He looked at the kids in the class. He began to wonder if they all thought he was a murderer.

Mr. Conklin continued his lecture, and Mitch again found himself watching the images on the board. Mr. Conklin froze the video on a grainy, black-and-white image of a Japanese American family standing behind barbed wire. "And this is one of the great atrocities of American history," Mr. Conklin said, pointing at the board with a yardstick. "The United States government authorized the confinement of Japanese Americans in internment camps during the war. This was a clear violation of their constitutional rights as American citizens."

Mitch found himself looking at the picture of the imprisoned Japanese Americans. He stared at the image of a little girl being held by her mom behind the fencing. It seemed sad, Mitch thought, that the little girl appeared devoid of any happiness.

"What does this picture say to you?" Mr. Conklin asked. "Look at these people. Was it fair what our country did to them?"

"Hey you," a guy with thick glasses, greasy hair, and a pockmarked face two rows over said softly to Mitch.

"Me?" Mitch asked, looking around.

"Mitchell," Mr. Conklin interrupted, "did you have a comment to make about the image we are analyzing?"

"No."

"Come on, Mitchell. You're not getting off that easy. Was it fair?"

"No."

"Why not?"

"The little girl."

Everyone turned and looked in Mitch's direction.

"What about the little girl?"

"She looks sad, like someone has taken something away from her," Mitch said, remembering the sadness he felt when his dad was taken away from him.

"What do you think was taken away from her?"

"Her childhood," Mitch continued. "I mean, she's only a kid. Did people really think she was gonna hurt someone?"

"Well, Mitch, many people assumed that Japanese Americans were going to help Japan during World War II."

Mitch listened.

"Our country made many assumptions based on these people's heritage, when they were in fact American citizens. We violated their rights out of fear, not logic."

Mitch absorbed Mr. Conklin's words while the class continued. The greasy-haired kid again got his attention. "Yeah, you're the guy accused of killing Rooney."

"I didn't kill anyone."

"Is there a problem, gentlemen?" Mr. Conklin said from the front of the class, again confronting the two.

"No sir," the greasy-haired kid replied. He waited for Conklin to turn back to the white board. "Here," he said, as he threw Mitch a note. It landed on his desk just seconds before Conklin turned around, still looking inquisitively at the two students.

Mitch covered the note with his hand and waited for Conklin to turn back to the video. When the time was right, he quickly opened the note and read it. In shaky handwriting, the note read:

I have information that you're not guilty.

Saturday 4 PM in the rec room look for me.

Mitch's heart raced, and he wanted to talk to the kid now, but he knew that would not be possible. He looked at the kid, who simply kept adjusting his glasses and looking forward without acknowledging Mitch again. Mitch took the note and began covertly ripping it into small pieces beneath the desk. Who was this kid and what did he know? Mitch wondered. He again focused his attention on Mr. Conklin, who continued his lecture.

"So as you can see, ladies and gentlemen, our lack of understanding and fear of those who are different from us led to the mistreatment of Japanese Americans during World War II. Of course, history has since taught us not to—if you will forgive the cliché—judge a book by its cover," Mr. Conklin said, only to be interrupted by the bell.

Kids rose to their feet and gathered their materials, obediently waiting for instructions from the guards to transition to their next class. Mitch immediately positioned himself in line so he and the greasy-haired kid would reach the door at the same time. The boy kept his head down as Mitch reached him.

"What's your name?" Mitch asked.

The boy did not acknowledge Mitch and continued heading for the door.

"Come on, man, what do you know?" Mitch asked.

"It's dangerous," the boy said, looking around nervously as the two exited into the hallway.

"What's dangerous?" Mitch asked, grabbing the kid's arm to stop him.

The greasy-haired kid looked down the hall, only to find the ever-watchful eyes of Dr. Brady upon him. With a sudden jolt, he nervously pulled his arm away from Mitch, diverting his gaze away from Brady. "It's dangerous!"

Dr. Brady's eyes followed the two down the hall. The greasy-haired kid put as much distance between Mitch and himself as possible. Brady watched, attempting to discern what their conversation had entailed. He stroked his beard and mumbled under his breath, "What do we have here?"

26

Mitch Blais sat in the far back corner of the rec room, one eye fixed on the entrance. He waited for the greasy-haired kid with the thick glasses. *What does he know?* Mitch asked himself. Clearly, whatever it was would help to prove Mitch's innocence, and he was anxious to talk to him. But what was dangerous? Why would proving that he was innocent be dangerous to anyone? Mitch sat and waited, unanswered questions swirling around in his head.

The rec room was filled with kids engaging in adolescent activities. The same predictable group gathered around the television, anticipating the *Dr. Bob Show,* excited to revel in the misfortunes of others. Another group of kids played pool, while yet others sat around playing video games. Isolated individuals dotted the recreation room, some reading while others sat talking to themselves. Mitch wondered how he had ended up in a place like Sherman Point.

Mitch grew impatient. Maybe he wasn't coming. Maybe it was, in fact, dangerous and something had happened to the greasy-haired kid. Mitch was beginning to wonder what the hell was going on. He continued waiting, his mind racing with thoughts of his impending court case. He thought of Charlie and Grandma Jackie.

Mitch looked around and saw Cassandra and Tina sitting at a table, talking. He liked Cassandra. She was feisty and certainly wasn't afraid to say what was on her mind. No games or bullshit, like he had dealt with in the past with other girls. He liked Cassandra's directness, but she thought he was an asshole. She had said so right to his face. He respected that.

A voice rang out from behind Mitch. "You know that I was just a small kid when the World Trade Center was attacked on 9/11."

Mitch spun around, caught off guard, to find Sameer standing over his shoulder, "What?"

"The World Trade Center," Sameer said, looking sternly into Mitch's eyes. "I was just a kid."

"Big deal."

"Big deal?" Sameer said, making his way around to the front of the table opposite Mitch. "You were saying some shit in group about people like me that bomb buildings, killing innocent Americans, and sleeper cells and some other bullshit."

"Yeah, well my father was in the war and he taught me to never trust a Muslim."

"Oh, that's right. I heard that. Your father was some sort of war hero or something."

"That's right."

"Well, killed in the war or not, he was wrong."

Mitch felt the anger boiling over inside at those words. He did everything he could to keep from jumping up and popping Sameer in the nose.

Sameer took half a step forward, "My family is from Pakistan, and we're not terrorists. Shit, I was born in Cambridge, Massachusetts."

"What?"

"Cambridge, Massachusetts," Sameer continued. "My father's a professor of Middle Eastern studies at Harvard."

"So what," Mitch said.

"So what?" Sameer said, clearly becoming increasingly annoyed. "So before you go around calling people terrorists, you should know what the hell you're talking about. I'm as much an American citizen as you are. I'm not locked up in here for being a terrorist. I'm in here for beating the shit out of a guy for hitting a girl I know in the face."

Mitch looked at the passion in Sameer's eyes. He thought back to what Cassandra had said about Sameer being her friend. He thought about what his dad had told him about never trusting Muslims. The Japanese girl from the history video flashed in his mind. Confusion set in as Mitch tried to sort out all the information he had been fed. He kept gazing toward the entrance for the greasy-haired kid.

"I hear you're telling people that you didn't kill your probation officer."

"I didn't."

"Oh yeah? We all think you did."

Mitch stared at Sameer, the anger mounting inside of him. "Go to hell, man. You don't know shit."

"What I do know is that it makes you feel like shit when someone accuses you of something you didn't do. Doesn't it?"

The two looked at one another. Mitch absorbed the words Sameer had just said. Sameer was right. Mitch did feel lousy when people said he killed Rooney. He knew he didn't, but everyone was treating him as if he was a killer. It wasn't fair.

"Before you cast stones at others," Sameer said, pointing a finger at Mitch, "you damn well better take a good, long, hard look at yourself in the mirror."

Mitch wasn't sure what to say to Sameer. The guy was making some sense. Words were about to leave Mitch's mouth when out of the corner of his eye, he saw the greasy-haired kid enter the room. He rose to his feet, Sameer taking a half step back in response. "I've gotta go, man," Mitch said as he walked away from Sameer.

"You gotta go. Just like that," Sameer said, watching Mitch walk toward the door. "This isn't over."

Mitch was glad to see the greasy-haired kid and quickly made his way over to him. *This could be what I need to prove my innocence and shut everyone up about me being a killer,* he thought. A sense of excitement rose within Mitch as he sat next to the kid at a round table positioned against the wall.

"Hey," the greasy-haired kid said.

"Tell me what you know," Mitch said.

"Shit, I never wanted to hear it," the kid said, looking around to make sure no one was listening.

"Hear what?"

"Rooney was my PO too, you know. I heard him arguing with Dr. Brady two days before he was killed," he said nervously, removing his glasses and cleaning them.

"Rooney worked here?"

"Yeah, he did. And I heard him and Dr. Brady arguing, and then poof—he's dead."

"What did you hear?"

The greasy-haired kid stopped talking and looked straight ahead as a guard walked by, looking down at the two as he passed them. He continued his trek around the rec room.

"Shit," the greasy-haired kid said.

"Come on, man. What did you hear?"

"I heard Dr. Brady saying something like, 'You don't know what you're talking about' and that Rooney should be careful saying such things," he said, stopping and looking around as if someone was listening. "Then I heard Rooney say a name."

"What name?"

"Christie Lambert," the greasy-haired kid said.

Mitch stopped and thought. What did a missing girl who ended up dead have to do with him? "It doesn't make sense," Mitch said.

"He told Dr. Brady that three girls had some things in common and that he had proof they were kidnapped. Some documents or some shit."

"Three girls? Kidnapped?"

"The three girls that disappeared," the greasy-haired kid said, and then stopped abruptly in midsentence. "I gotta go, man. It's dangerous," he said, as he jumped up and turned from the table, looking over at Felix, who was barreling toward him. "Check the names."

"Check the names?" Mitch repeated.

Then it was too late. Felix approached Mitch at the table where the boys had been sitting. He stood, hovering over Mitch so he was unable to rise from his chair. "What was that all about?" Felix asked, keeping an eye on the greasy-haired kid, who was now walking to the other side of the rec room.

"What was what?"

"Listen, asshole, don't mess with me. I don't care who they say you killed. Mess with me and you'll find yourself in deep shit. You got it?" Felix said, puffing his chest out in a show of authority.

"Yes sir," Mitch said, raising his hand to his forehead and saluting Felix.

Felix leaned forward, placing his face within inches of Mitch's. "You're a real wise ass, aren't you Blais?" he said, his spit spraying Mitch in the face. "Well, I'm watching you."

"OK then," Mitch said, as Felix leaned backward and adjusted his pants around his protruding stomach. He turned and walked away.

Mitch watched Felix head back to his assigned post. *Check the names? The three girls?* he said to himself. *Documents? What documents?* Mitch thought back to the day at school with Rooney. Rooney had been nervous and kept looking out the window as if he was scared. Then he ended up dead. Check the names? Then it came to Mitch in a jolt of recognition. He sprang up from the table. "Holy shit, I need to call Charlie!"

27

Afternoon basketball at the outside court on Saturday was a social event at Sherman Point. Players were divided into teams as equally as possible, and those who didn't play cheered and mingled. The air was crisp, and the trees around the court wore the yellow and red leaves of a New England autumn.

Mitch ran down the court, watching the game with one eye and gazing in Cassandra's direction with the other. She looked good, and there was no denying it. Mitch was attracted to her, but he was confused about how to approach her to tell her. He'd never had trouble talking to girls in the past, but Cassandra was different, and he knew it. He also knew that she wasn't his biggest fan.

The game came down to the last basket. Mitch's team was playing against Sameer's team, and the score was tied at eighteen points.

"Next basket takes it," Sameer yelled. He pushed the ball down the court in Mitch's direction. Mitch stepped up aggressively to defend against Sameer, and Sameer passed the ball to one of his teammates. With a burst of speed, Sameer passed Mitch and ran toward the basket as his teammate threw the ball back to him. In one fluid motion, both Mitch and Sameer jumped to get the pass. Mitch stretched his body as much as he could, but the ball slipped past his fingers and landed in Sameer's hands. As the ball reached Sameer's palms, his body collided with Mitch's—but not until Sameer was able to roll the ball off his fingers and into the hoop. The two players bounced off one another and plummeted to the ground with simultaneous thumps.

Everyone around the court jumped up to see the spectacle. Supporters of the winning team were yelling, and everyone's eyes were fixed on the two players below the net, their bodies scraped up from landing on the cement.

Mitch was the first to bounce up, bleeding slightly from his arm. He looked around, confused, and then realized that his team had just lost.

"What the hell, man!" Sameer protested, his head still foggy from smashing it on the concrete.

All eyes were glued to the two in anticipation of a fight. Their brief history of not getting along had spread through the campus like wildfire, and onlookers were ready for some of the best entertainment they'd had in a long time.

Mitch walked over and stood above Sameer, who was still on the ground, his head throbbing from the contact it had made with the court.

"What the hell, man, take it easy," Sameer protested, preparing to retaliate against Mitch.

To Sameer's surprise, Mitch extended his hand in an offer to help Sameer off the ground. Neither spoke, but everyone in attendance witnessed the sportsmanlike gesture. The two walked in different directions toward their respective teams.

Mitch headed off the court, wiping the blood from his arm. He slowly looked over in the direction of Cassandra, who flashed him a tentative smile. She was impressed with his gesture of respect toward Sameer. Mitch smiled back and felt a strange feeling inside him. It felt like the first time he kissed a girl. It was a nervous and exciting emotion all wrapped up in uncertainty. It was at this point that Mitch realized that he was falling hard for Cassandra.

"Hey look, the blue van!" someone suddenly yelled from the crowd.

The blue van from the courthouse usually meant one thing—new residents had been sent to Sherman Point from the bench of Judge Jeremiah Butler. Everyone watched as Felix rolled out of the driver's seat and waddled to the back of the van with the two Doberman Pinschers—Damian and Deuce. Both dogs barked viciously until Felix silenced them with a backhand across their snouts. "Shut up, you stupid mutts," Felix commanded.

Everyone on the court waited with great anticipation to see the newest residents of Sherman Point. As far as entertainment was concerned, the arrival of new inmates was right up there. First, a small, frail-looking kid exited the van, looking around nervously.

"Down here, shit for brains," Felix barked, pointing to a spot behind the van.

"OK, yes sir," the kid said, following every order.

"You too, tough guy," Felix yelled into the back of the van. "Get your dumb ass out here. Now."

The second new inmate stepped out of the back of the van with a smile fixed upon his face. He inhaled deeply, looking around at his new home.

"Get down here," Felix said.

The large, bulky guy stepped off the back of the van and turned toward the basketball court, revealing a burn mark on the left side of his face. The smile he was sporting instantly disappeared when he saw Mitch Blais.

“Holy shit,” was all that Mitch said as his eyes met those of the newest inmate at Sherman Point: Steve Grabowski.

28

The greasy-haired kid shoved the mop back into the bucket, wrung it out, and then plopped it back on the floor, repeating the same back-and-forth motion, just as he was taught. The chore of mopping up the cafeteria after dinner had been his for three months now. It had become routine. He methodically repeated the back-and-forth motion as always, but tonight something was different. Tonight he found himself looking over his shoulder a little more often.

The chore was solitary, to be sure. The greasy-haired kid had become accustomed to being left alone in the cafeteria. After all, he was a trusted inmate who never caused any problems. *Why would anybody want to bother with me?* he thought.

He had information for the new kid who was accused of killing his PO. He was doing the right thing. He didn't know the new kid, but the guy shouldn't go to jail for something he didn't do. He wished he hadn't overheard what he had, but how could anyone possibly know what he heard? *I'm being crazy,* he thought. *Thinking too much when really I should be focused on the floors.* "Stay focused," he said to himself under his breath. Anyhow, what was the big deal? As soon as he could, he would tell the new guy everything else he knew. But first, he had to finish the floors, just as they had taught him to do.

The floors really shone nicely under the overhead lights, the greasy-haired kid thought. He did the same routine over and over, and each morning the staff would tell him how nice the floors looked. He was proud of his work and was really staying on rhythm—back and forth, back and forth. He looked around and realized he was more than halfway done. This made the greasy-haired kid happy.

Suddenly, the sound of a door clicking closed across the cafeteria caught his attention. The mop stopped involuntarily, and the kid stood motionless, listening.

"Hello," he said across the room. "Anyone there?"

No reply was forthcoming. *Damn, I'm getting paranoid*, he thought as a nervous grin flashed across his lips.

He continued mopping his way back toward the stairwell, just as they taught him. Taking a reprieve, the greasy-haired kid stopped and removed his glasses. He cleaned the lenses on the bottom of his T-shirt and then held them up to the fluorescent lights to check for spots. None. *Another good job done*, he thought. He placed his glasses on the bridge of his nose and listened for any unfamiliar sounds.

Nothing.

The floors sure sparkle again tonight, he thought, looking at the bright luster, when suddenly the lights snapped off and everything went black. His heart raced while his other senses heightened. The greasy-haired kid waited several seconds without moving a muscle. Slowly, his eyes adjusted to the darkness. He could see the exit signs powered by the generator, and he knew the electrical box was in the utility closet where he got the mop and bucket. He'd simply make his way back there and check the box to see if a circuit had popped. *Simple*, he thought.

The night was oddly quiet as he made his way toward the utility closet. Deliberately, the greasy-haired kid placed one foot in front of the other, looking as far ahead as possible and listening intently. *There, what was that*? he thought. The greasy-haired kid swore he heard the distinctive sound of footsteps scurrying across the floor. "Bobby, is that you?" he said, hoping for a response from a friend.

Nothing.

Picking up his pace, he headed directly for the utility closet and opened the door. Tripping over several bottles of cleaning fluid, he made his way to the electrical box, opened it, and frantically began popping circuits. Then, with a great sense of relief, he saw the lights in the stairwell power back up. Letting out a long, heavy breath, he turned away from the electrical box to make his way back to the cafeteria to finish his job.

Unexpectedly, out of the corner of his eye, the greasy-haired kid noticed a black flash reveal itself from behind a large stack of boxes. The black object jumped straight for his head, knocking him backward over a trash can and into a wet wash bucket on the floor. Mops fell on top of him from all directions. Scrambling, he threw the mops aside and prepared to take flight. He looked to see who his assailant was, and with relieved laughter, he saw a black cat hissing as it ran out of the utility closet.

"You really need to relax," he said to himself. He pulled himself up and replaced the mops in their original positions. Water dripped from his backside.

The greasy-haired kid headed out of the closet and into the stairwell, alleviated of his fear as he realized that he was being paranoid about a cat. *That's funny*, he thought as he closed the closet door, water continuing to drip off his pants, onto the floor. Firmly, as they had taught him, he secured the latch on the door and turned toward the cafeteria.

It took a second for the image to come into full focus—the outline of a man standing between him and the door to the cafeteria, a black ski mask concealing his identity.

Panic shot through the greasy-haired kid, and with overwhelming trepidation, he turned and raced up the stairs, quickly looking back to see if he was being pursued. The man in the black ski mask took off after him, running swiftly until his feet hit a wet spot, causing him to slip and slam his head on the floor.

The greasy-haired kid kept ascending the staircase until he reached the top floor. Approaching a door, he threw all his weight into it, forcing it open; his forward momentum propelling him onto the surface of the building's roof. He stopped briefly to listen, and heard the sounds of footsteps running up the staircase.

Sweat poured down the greasy-haired kid's forehead and his glasses began to fog up. The night air was cold and his breath was visible with each desperate exhale. He scrambled to his feet, looking at all four sides of the roof. No plan came to mind.

Running to the edge of the roof, he cautiously looked over the side. A queasy feeling overtook his stomach when he realized it was at least a fifty-foot drop. *Think! Come up with something*! he thought. With nowhere to go, the greasy-haired kid spun around, thinking he could head back to the stairwell, but it was too late. In the doorway stood the figure of the man, a black ski mask hiding all except a pair of angry eyes.

Realizing his prey was trapped, the man in the black ski mask slowly made his way toward the boy without saying a word.

"What do you want?" the greasy-haired kid pleaded. "I didn't do anything!"

No reply from the man in the black ski mask, who continued in the direction of the greasy-haired kid.

"Please, no," he said, slowly walking backward. He continued backpedaling until he realized he was at edge of the roof. Looking back over his shoulder, fear engulfed him. He knew that there was nowhere to go.

The figure now stood two feet from the greasy-haired kid. The silence of the night air was only broken by the terrified pleas of the kid. "I didn't say nothing. Please don't," he said, looking down at his shoes, only to see urine running out of the bottom of his pant leg. "Please don't."

The man in the black ski mask reached up and placed his hand on the shoulder of the greasy-haired kid. Then, with no more than a slight shove, the hand pushed backward on his shoulder.

In an effort to save his life, the greasy-haired kid reached out and grabbed the black ski mask with his right hand. As the boy fell backward, the man in the black ski mask felt his head jerk forward, the boy's momentum pulling him downward. At the last second, the greasy-haired kid lost his grip on the ski mask and he plummeted toward the ground.

A panicked scream escaped the mouth of the greasy-haired kid, only to be terminated by a vicious encounter with the ground. The man on the roof picked himself up and adjusted his black ski mask. He looked over the side of the building and saw the greasy-haired kid lying awkwardly on the ground, his body contorted in an unnatural position.

"That will teach you to eavesdrop on other people's conversations," the man in the black ski mask said. He turned and walked toward the stairs, a sinister laugh filling the night air.

29

The cell phone beeped just once, and the hand knew what question was coming:

Did the package get delivered?

The hand began pecking out the response, sure they would be happy.

Yes. Without a return address.

The hand gripped the cell phone, waiting for confirmation response.

Good. We have talked and it would be best if we put our project on hold. There are too many interested parties out there now.

The hand replied:

Agreed.

Several seconds later, a response came.

And what of the lost papers that link all the packages? Have they been secured?

The hand trembled slightly, knowing the answer would not be agreeable.

Not sure.

A nervous minute passed as the hand waited.

This is not good. These packages must not be linked, or else.

The communications ended. The hand put the cell phone down on the table.

30

The group therapy session was solemn after the news of the suicide of Myles Harwich—the greasy-haired kid. Mitch sat off to the side, not willing to talk about the events that took place the day before his death. What was the kid trying to tell him? He knew there was a link between Rooney and the missing girls, but what was it and how did it relate to him? Mitch sat in confused disbelief as he tried to piece together what had happened. One thing that the greasy-haired kid said was certain—it's dangerous. Mitch knew exactly how dangerous it was now and he knew the greasy-haired kid didn't commit suicide.

"Well guys, we all know what we need to talk about today," Dr. Cav said, looking at the blank faces in the room. Cassandra sat motionless next to Sameer, as the two stared forward at Dr. Cav. "Although Myles wasn't part of our group, he was certainly part of our larger community. Does anyone have any thoughts?"

Suicide, my ass, Mitch thought. But no way would he share that thought, knowing what had happened to Myles Harwich when he opened his mouth. He looked around the room. Turtle was paralyzed with silence, the oversized chair seeming to swallow him. Tina curled up in a ball in her chair. Makeup ran down her face, the tears falling freely.

"Anyone?" Dr. Cav probed, again looking for participation.

"At least he had the balls to do it and do it right," Tina said as she looked at her wrists, where scars revealed her past efforts at ending her life. She shifted in her seat and looked around at each member of the group. "That's right, take a look," she said, holding her wrists up for everyone to examine. "Maybe next time I'll get it right."

Mitch looked at her wrists and felt a lump develop in his throat about his own secrets, yet to be revealed.

"I tried but I screwed it up—like I screw everything up," Tina continued, wiping mascara-blackened tears on her hospital gown. "That's why they keep such a close eye on me. Because they know I'll do it."

Turtle looked at Dr. Cav, shaking, as Tina continued crying and talking.

"Best thing he could have done. Now all his problems are behind him," she said, her eyes swelling from the unstoppable tears.

"Suicide is never the answer, Tina," Dr. Cav said, walking a box of tissues over to her.

"Yeah, Tina," Cassandra said, joining the conversation. "Think about how many people would miss you if you died."

"Shit, no one would miss me if I killed myself. Who? My parents? They're happy I'm in this shit hole now so I can't bother them. They'd be happier if I were dead."

"I'd miss you," Cassandra said, trying to reassure Tina that she had people who cared about her. "Who'd make me laugh every day?"

"That's right," Sameer said, clearing his throat slightly. "You're one of the funniest people I know, Tina. Why would you say such a thing?"

"Because it's true. My parents would hold a party if I died. They'd be so happy that they'd invite everyone. They would never even miss me."

"That's not true," Mitch interjected from the other side of the room. Everyone turned toward him, surprised he had something to offer on the topic.

"What the hell do you know about it?" Tina asked.

"Mitch, do you have something to add?" Dr. Cav asked, excited to see Mitch participating more openly in the group therapy sessions.

"You don't think people will miss you because of the pain you're in, but they will, believe me. Whether you know it or not."

Cassandra looked at Mitch, interested in what he had to say. She was happy to see him speaking so freely and participating. She was curious. "Why do you say that, Mitch?"

"Yeah, Mitch, what makes you such an expert?" Tina added.

Mitch's face got red, and his mouth went dry. He wasn't sure why he was going to say what he was about to, but he thought it could help Tina in some way. He'd never talked about this with anyone. Not Charlie, not Grandma Jackie. No one. He looked around, his uneasiness growing. He felt sweat developing under his arms. He took a deep breath. "I know because I miss my dad."

"Come on, man, not more of this war hero, hate Muslims shit," Sameer said. "We all know your father was killed in the war."

"The war killed my father all right," Mitch said, looking back at Sameer.

"Easy, guys. Let's focus on Tina and not our own differences," Dr. Cav said. "Do you have anything else to say to Tina, Mitch?"

"Yeah," Mitch said, hesitating slightly to collect his thoughts. "I'm just saying, Tina, that you may not think people care, and then bam, you're gone. Just like that and it affects everyone around you. I would do anything to have my dad back, but that will never happen, and every day I wish he was here."

"Bullshit," Tina said, tears rolling down her cheeks. "No one would care and everyone would be better off."

"Not me," Cassandra said. "I'd miss our time talking about boys and what we're gonna do when we get out of here. You don't want to give up on that, do you?"

"Me too," Turtle said, surprising the group.

Cassandra looked in Mitch's direction. She could detect a sense of pain in his words. She could see it in his face. A long silence filled the room until Cassandra spoke up. "Mitch, you told me to trust you before, now it's time to start trusting us."

Mitch slowly raised his head and looked at Cassandra. The genuine warmth in her words and the sincerity in her eyes made Mitch feel welcomed. It made him feel safe and part of their small community.

"My dad," Mitch began, a lump instantly forming in his throat, "my dad was my hero and he was a good man." The words barley made it to his lips, causing him to take a deep breath and pause.

The group looked at one another, confused, as they tried to make sense of what Mitch was saying. Finally, Sameer spoke up. "Yo, Mitch, you know we're all sorry that your dad was killed in the war, but you can't hate every Muslim because of that."

Mitch sat silently for a second and then mustered the courage to speak. Tears filled his eyes. He swallowed hard. "I never said that my father was killed in the war, I said the war killed my father."

The room fell silent.

"What do you mean, Mitch?" Cassandra said in a soft voice, encouraging Mitch to say more. "I thought he died in Afghanistan."

"Go on, Mitch," Dr. Cav said. "You're in a safe place here, and we're here to help. You can trust us."

"Yeah, Mitch, what are you talking about?" Tina asked, still sobbing.

Mitch looked at Turtle, who looked blankly back at him. "My dad used to come home from the war when I was young," Mitch began. "He'd show up at school in his uniform and surprise me. I'd show him off to all my friends. He was a superhero to me, larger than life, like something out of an action movie. He was the biggest, strongest man on the planet—a war hero. Everything was fine until he came home the last time, and the changes happened."

"What changes, Mitch?" Dr. Cav pressed.

"Yeah, changes. I always looked forward to my dad coming home. He would take me on great adventures fishing and camping, and we worked on junk cars together," Mitch said, taking the time to clear his throat. "But the last time he came home, he was a different person."

"How, Mitch?" Dr. Cav said.

Mitch looked around and saw everyone looking in his direction. He was going to stop, then he saw the reassuring look in Cassandra's eyes. He wanted to trust her. He wanted her to know she could trust him.

"Mitch, we want to help you. It's OK," Cassandra said with the softness in her voice that Mitch had come to appreciate. Mitch took a deep breath and closed his eyes.

"Go ahead, Mitch," Cassandra said one more time, hoping he would share with the group.

"The last time my dad came home, he was different. He didn't smile and he would sit for hours drinking beers and just staring at nothing—like he could see something in front of him that no one else could. Anytime we went out to the store or anywhere with people, he would get jumpy and he'd start yelling and swearing. I didn't understand why he was different. My Grandma Jackie told me that he suffered from post-traumatic stress disorder because of what he saw in the war. She said he just needed time and it would be OK. I waited and waited, but my dad never came back to me. His body was with me, but his mind was somewhere else." Mitch stopped and opened his eyes, realizing what he was saying. He had never spoken about his dad to anyone before. He felt unsure.

"Go ahead," Turtle said, again surprising everyone in the group.

"He just got quieter and quieter," Mitch said, closing his eyes again. "He would sit me on his lap and not say anything for a long time, then he would rub my hair and say, 'They did this to me, son,' and then he would cry and tell me he was sorry. I had never seen my dad cry until that moment and I knew then that he was a different person."

"Who did what to him, Mitch?" Tina asked, seemingly more interested in what Mitch had to say than in her own pressing, emotional issues.

"My dad always told me never to trust a Muslim. My *hero* told me never to trust a Muslim," Mitch said, hesitating slightly and looking at Sameer.

Sameer simply looked away, knowing that saying something back wouldn't help anything.

"He told me that his best friend was killed in Afghanistan by an Afghan police officer the U.S. military was training. They were training these people so they could have a better life. They were there to help these people. They trusted them until one day the Afghan guy opens up on his so called 'friends' and kills a whole bunch of US Marines. He killed my dad's best friend. My dad's best friend died in his arms. Later, I learned they call this a blue-on-green attack," Mitch said, hesitating and looking down, searching for words. Without looking up, he said, "This is why I don't trust you, Sameer."

Sameer said nothing as he listened to Mitch.

"He served in Iraq and Afghanistan and when he came back, he was never the same. Then, about six months after he returned for the last time, I came home from school and my Grandma Jackie was waiting for me. I could see she had been crying, and right away, I knew something was wrong. She held me so tight and told me that my dad was gone. He had killed himself that morning, and I would be living with her now. It felt like someone had ripped my heart out of my chest, and I never cried so hard and long in my life. My dad was my hero and now he was gone."

A stunned silence filled the room. Tears welled up in Cassandra's eyes as she suddenly realized that Mitch, too, had been living with a painful past that had shaped his life and his beliefs. Like her, deep, down inside, in a protected place, he still existed as a small child, unable to process the raw emotions that held him back from becoming his own, autonomous person. Bottled up deep inside, the pain had lingered and shaped his life. No longer did she see him as an insensitive thug. He was a person who needed help and guidance, as everyone else did, to navigate a confusing and challenging world that had been shaped by the actions and opinions of people who came before him. A compassionate attraction to Mitch came over Cassandra; she was proud of him for opening up his heart to the group.

Dr. Cav looked with a kind eye at Mitch and simply said, "I'm sorry."

Mitch held back his tears as he tried to regain his composure. "My life changed forever that day, and I swore then that I would someday join the military and get back at those people that took my hero from me. I swore that I would never trust a Muslim—any Muslim. I'm not really sure what that means anymore."

Sameer sat up in his chair. "Mitch, I'm really sorry about your dad. I mean it. That shit's just messed up. He fought against Muslims, but not Muslims like me. There are radical Muslims that take our holy book, the

Koran, and use it for their own evil purposes," Sameer continued, convinced he could help Mitch understand. "The religion of Islam is one of peace. There is a saying that whoever solves someone else's problem, Allah will make things easy for him in this world and the hereafter…Allah is ever assisting his servant as long as that servant is helping his brother. I don't want to hurt anyone, but if I see my brother in distress, I will help him. I'm not as religious as my parents are, but that is the religion I know. It's not about killing Americans and sleeper cells and all that other shit, and it is not that way for the majority of Muslims. Some people are good and some people are bad. It doesn't matter about their religion or skin color. What matters is what's inside."

Mitch sat speechless, trying to accept the depths of his ignorance. "My dad was not a bad man," he said, hoping to convince everyone. "He was my hero." That was all he could manage.

"No one is saying that your dad was a bad man, Mitch," Dr. Cav said, breaking the silence. "He served in a war zone and saw terrible things—things that caused his PTSD—and maybe if he had gotten some help things would have been different."

"Maybe."

"Yeah, Mitch," Cassandra said, wiping the tears from her eyes. "I've told you some heavy things about me and trusting people, but we have to move forward and think for ourselves. You know, make our own lives. One thing I've learned here is that we can't live in the past or else we won't grow. It isn't easy, but I'm starting to trust again and let people into my heart," she said, smiling in Mitch's direction.

"That's funny," Mitch said.

"What's funny?"

"About letting people into your heart. Not too long ago, someone told me you must open your heart and the goodness within will be seen by all."

"That's great advice, Mitch. Who told you that?" Dr. Cav asked.

"Just an old friend," Mitch said with slight smirk, thinking about the vision of Therese Harriet Coleman.

Tina got up and walked across the room, wiping the last of the tears from her face. She made her way over to Mitch and leaned over, giving him a soft kiss on the cheek. "Thanks, Mitch. Thanks for listening and sharing."

"Thanks for trusting us," Cassandra added.

Mitch had no response to offer. He was glad that he helped Tina, and it felt good to talk about his dad. It was the first time he had talked about his dad with anyone. He felt better. He looked over at Cassandra, who gave him a warm smile.

Mitch thought about the things Sameer had said to him. He was no longer sure of whom to blame for his dad's death. Maybe it was the Muslims' fault. Maybe it was no one's fault. He wasn't sure, and he knew he didn't have all the answers. The one thing he did know for sure—and he wasn't going to talk to anyone about it—was the fact that the greasy-haired kid told him that it was dangerous, and now the greasy-haired kid was dead. He was dead, and Mitch knew it wasn't suicide. It truly was getting dangerous.

31

Robin Clarkson turned the government-issued police vehicle into the entrance of Sherman Point and came to a stop at the security booth. Annoyed that the guard didn't automatically open the gate upon noticing the police car, she pressed the button to lower her window and didn't offer any words to him.

"Can I help you?" the guard asked, looking down into the vehicle.

Clarkson held her police badge up without further explanation.

After a symbolic scrutiny of the badge, the guard said, "OK, ma'am," and the gate went up. Clarkson pressed the accelerator and sped through the opened gate.

Robin Clarkson took her job seriously and prided herself on doing the best investigative work possible. Being a police officer had been her only goal in life, and when the opportunity came to join the military as an MP after her high school graduation, she jumped at the chance. She was a good soldier—above average, according to her evaluations. After two tours in Afghanistan, she found herself taking the civil service exam back home and applying to the police department. The brass jumped at the chance to hire a woman with military experience, and neither they nor Robin Clarkson had any regrets.

A suicide at Sherman Point was not completely out of the ordinary. Clarkson had investigated several before, and they had all been routine. As a prison for offenders with mental health issues, escape attempts, assaults, and the occasional suicide were not uncommon. As far as Clarkson was concerned, the majority of the inmates here got what they deserved. Mental health issues or not, the law was something that everyone had to abide by, and when people didn't, they got what was coming to them.

Clarkson made her way into the reception area and again flashed her badge, indicating she had the universal pass to go anywhere she wanted to go. As the receptionist instructed, she sat on a couch and opened her leather file folder to review the particulars of the case. After several minutes of waiting, she walked back up to the receptionist, wearing an impatient expression.

"Excuse me," she said to the young receptionist, who was watching television on a small, portable TV, "how much longer will Dr. Cavanaugh be?"

"Not long at all," a man's voice said from behind Clarkson. "I'm sorry to keep you waiting, Detective Clarkson. I'm Dr. Paul Cavanaugh." He extended a hand to Clarkson.

"Nice to meet you, Dr. Cavanaugh. Can we get started?" Clarkson said exchanging a firm handshake with him.

"Yes, of course. Please come into my office."

Clarkson's investigative intuition took over when she sat in Dr. Cavanaugh's modest office. She surveyed the room and noticed many pictures of kids hiking, playing at water parks, and in group photos, all with Dr. Cavanaugh in the middle. "Interesting," Clarkson said as she finished her informal inspection.

"What's interesting?" Dr. Cavanaugh asked.

"All these kids in the pictures. They're all out in public."

"That's right," Cavanaugh said.

"Shouldn't they all be in behind bars—away from anyone they can harm?" Clarkson said.

Dr. Cavanaugh looked at her curiously, wondering where she was going with this. "Well, as the chief therapist on the adolescent unit, it's my determination that teenagers need to get accustomed to the demands and expectations of society. What better way to do that then to supervise them on trips in public?"

Clarkson continued to look around the room, searching for anything that might spark her inquisitive intuition. She turned her attention back to Dr. Cavanaugh. "Doesn't it make more sense to let them serve hard time and suffer for the crimes they've committed? Wouldn't that stop them from repeating their mistakes?"

"Detective Clarkson," Cavanaugh said, adjusting himself in his seat, "research has shown us that the rate of recidivism drops considerably when adolescents are treated with respect and given the opportunity to be exposed to society rather than locked away and alienated."

"Tell that to their victims," Clarkson said.

"We also teach the residents of Sherman Point to have empathy for their victims—"

Clarkson cut him off midsentence. "Let's take a look at your safety record, since we're on the topic, Dr. Cavanaugh." She pulled a document from her leather-bound file folder. "Correct me if I'm wrong, but in the last year, you've had several escapes from Sherman Point, the most recent ending in the tragic death of a Christie Lambert." Clarkson paused, looked up at Cavanaugh, and then immediately back down to her notes. "And now, just weeks after Ms. Lambert's death, a Myles Harwich does a swan dive off one of your buildings. Not a very good record. Wouldn't you agree?"

Dr. Cavanaugh felt his pulse begin to pound. “Detective Clarkson, we are a staff-secured facility here at Sherman Point, not a federal prison. We have a secure front gate with guards, and each of the dormitories housing the residents is under twenty-four-hour lock. Kids aren’t housed in cages, but share dormitory rooms with others. Due to budget cuts, we have limited resources and we do the best we can with what we have.”

“How’s that working out for you, Dr. Cavanaugh? Maybe if you folks here took the crimes of these kids more seriously, and you were a little more attentive to security, you wouldn’t have such issues.”

“Detective Clarkson,” Dr. Cavanaugh said, inhaling a deep breath in an effort to remain calm, “we have many adolescents here with some serious mental-health issues.”

“Yeah, I know.”

“May I finish, Detective Clarkson?” Cavanaugh said, increasing his volume to indicate that he was a professional and had a right to be heard.

“Certainly,” Clarkson said.

“We have teenagers here with many issues that are out of their control. Besides having some mental health issues, many of our residents have suffered terrible abuse, both physical and psychological. Much of their behavior stems from these abuses, and much of it has been learned in the environments in which they grew up. If a kid sees his father abuse his mother daily while growing up, what do you think the chances are that that kid will grow up to abuse his spouse? Our job is to break that cycle and teach new behaviors. We don’t just lock these kids up and hope for the best when they get out.”

Clarkson listened intently to Dr. Cavanaugh, wondering if all the doctors at Sherman Point were bleeding hearts as he was. She had been a cop for years and she knew that criminals needed to be behind bars and made to suffer, but arguing with this guy would be a waste of her time. She decided to move on. “In the matter of the boy that jumped off the roof, Myles Harwich. Can I take a look at his file and see where the crime took place?”

“Crime?” Dr. Cavanaugh said, a surprised look coming over his face.

“Oh, I’m sorry. Force of habit. May I see the building he jumped off of?”

“Of course. I’d be happy to help in any way I can,” Dr. Cavanaugh said as he stood up, motioning toward the door.

Dr. Cavanaugh led Detective Clarkson across the campus of the adolescent unit of Sherman Point. She looked skeptically at the kids walking to-and-fro in the early autumn air under the watchful eyes of the guards. *Rent-a-cops,* she thought. *Under-qualified rejects who couldn't make it on a real police force. No wonder kids escaped from this place.* Cavanaugh continued to lead her to the building that housed the cafeteria. The two entered and ascended the staircase to the roof.

Clarkson walked the perimeter of the roof, notebook in hand, jotting down notes. She leaned over, above the spot where the body had been discovered. "Did Myles Harwich leave a suicide note, Dr. Cavanaugh?" Clarkson asked.

"No."

"No? Do you find that strange?"

"Sometimes it's difficult to tell what kids are thinking," Dr. Cavanaugh explained. "In this case, the stressors of life just caught up with him, I guess."

"Interesting," Clarkson said, as she continued to examine the roof. "And the official report said that this kid was mopping the floor in the cafeteria, finished more than half the job, took a break, walked up to the roof, and decided to jump off of it."

"In less dramatic terms, but yes, that is what the report says."

"Does that make sense? Why mop any of the floor if you plan on doing yourself?" Clarkson said, writing something on her small pad. "Why not just come up and do it?"

"I'm afraid the only one that could answer that is Myles Harwich."

"Maybe, but he can't tell us what happened, can he."

"Unfortunately no," Dr. Cavanaugh agreed.

"May we look on the ground now?" Clarkson asked. As she turned toward the door with Dr. Cavanaugh, her attention was diverted by something on the ledge. Squatting down to get a better look, Clarkson noticed several small, black threads. "Interesting," she said, as she extracted a plastic bag and a small pair of tweezers from her inside coat pocket. Picking the threads up with the tweezers, she neatly placed them in the plastic evidence bag, and then turned and followed Dr. Cavanaugh, who was already making his way down the stairs.

32

The visiting room at Sherman Point was not somewhere Charlie wanted to be. He had never been inside any type of prison before, and he found the strictness of the guards intimidating. He made his way to the first checkpoint, knowing he was doing something he probably shouldn't. His hands trembled with fear.

He never asked Mitch why he wanted him to go to Grandma Jackie's house and go through his dirty laundry, but he did it because he trusted Mitch. Mitch had gotten him out of countless jams, and now that his buddy was in trouble, he was going to do what he could for him. He didn't even ask Mitch why when Mitch told him that for his own safety, he shouldn't look at the paper that he was retrieving from Mitch's jeans pocket. He only knew that Mitch said it could help prove that he was innocent, but it could be dangerous. "It's not safe," is what Mitch told him. Safe or not, Mitch had always helped Charlie in the past, and now his buddy needed him.

"Hold it right there," a guard said, holding his hand up to stop Charlie from proceeding. "Take off your belt and shoes and lean against the wall and spread your legs."

Charlie complied and thought for a second that they were onto him and he was being arrested. He stood motionless, hands against the wall, his feet spread apart. The guard took a metal detector and ran it up and down his arms and then up and down his legs, lightly touching his crouch. Charlie flinched in fear. The metal detector briefly touched his crouch exactly where he had concealed the paper in his underwear. He felt awkward and stood waiting in the same position for what seemed like an eternity.

"OK, here's your shoes and belt," the guard said, as he jotted information on his clipboard. "No embracing, no touching, nothing passed across the table. You stay on one side; the inmate stays on the other. No food, no gifts, no electronic devices. Understood?"

Charlie nodded.

"Good. You have one half hour. Any questions?" the guard said.

"No sir."

"Good, open door six to the visiting area."

"Opening door six," a voice rang out from a control area.

With that, door six opened, revealing the visiting room to Charlie. The room was devoid of anything decorative except signs that spelled out the rules that the guard had just reviewed with him. Rows of tables stretched across the entire room. Inmates sat in their standard blue pants and white T-shirts talking to friends and loved ones, who sat on the opposite sides of the tables. In each corner of the room, guards were perched about four feet off the floor on platforms in order to scrutinize all of the activity that took place. Charlie began to think that this was a really bad idea, and he wondered how he was going to get the paper to Mitch.

Charlie waited as a guard approached him. "Inmate's name?"

"Excuse me?"

"The inmate you are visiting. Does he have a name?" the guard said, slowing his speech in a mocking manner.

"Mitchell Blais," Charlie said, his hands shaking as he thought once again that this was a terrible idea.

"Blais," the guard yelled to another guard on the platform. "Let's go. Follow me."

The guard led Charlie to an empty table, "Sit here," he said, pointing to a vacant chair. Charlie complied with the command and sat. He waited for several minutes. He looked around the room at the other inmates and felt like he shouldn't be there. Two tables over, a girl with black hair sat talking to a guy. She didn't wear the blue pants and white T-shirt like everyone else. Instead, she wore a white hospital gown. Charlie's eyes caught hers and when she noticed, she winked at Charlie. Immediately a flood of embarrassment came over him and he looked away, lowering his head.

"Charlie, my boy," Mitch said in a playful tone. A guard directed him to the seat by pushing down on his shoulders.

"Mitch, man, it's great to see you. How are you?" Charlie asked.

"Doing great, Charlie. How about yourself?"

"I'm OK. Everyone's asking for you. Your grandma wanted to make sure I said hi and tell you she loves you. She said she just can't come down and see you in a place like this."

"I know," Mitch said, wondering how embarrassed Grandma Jackie must be, explaining to everyone why he's here. "Charlie, tell her I love her and I'm gonna prove that I didn't do it."

"I know you didn't, Mitch."

Mitch looked around, making sure no guards were in range, and then asked, "Did you get the paper?"

"Yeah, but how am I going to get it to you, Mitch?" Charlie said, looking around at all the guards.

"Don't worry, Charlie," Mitch said. He looked two tables over at Tina, who was wearing the white hospital gown. "It's all taken care of…three, two, one…"

"You son of a bitch!" Tina yelled across the table at the guy to whom she was talking. "I'll kill you!" she said, as she catapulted across the table, sending it, the chairs, and the guy to the floor.

"Code blue in the visiting room," a guard yelled into the phone. The screeching noise of a siren filled the air, and all the guards in the room converged on the chaotic scene. Charlie sat horrified, trying to figure out what was going on.

Tina continued to scream as she slapped the guy on the floor below her, "You cheating son of a bitch, I'll kill you!"

Mitch looked calmly across the table at Charlie as the bedlam unfolded around them. "Now would be a good time for you to throw that paper under the table," Mitch said.

It took a moment for Charlie to comprehend what was going on. He bent forward slightly to conceal his midsection and then he reached swiftly into his underwear, extracting the folded paper and throwing it on the ground.

Additional guards swarmed through the doors, grabbing Tina, trying to restrain her arms. The mass of bodies moved in the direction of Charlie and Mitch, slamming into their table, throwing it askew, and revealing the paper on the floor. Instinctively, Mitch dropped to the ground feigning being mauled by the group. Falling directly on the paper, he curled up in the fetal position and shoved the paper into his pants.

"All visitors out!" a voice boomed over the intercom. "And all inmates against the wall!" By now, the room was filled with guards and doctors. Charlie stood up and obediently headed for the exit. A guard grabbed Mitch and ushered him to the wall.

As the mayhem subsided, Tina was raised to her feet and handcuffed. Guards were on both sides of her. Charlie looked at her. Her hair stood up in all directions and her white hospital gown was ripped on the side. Charlie looked directly into her eyes. She looked intensely crazed as she stared back at Charlie. Then, with a crooked grin, she again winked at Charlie. At that moment, Charlie knew his friend, Mitch Blais, was responsible for all this chaos.

33

Going to the county morgue was the least favorite aspect of Robin Clarkson's job. Death was something she saw a lot of when she was in the war, so she tried to avoid trips to the morgue at all cost. But something wasn't sitting right about the suicide of this kid at Sherman Point. Whether it was police intuition or her woman's intuition, something was off. With the autopsy completed that morning, she knew the chief medical examiner would have some insight into the cause of death, and she was interested in getting his input.

"He jumped from a building, Robin," Dr. Victor Radcliffe said as he reread his notes from the morning. The two had worked before on various cases, and Dr. Radcliffe had an unspoken appreciation and a clear attraction to Clarkson.

"That's it? Something seems fishy about it," Clarkson said.

"Fishy? I'm not sure what else you're looking for. The kid was an inmate in an adolescent facility for offenders. He had enough and he jumped," Radcliffe said, scratching the top of his bald head and taking a long swig of his energy drink.

Victor Radcliffe was the type of guy who belonged in a morgue with dead people. His social ineptness was evident in all interactions he had with the living—especially women. He was creepy, to say the least, but Clarkson had worked with him for a long time. The two had developed a playful relationship accented by mutual professional respect. Victor Radcliffe knew where the line was with Robin Clarkson, and he constantly tried to cross it in hopes that she would someday give in to his awkward advances. Admiring her well-maintained physique, Radcliffe inquired, "By the way, are you still swimming all the time?"

"What? Yeah, I still swim," Clarkson replied, quickly dismissing the comment and getting back to the business at hand. "Did you look for any defensive wounds?"

"Defensive wounds? Robin, the kid jumped. And guess what the cause of death was?" Radcliffe said, waiting in vain for a response. "Going splat on the ground." Radcliffe smiled, displaying a sense of humor reserved for those who work with dead bodies all day.

"No shit, Victor. Can I look at the body?" Clarkson asked, knowing this would mean retrieving the remains and there would be a cost for such a request.

"See the body? Come on, Robin, the kid jumped."

"Victor, let me see the body. Five minutes and I'm out of here."

"Dinner," Radcliffe said.

Clarkson paused for a moment, knowing that no romantic future existed for her and a guy who lived on caffeine and sugar and spent the majority of his time with dead people. "I'll tell you what, Victor, you let me look at the body, and if I don't find anything, then it's dinner."

"Sounds good," Dr. Radcliffe said, knowing there wasn't anything to find.

"I'm not done," Clarkson continued. "If I find what I'm looking for, then the deal's off."

"Fine," Radcliffe said.

Radcliffe and Clarkson made their way through double doors into a room housing about a half-dozen bodies. Immediately, an uneasy feeling came over Clarkson. It was the same uneasiness that she experienced every time she was in the vicinity of multiple dead bodies. She hesitated slightly as the two walked to the end of the room where Myles Harwich's body was housed.

"What's the matter, Robin? You've seen dead bodies before," Radcliffe said, pausing to give Clarkson a second.

"I know. It's the smell," she said.

"Remind you of Afghanistan?" Radcliffe asked, knowing that Clarkson was a combat veteran.

It had been a number of years since she served in a combat zone, but for Robin Clarkson, it was the smell that always brought the memories back. After seeing the death and destruction she had seen, she'd made a promise to herself to devote her life to doing good and helping others in need. This journey had led her directly to the police force after her service to her country.

Clarkson took a second to get acclimated to the odor and then she continued to the body bag holding Myles Harwich of Sherman Point. "I just need to see the hands, Victor, if you would."

Dr. Radcliffe extracted the left hand from the bag and exposed it for examination. Pulling latex gloves onto her hands, Clarkson gingerly took the hand and turned it over to expose the palm. Taking a surgical instrument from the nearby table, she began scraping methodically under each fingernail.

"Anything?" Radcliffe asked.

Clarkson finished the last fingernail, disappointed that nothing turned up. "Nope," she said.

"Well, I'm thinking Italian food—or wait a minute, maybe you're more of a Chinese-food girl," Radcliffe said, giving a jovial laugh. "All in favor, raise your hand." Radcliffe put his hand in the air and grabbed the lifeless hand of Myles Harwich, raising it in the air also.

"Very funny. Can I see the other hand?" Clarkson asked.

"Come on, Robin. What is it you're looking for, anyway?"

"I'll let you know when I find it."

Radcliffe reached into the bag, this time pulling the right hand out. "We can always do takeout at my place," Radcliffe said, while he watched Clarkson perform the same scraping routine under the fingernails. "You know, I make a mean omelet and—"

"Bingo!" Clarkson said interrupting Radcliffe in midsentence.

"Bingo?" Radcliffe said, looking at Clarkson and wondering what she could possibly have found.

"I guess I'll have to take a rain check, Victor," Clarkson said as she held a pair of tweezers up to the lights and examined the contents secured between them. Dr. Radcliffe moved in closer to see what she was looking at, and the two stood for a moment, staring at a small piece of black fiber that matched the black fiber she had found on the ledge. "Something isn't right at Sherman Point," Clarkson said as she hustled for the exit, kissing Dr. Radcliffe on the cheek as she passed him. "And I plan to find out what it is."

Bringing all the kids together for a night of fun at the Oktoberfest Dance was something new to Sherman Point since the arrival of Dr. Brady. He said it was part of his innovative approach to rehabilitative treatment that emphasized practicing appropriate social interactions prior to being released back into society. Although many of his staff balked at the practice, Dr. Brady simply dismissed their arguments as coming from those with less education than he had. For those incarcerated at Sherman Point, it was the only chance to have physical contact, albeit supervised, with the opposite sex.

The guards at Sherman Point enjoyed the dance more than the inmates did. The one stipulation that Dr. Brady conceded to was their request to have additional personnel working to help supervise the activity. For the guards, led by Felix, whose decision-making was questionable, this didn't mean increased scrutiny and monitoring of those in their charge. Rather, the increased personnel level meant they could take a more lax approach to their duties, including consuming a homemade concoction of various liquors that Felix smuggled in and called "jungle juice." Needless to say, several hours into the evening, the guards were more concerned with their own selfish endeavors than with the safety and security of Sherman Point.

Turtle and Mitch sat in the far corner of the rec room, watching the mingling taking place in front of them. Turtle was made nervous by the size of the crowd, but took some comfort in knowing that Mitch was nearby.

"Come on, Turtle, let's go dance with some honeys!" Mitch said enthusiastically, allowing his body to move to the beat of the music blaring from the speakers.

"No."

"Come on, Turtle, we got to get you a lady friend to loosen you up a bit."

"I'm loose."

Mitch looked out to the dance floor, noticing Sameer dancing with a cute blonde girl from the female unit. The two moved in beat with the music, smiles permanently affixed to their faces. They seemed to be caught up in the moment, just being teenagers.

Cassandra walked through the door with a group of girls who all looked ready to take on the night. Their hair and makeup were perfect. They might as well have been walking into a New York City nightclub.

Mitch stopped in his tracks and followed Cassandra with his eyes as she made her way across the room, stopping periodically to interact and laugh with others. *She's tight*, Mitch thought. *A beautiful body with long, perfectly proportioned legs.* Her body took a back seat to the natural beauty of her face. Delicate, soft lips accentuated her light-brown skin. Mitch wanted to touch her. He wanted to kiss her.

But there was more. Something Mitch hadn't found in other girls. Within Cassandra, there existed a kindness and an obvious concern for others that superseded her own personal wants and needs. She was available for everyone and offered up friendship and support to all those who would accept it. She expected nothing in return; it was simply her purity of heart that made her so genuine. Yet she was suffering too with her own demons from the past. They didn't define her or encompass her whole being, but they lingered and they affected her. Mitch wanted to be there for her. To listen to her. To hold her when she felt empty and alone.

Cassandra made her way over to Mitch and Turtle. "Hey, Turtle."

"Hey."

Cassandra looked at Mitch. "You wanna dance?"

"I thought you'd never ask," Mitch said, extending his hand to Cassandra. The two walked onto the dance floor and found an open spot next to Sameer and the blonde girl.

The music dictated the tempo. Mitch moved around Cassandra, watching her body gyrate perfectly with the music. She glided on the floor gracefully, as if she was a trained Broadway dancer, but with a hint of raw sexuality in every movement. The flashing lights created a surreal atmosphere, offering up a new view for the senses with each passing second. The pounding of the bass through the speakers increased the dancers' intensity. Mitch and Cassandra moved in perfect harmony, their movements hard and unscripted. They continued back and forth, their heightened heart rates matched only by the heaviness of their breathing. The song approached its end, and a collective yell of satisfaction resonated from the crowd when the music climaxed and stopped on one last, hard note.

A mellow glow fell upon the room as the lights were lowered in preparation for the slow song that followed. No words were spoken. Mitch simply pulled Cassandra into him and the two moved softly. Their heart rates slowed back to normal, easing them into an unforeseen comfort that felt natural to both. Mitch was consumed by his thoughts. He had opened up his heart to Cassandra, shared things with her. He wanted to tell her more and to be there for her.

He touched the side of her face. The two looked deep into one another's eyes. He wanted to be closer—together. Cassandra did not protest his advances. Warmth engulfed Mitch and a euphoric peacefulness came over him. He put his hands on her neck softly, but with enough authority that she understood that he wanted her, longed to touch her, to hold her, to feel her heart. He wanted her to trust him. He wanted to promise that he would never hurt her.

Arousal filled Mitch's being as he explored Cassandra's neck, caressing her with his hands. Mitch trusted her, felt safe with her, and wanted her close. He pulled her waist into his with a gentle intensity. She didn't resist. Mitch felt the small of her back, further excitement building with each passing moment.

He wanted her to be his girl, and he hoped she felt the same way. On impulse, Mitch pulled Cassandra's lips to his. She didn't resist. The two met with a mutually passionate aggression that answered Mitch's questions. As their lips touched, their lustful appetites continued to grow. Cassandra's moans of acceptance filled Mitch's ears. He could hear a sound from her lips that was barely recognizable as words. He wasn't sure, but then he heard it again.

"I want you, Mitch," Cassandra whispered in his ear. "I will never give up on you."

Mitch felt an elation come over him that words couldn't describe. His heart pumped with excitement, and without hesitation, the words flowed from his lips. "I'm here for you, Cassandra. You can always trust me."

Their lips found each other again in a natural unity, and from that moment on their souls became one.

35

Turtle sat at his desk drawing a picture of Sherman Point to add to the collection on his wall. He did not acknowledge Mitch. It was peculiar, Mitch thought, but the only thing that seemed to interest Turtle was Sherman Point itself. The kid seemed strangely obsessed with the facility, and he spent hours drawing maps and pictures of the very place that kept him imprisoned.

The two sat in silence, as they often did, until Mitch asked a question or made a comment. It seemed to Mitch that Turtle would be happy remaining silent and never talking to anyone. Mitch wondered what it would be like to live in the quiet.

Mitch looked out the door to see if the guards were making their rounds. To his satisfaction, the hallway was clear, so he reached deep into his mattress, through the small slit he had made in the fabric, and pulled out the piece of paper Charlie had brought to him. He unfolded it to find three names written in pen:

Kathy Hurley
Tanya Gomes
Christie Lambert

Mitch looked at the names, only recognizing the last one—Christie Lambert, the girl who was hit by a car after running away from Sherman Point. The other two didn't sound familiar.

"Hey, Turtle, do the names Kathy Hurly and Tanya Gomes mean anything to you?" Mitch asked, not expecting much of a reply.

"Yes," Turtle said, not looking up from his rendition of Sherman Point.

"Well?" Mitch said.

"Well what?"

"Who are the two girls?" Mitch asked.

Turtle stopped and put down the pencil he was using. Spinning his chair around, he looked in Mitch's direction. "Kathy Hurley was admitted two years ago on December 15. She was a foster child and was charged with breaking and entering into a store when she ran from her foster family. She denied doing it. She served two years, took off sometimes to see her boyfriend, but always came back. Two months before she was to be released, she escaped and ran away. No one ever heard from her again."

Mitch's mouth hung open. He was amazed at how much Turtle had just said and the facts about Kathy Hurley he possessed. Turtle sounded like a talking version of Wikipedia. It was the most Mitch had ever heard him say at one time—if not in one day. Mitch was about to say something, but didn't get a chance.

"Tanya Gomes," Turtle continued, "not here as long as the other one, only eight months. Admitted a little over a year ago. She was also a foster kid and was arrested for causing trouble and running away from her foster parents. She was sentenced to three years but took off after eight months. She wasn't such a model prisoner. She had three major infractions on her record—assaulting a guard, smuggling in food, and telling Dr. Brady to go you-know-what himself. She escaped too, and I don't think anyone ever heard from her again." Turtle turned back to his drawing.

Mitch was astounded. "Turtle, how do you know all this stuff?"

"Just do."

"Just do? Just like that?" Mitch said.

"They say I have a photographic memory."

"Photographic memory?" Mitch said. "Like you see something one time and just remember it?"

"I guess," Turtle said. "I just remember stuff."

"Who told you that you have a photographic memory?"

"The same people that say I have autism."

Mitch continued to stare at Turtle in amazement. He wondered how this guy could know all this information, and he began to realize that he didn't know a thing about his roommate. "Turtle, why are you here?" Mitch asked.

Again, Turtle didn't look up from his illustration. In a barely audible voice, he muttered, "I have autism."

"Autism?"

"Have you heard of it?" Turtle asked.

"Well, yeah, I've heard of autism, but they don't lock people up for having autism," Mitch said with some confusion. "What did you do to get here?"

"Where, this room?" Turtle asked, his voice devoid of expression.

"No, Turtle, Sherman Point," Mitch said.

"They put me in Sherman Point for bringing a knife to school," Turtle said.

"A knife?" Mitch said, unable to imagine Turtle trying to hurt anyone. "Why would you bring a knife to school?"

"To stop the bullying," Turtle said.

"Did you use it?" Mitch asked, his curiosity piqued.

"No, they found it and sent me here."

"Would you have used it?"

Turtle didn't offer a response, and Mitch decided to infuse a little humor into the situation.

"Hey, Turtle, am I safe?" Mitch asked, remembering his first conversation with Turtle.

"Safe?"

"Yeah. Am I safe?" Mitch continued. "After all, I'm in here with a guy that carries knives around. Am I safe?"

Turtle turned in his chair, confused by what Mitch was saying; unable to understand that he was being facetious. He looked directly into Mitch's eyes and said, "You don't pick on me. You're nice to me."

"OK, so I'm safe?" Mitch said again, this time with a slight smile on his face.

"Yes. We're both safe," Turtle said, offering a rare smile.

Mitch laughed, happy to share a lighter moment with Turtle. He liked his roommate and wondered what kind of jerk someone would have to be to pick on him. He was impressed with the amount of hidden information Turtle had in his brain. He decided to press for more. "What about the three girls that escaped, how do you think they did it?"

Turtle stopped and turned toward Mitch. Getting up from his chair, he went to the door and looked to see if any guards were coming. When he was sure they were alone, he went back to his chair and sat down. "I don't know how they escaped, but it's easy."

"Easy?" Mitch said looking at Turtle, wondering how it could possibly be easy.

"I know how to get all around Sherman Point without getting caught. I can get you in and out and to other units or off the point and back. It's really easy," Turtle said. There was no emotion on his face. "Do you want me to teach you?"

"Hell, yeah," Mitch said, excited to be exposed to freedom. "But how do you know all this?"

"I did a report for school on the history of Sherman Point," Turtle said, pointing to a binder on his desk.

"You have all the information about Sherman Point in that binder?" Mitch asked, truly beginning to understand the depths of Turtle's obsession with the place.

"Not the good stuff," Turtle said.

"Where's the good stuff?"

Turtle looked at Mitch, allowing a slight grin to become evident on his face. With his index finger, he pointed to the side of his head, and the grin became a full smile. "Remember, photographic memory."

Mitch looked at Turtle with new respect. Dr. Brady and Dr. Cav had no idea that behind the isolation and silence lived and breathed a walking encyclopedia of Sherman Point. Mitch now knew the secret and realized that he had misjudged Turtle. Turtle, the kid with autism that most people walked by without noticing, was in reality some sort of genius and no one gave him the attention to realize it. They formed their opinions and closed the book on him. Mitch knew it wasn't fair for people to jump to conclusions about Turtle. They were wrong, and Turtle deserved better.

Mitch wondered who else he had misjudged. Cassandra had been wrong about him at first, but rightfully so, because of the way he treated Sameer. And what about Sameer? Mitch didn't even know the guy, and he never gave him a chance. Now it seemed like Sameer was a good friend to the people around him. Maybe he should give the guy a chance. After all, Cassandra had been brave enough to give Mitch a chance and learn who he truly was, and now they were together. She inspired him to be a better person, and he was going to start looking deeper into people before judging them.

Mitch was about to thank Turtle when he looked up to see the belly of Felix forcing the buttonholes on his shirt to stretch to their max. He stood in the doorway, his frame taking up the entire space. "Blais," he barked, "let's go. Dr. Brady wants to see you in his office right now."

"Ah, OK," Mitch responded, turning his back to Felix and covertly placing the piece of paper with the girls' names on it in his mouth. He began chewing rapidly while Felix made his way into the room. Turtle stared intently at his work, never acknowledging Felix's presence.

"What do you have here, Turtle?" Felix asked looking down at his depiction of Sherman Point.

No response.

"Very nice," Felix said in a sarcastic tone, picking up the drawing. Then, for no apparent reason, he began ripping the picture into pieces.

Turtle said nothing.

Felix turned his attention back to Mitch. "Now, Blais," he barked walking up behind Mitch and giving him a shove in the back.

Mitch jolted forward slightly and chewed a few more times. Then, just as Felix spun him around, he took a long, hard swallow, forcing the paper down his esophagus. He winced from the uncomfortable feeling and briefly closed his eyes. When he opened them, Felix was standing directly in front of him.

36

Mitch waited in front of Dr. Brady while he diligently read a file. No words were exchanged. Dr. Brady went about his business as if Mitch wasn't even there. Closing the file, Dr. Brady got up from his chair and headed for the long row of file cabinets in the back corner of his oversized office. After replacing the file, he turned toward Mitch.

"Mr. Blais, do you know what this is?" Dr. Brady asked, turning halfway back to the file cabinet and gesturing with his hand as though he were a model at a car show. "This cabinet, Mr. Blais, contains the permanent records of all inmates at Sherman Point for the last decade."

Mitch looked toward the file cabinet, wondering where Dr. Brady was going with his speech.

"Mr. Blais, do you know that you have a file in here?" Dr. Brady asked, extracting a file folder from the cabinet and heading back to his desk. Sitting down, he opened the file, exposing a neat, packaged history of Mitchell Blais.

Mitch adjusted himself in the chair and waited with some apprehension, not knowing what was coming next.

Dr. Brady cleared his throat. "I won't bore you with all the details. After all, it is your life and you are more aware than any of us what it has entailed, aren't you, Mr. Blais?"

"I guess so."

"Today, Mr. Blais, I would like to focus on your diagnosis—ADHD with issues with impulse control." Dr. Brady looked up, expecting a comment, but Mitch remained silent. "We have been giving you medication to help control this issue, but it doesn't seem that the dosage has been appropriate for a young, excitable man like yourself."

Mitch looked at Dr. Brady and his file. He offered no response.

"You're accused of murder, Mr. Blais, and as far as I know, the state is pursuing those charges." Dr. Brady said, looking at Mitch and hoping for some sort of reaction. "It seems that your impulses have more control over you than you do over them. Is this what drove you to killing Rooney?"

"I didn't kill Rooney and I plan on proving it."

"Well, that sure will be difficult to do while you are incarcerated at Sherman Point, won't it, Mr. Blais? The state still has no proof, but I'm anticipating it will just be a matter of time," Dr. Brady said as he shuffled papers on his desk and turned his computer monitor slightly toward Mitch.

"How was your visit with your friend? What is his name? Ah yes, here it is, Charlie."

A wave of uneasiness washed over Mitch as he realized that Dr. Brady might know something about the paper Charlie had smuggled to him. He took a quick breath and said, "Oh yeah, that girl, Tina, went nuts or something on her boyfriend. Ruined my visit, you know."

"Yes, Mr. Blais. Ruined your visit, did she?" Brady said as he pecked away on his keyboard. "What I'm most interested in talking about, Mr. Blais, is this right here." Dr. Brady hit a button and a view of the visiting room popped up on the screen. Mitch again took a deep breath as he saw the image of himself lying on the floor of the visiting room, his table pushed aside, and guards restraining Tina.

"Here it comes, Mr. Blais, your indiscretion, if you will," Dr. Brady said, not averting his eyes from the screen. Then, as clear as day, the camera captured Mitch grabbing something on the floor and quickly shoving it in his pants. "Oh, let's play that again," Dr. Brady said, clicking his mouse several times and replaying the scene.

Mitch silently watched the scene play out on the computer screen.

"What was it, Mr. Blais, that you smuggled into Sherman Point?" Dr. Brady asked, peering over the rims of his glasses at Mitch.

"Nothing."

"Mr. Blais, you have already learned that there are two ways to do things—the easy way and the way that will lead you down a further path of deceit and lies and swift punishment," Dr. Brady said, waiting for Mitch to give in to his request for the truth. "As we speak, Mr. Blais, your room is being searched for contraband. Now, last chance: what did you smuggle into Sherman Point?"

Before Mitch could answer, there was a loud knock on the door.

"Enter!" Dr. Brady said, raising his voice to be heard.

The door opened and Felix took two steps forward, holding some large, rolled-up papers in his hand. He flashed Mitch a condescending look. "We didn't find nothing in the room for him, sir, but that other kid, Turtle, he had these maps and diagrams of this place under his bed. You should take a look at these. They're pretty good."

"Thank you. Throw those things in the corner. My concern is not with drawings and maps at this time. Wait here," Dr. Brady said to Felix. "What, Mr. Blais, did you smuggle into Sherman Point?"

Silence.

"Don't say I didn't give you a chance, Mr. Blais," Dr. Brady said, motioning to Felix.

Felix looked back toward the door. "Come on, boys," he said, and three other guards followed his lead as he moved toward Mitch. Mitch jumped to his feet in an effort to get away, but it was in vain. The guards quickly secured Mitch's arms, repositioning their grips until they had complete control of him.

"Screw you!" Mitch said. He convulsed his body and violently struggled until his left arm popped free. He immediately reached over and hit Felix in the face, making contact with his nose and sending him to the ground. A guard quickly jumped on Mitch's back, the momentum forcing everyone to the ground. Mitch lay on the floor, unable to move under the weight of the three guards. Out of the corner of his eye, he could see blood pouring down the front of Felix's shirt. He tried to yell but nothing would come out. The feet of Dr. Brady suddenly came into his view, and he could hear the man's voice.

"Perhaps, Mr. Blais, another stint in the Chamber will help refresh your memory." Dr. Brady leaned down so he was completely within Mitch's field of vision. "And Mr. Blais, I will get my answers one way or another," Dr. Brady said as he extracted a needle from his pocket. It was filled with liquid. He tapped on it twice, sending droplets into the air. Without hesitation, Dr. Brady stabbed the needle into Mitch's shoulder.

Mitch felt a burning sensation enter his arm, but he continued to struggle in an effort to get the guards off him. He strained every muscle, only to feel the energy leave his body. Motionless, the fight inside of Mitch subsided, and he felt his eyelids getting heavier and heavier. He told himself to keep them open, but his body didn't register the command. With two short blinks, Mitch's head rested on the ground and everything went black.

37

Mitch lay on the hard, cement floor of the Chamber while his dreams struggled with reality for dominance in his mind. A surreal existence won out, and from the top of the Chamber, Mitch looked down to see a body lying on the floor, motionless. He wondered how long it had been there. Swirling around the Chamber ceiling, Mitch watched the muscular body begin to move. He moved down for a closer look, hovering just feet above the form. In a swift movement, the physical structure pushed itself upward from the floor, muscles popping out all across the upper torso. The body sat up, realizing it was awakening, and in seconds, its eyes focused. Mitch quickly inserted himself into the body and became one with his dreams.

Mitch looked around the Chamber to see water dripping down the walls. Slowly, he got to his feet, shaking his head in an effort to regain some focus. A chill filled the air and Mitch shivered slightly from it. He could see his breath. He looked up, and to his surprise, noticed that the security door of the Chamber was open. *What the hell*? He moved toward the door, sure that he would encounter a guard. Tentatively, he stuck his head out the door and said, "Hello?"

There was no response.

He looked to his left, seeing nothing but the end of the hallway. Turning to his right, Mitch saw something at the end of the hall. Unsure of what it was, he walked through the doorway and proceeded in that direction. As Mitch got closer, he saw the familiar figure of a young girl in a worn hospital gown. It was Therese Harriet Coleman. Mitch stood still, staring at the apparition, confused about what he should do. With a single motion of her index finger, Therese Harriett Coleman indicated that Mitch should follow her.

An impulsive curiosity filled Mitch as the figure made its way down the hallway toward a door marked "Maintenance Closet." Without stopping at the door, the vision seemed to pass right through it, disappearing from Mitch's view. Perplexed, Mitch ran down the hall to the door. He felt it, finding it solid—no different from any door he had encountered in his life. He wasn't sure how to get through it, so he reached down and put his hand on the knob. "How about that," Mitch said with a chuckle as he turned the knob all the way, opening the door.

The closet was dark, illuminated only by the dim light that spilled in from the hallway. Mitch looked around curiously, wondering where the girl had gone. Several mops rested against the wall, and a shelf housing cleaning supplies stood deep in the closet. There seemed to be no way in or out, except the door.

Mitch backed up, resigning himself to the fact that the girl was gone and he must be dreaming—or worse, losing his mind. He decided that the best course of action would be to stop chasing ghosts. Maybe that was it. Maybe Therese Harriet Coleman was a ghost. Maybe the shot they gave Mitch was making him see things that weren't there. Either way, Mitch had seen enough and he was ready for the craziness to stop.

Backing out of the closet, Mitch looked down the hallway leading back to the Chamber. He began thinking about where he could go other than back to the maddening isolation of the Chamber. He took a half step out into the hallway when he heard a crash behind him. Startled, Mitch spun around to see the shelves on the ground, cleaning supplies and rags strewn about the floor. On the back wall, previously obscured by the shelving, was a damaged ventilation grate, three feet by three feet in size. Mitch noticed that the grate was held in by only one screw, and its lopsided tilt exposed an opening behind it. Mitch made his way to the grate mostly out of curiosity, and bending down, he stuck his head through the opening.

Mitch looked into the gap expecting to see the metal ductwork of a heating system, but to his surprise, he was looking at the rocky walls of a tunnel. He looked around on the floor of the closet and gathered up as many cloth rags as he could wrapping them around a broom handle. He opened up a can of paint thinner, soaked the rags and set them ablaze with a lighter he found in a metal toolbox.

Mitch placed the makeshift torch into the entrance of the tunnel and was surprised to see that it descended. Inquisitiveness took over. Mitch instinctively decided that he needed to see where the tunnel went and whether it would lead him to Therese Harriet Coleman.

Mitch's heart raced and perspiration dripped off his forehead as he negotiated the narrow opening and made his way into the tunnel. He was beginning to feel nervous, unsure as to what was ahead. He noticed a familiar, sweet, smoky aroma in the air but couldn't quite put his finger on it. The smell increased in intensity, as did the smoky mist that surrounded him. Mitch struggled to see, but the mist obstructed his view. He had to rely on his other senses to navigate the tunnel, feeling his way by touching the walls.

The tunnel became smaller and twisted in a serpentine path that led around a wall. Mitch doubted that he could continue as the tunnel narrowed to no more than two feet in height. *Where the hell am I?*

Mitch's heart was pounding. The smoke made his breathing labored. He attempted to look for other routes, but the sweet smell in the air was clearly coming from the narrow opening. Mitch debated whether to explore further. He tore off a piece of his shirt, added it to the makeshift torch, and inched forward. Mitch slowly got his footing and crouched down, trying to see into the black labyrinth in front of him.

He threw his torch through the opening to illuminate the area. Then, grabbing a large stone, Mitch pulled himself into the void, popped up, and grabbed his torch. The smoke had subsided, allowing him to see better. Mitch continued forward without looking back, following the path until the tunnel floor in front of him dropped off sharply. He crept to the edge and, judging the drop to be only about three feet, he jumped down into what seemed to be a cave. Immediately he felt the ground change beneath his feet. Scanning the roof of the cave, Mitch could see no openings. Nor were there any passages besides the path forward.

But the ground was soft and uneven, and Mitch could swear it was moving under his feet. Wondering why the floor was no longer solid, he lowered his torch and quickly got his answer. Rats! Hundreds of them!

"Oh shit," Mitch said, the air leaving his lungs. He ran across the cave, crushing squealing rats with each step. Mitch felt sick. Then, without warning, a rat fell from above and landed on his shoulder. He began swatting at it with a frantic urgency as the rat attempted to penetrate his skin with its teeth. Several more rats landed on Mitch's head, and he swatted them away with his hands. He felt one crawling up his leg and he kicked in a panicked rhythm until the rodent was dislodged. Thrashing in all directions and slamming against the wall, Mitch eyed a small gap in the tunnel wall and dove through it in an attempt to escape the rodents' attack. With that, he was again on safe ground. The rats behind him, Mitch sat looking back in shocked relief. "I hate rats!" he said aloud.

Out of breath, confused, and alone, Mitch collapsed to the ground behind a rock. He tried to slow his breathing, still inhaling streams of smoke. He listened for anyone or anything coming his way.

Nothing. Silence.

Retrieving his torch, Mitch surveyed his situation. Looking back, he saw nothing but a wild riot of scurrying rats. He spun slowly around, and that's when he saw it. Mitch couldn't believe his eyes.

He gazed up at an old, wooden door, standing at least fifteen feet in height. The ceiling of the cave rose at an incline from the top of the door, forming the natural, rounded, hill-like structure of the underground cavern. The smoke was streaming through the slight crack at the bottom of the door.

Mitch pushed against the massive door, but it wouldn't budge. He tried several more times unsuccessfully, the desperation of his situation becoming clear. He couldn't move forward because of this insurmountable obstacle, and he would not go back and face the rats again.

Mitch ran through his options. No answers were evident, and a terrible realization came over him. Maybe he would be down here for eternity, like the ghost of Therese Harriet Coleman. Maybe he would die a slow, agonizing death in a cave, his corpse becoming nourishment for a colony of crazed vermin. Mitch's thoughts became increasingly scattered, and he found it difficult to concentrate on any one thing. Suddenly, a noise echoed from the tunnel that Mitch had just exited. It was the sound of running footsteps, and they were getting closer. Paranoia raced through Mitch. He suddenly realized an unknown assailant was pursuing him.

38

Robin Clarkson waited impatiently in the office of Dr. Wes Brady, not really sure what direction her investigation would take. Something wasn't right about the suicide of the kid here at Sherman Point, and she wondered what the black fibers meant. She didn't like to be kept waiting, and it had now been fifteen minutes. It was nice that the receptionist let her wait in the doctor's office, but she thought it would have been more cordial if the good doctor had been on time for the appointment, which she'd made two days earlier.

Robin Clarkson scanned the room, trying to get a feeling for the type of man Dr. Brady was. His office had all the trappings of a doctor in charge of a large facility—books, file cabinets, and pictures and diplomas on the wall. She began to look at the pictures and noticed that, as in Dr. Cavanaugh's office, there were many pictures of Dr. Brady doing exciting, adventurous things. The only difference was that Dr. Brady's pictures were devoid of kids. He had photos of himself in outdoor settings with what appeared to be friends, family members, or colleagues, but no kids. There were pictures of him holding up a swordfish, rock climbing, and skydiving. Clarkson wondered where the guy found all the time to be such an adventurer.

"Oh, Detective Clarkson, I see that Kathy showed you in," Dr. Brady said, walking over to Clarkson and extending a hand. "I trust I haven't kept you waiting too long."

Clarkson stood up and although irritated by the wait, she extended her hand. "No, it's fine Dr. Brady. I know you're a busy man."

"That I am, Detective Clarkson. I'm sure you're also busy. You know, we have over three hundred inmates here on the adolescent unit, most of whom require maximum attention, and with the current fiscal issues we find ourselves in today, well, it's not easy," Dr. Brady said, letting out a long sigh.

"Yes, I'm aware that you have many patients to attend to here, but I'm really only interested in one—Myles Harwich."

"Terrible tragedy," Dr. Brady said.

"Yes, a tragedy."

"Yes, I was reviewing his file this morning, and it seems he had a long history of depression. A shame, actually. If only people would give us a chance to help them before they gave up," Dr. Brady said, shaking his head.

"Let me ask you a question, Doctor. Do you think something else may have happened to him?"

"Excuse me?"

"You know, Doc, could somebody have helped him dive off the roof?" Clarkson asked, making a diving gesture with her hands.

"Dive…whatever are you suggesting?" Brady said, caught off guard by the question.

"Well, sure. Here's a kid who, from my research, seems to be doing well in your program," Clarkson said, never taking her eyes off Dr. Brady. "Wasn't he scheduled to go home in several months?"

The expression on Dr. Brady's face changed instantly to one of annoyance as he realized that this was less a friendly visit prompted by professional courtesy and more a probe of the inner workings of Sherman Point. "Now you listen to me, Detective. If you are suggesting that somehow Myles Harwich was pushed off that roof, and therefore was murdered…" Dr. Brady paused and then said, "That's just preposterous!"

"Is it, Dr. Brady?" Clarkson asked, feeling as though she had the good doctor on the defensive. "What about the three girls that have disappeared in the last year and a half?"

"What of them?"

"Well, how do three girls just walk out of a facility like this and nobody notices?'

"You have some nerve coming in here and slinging unsubstantiated accusations in my direction," Brady said, his face turning red and his tone intensifying. "As I explained, Detective, we have had many fiscal issues in the last several years that have affected all aspects of our operations, and for your information, that includes security."

Clarkson watched as Brady clearly became angry at her line of questioning. It was difficult to tell if he was just defending the integrity of his facility or if he was trying to hide something. She paused and waited until she was sure Brady was done talking before she asked her next question. "The Lambert girl. She was killed. Isn't that correct, Dr. Brady?"

"Killed?"

"Yeah, Doc, she's dead, isn't that right?"

"Dead, unfortunately, yes. Killed, no. When she chose to run from the facility, she was hit by a car and expired," Dr. Brady said.

"Expired?" Clarkson said, surprised the doctor would use a term that she reserved for food in her refrigerator that was no longer fresh.

"Yes, she died. Is there anything else I can help you with?" Dr. Brady said, standing up to indicate to Clarkson that her time was up. "I have many people to see this afternoon."

"No, I guess that's it for today, but I know you'll call me if anything comes to mind that may help," Clarkson said, handing Dr. Brady a card with her number on it.

"Of course. Let me show you out."

Clarkson got up and walked toward the door, again noticing the pictures of Dr. Brady on his various adventures. "You seem to be quite an outdoorsman, Dr. Brady," Clarkson said, stopping to look at a photograph of skiers at the top of a snow-covered mountain. The picture was labeled "Sunday River, Maine."

"That's correct, Detective," Dr. Brady affirmed, not interested in making small talk with Clarkson.

Clarkson stood for a second, studying the faces in the photo. "That's funny, Dr. Brady, I don't see you in this photo."

Brady stood at the door, holding it open, ready for Clarkson to leave. "That's correct, Detective. Your deductive reasoning certainly seems sharp," he said in a condescending tone. "I'm the one on the far left. I get terribly dry skin in the winter and try to protect it as best I can."

"That's interesting," Clarkson said. "You're right here, Dr. Brady?" she asked, pointing to a figure in the picture.

"That's correct."

"Interesting," Clarkson said again as a chill came over her. All the way to the left of the picture stood a man in full ski attire, his face concealed by a black, woven ski mask.

39

The sound that Mitch perceived as feet running prodded him back into action. He jumped up and began to work at the door. It was heavier than he thought it would be. In one final act of desperation, Mitch mustered all his strength and attempted to force the door open. Nothing. The door refused to cooperate. Mitch quickly ran his hand over the surface of the door to determine if it had any weak points that he might be able to manipulate, but he found nothing vulnerable about its construction. It seemed the secrets behind the door would be kept for many more years to come.

Angry, frustrated, and tired, Mitch sat on a rock adjacent to the door and began to develop a strategy for dealing with his unseen foe. He listened intently, but no longer heard footsteps. Mitch looked all around, expecting to see someone.

Nothing.

Mitch thought he was losing his mind. Contemplating his alternatives, he decided that he had no choice but to retrace his steps and head back. *Shit! Not the rats again!* Mitch felt sick to his stomach. "I hate rats!"

Mitch wrapped the last of the fabric he had around the top of the torch, sending a newly ignited flame into the air in front of his face. He wondered where Therese Harriet Colman had gone. Below him, in front of the rock he sat on, was a small hole in the ground. Mitch thought that he could stick the unlit end of the torch in the hole to support it while he prepared a strategy for exiting the bowels of Sherman Point. He pushed the torch down into the hole and was surprised to find that its staff penetrated a good foot into the ground. Suddenly, a loud, cracking sound filled the air, and the ground shook. Mitch jumped up and braced himself against the stone wall in an effort to maintain his balance. Rocks plummeted from above, and now Mitch was certain that he would die down here, never to be seen again. He wondered if this was what happened to all the other missing kids from Sherman Point.

Mitch decided that he would take a chance and make a run for it. At least he would know he had tried to cheat death. He would give himself a three count and then bolt through the falling rocks into the rat haven in a last-ditch effort to save his life. Taking a deep breath, Mitch started to count. Three…two… Before he could reach one, a placid feeling came over him. The ground settled and the last of the rocks dropped from above. He was safe!

Mitch looked around, slowing his breathing. The sweet-smelling smoke was heavy again—the door was no longer visible. He groped his way tentatively through the haze until he could see the door again, and then stopped in disbelief. Amazed, he could not believe what he saw.

The door had come ajar, leaving a gap just wide enough for an average-size person to squeeze through. Working his way past the door, Mitch entered a tunnel, smoke obstructing any meaningful view. The flame from the torch illuminated the smoke and turned it a sunset red. Still breathing heavily with a combination of fear and adrenaline, Mitch could feel the smoke expanding his lungs with each breath. He could feel himself becoming calm. It seemed as if everything was slowing down. His vision became more intense directly in front of him and less so peripherally. It was as if his eyes were showing him the direction in which he should move: straight ahead.

Mitch continued, his thoughts slowing and becoming scattered. He thought of Cassandra. He thought about Charlie and Grandma Jackie. Tears welled up in his eyes, but he realized that they were becoming irritated and itchy because of the smoke. His eyelids drooped and became small slits. He thought they might close.

Mitch ventured forward, following the orangey haze in front of him as his torch shot amber flames into the smoky mist. As Mitch watched the display, hundreds of tiny, red bursts of flame shot upward, swirling, and circling about the tunnel. Mitch had no concern for anything but the present moment. A childlike smile came across his face, and he thought he would be happy just staying right here, in this spot, forever. No past, no future, just now. The smile grew bigger, and Mitch spun around, waving his torch in all directions, looking for an exit. Flames and flickering fire encircled him. Brilliant flashes of orange filled the tunnel, leaving yellow streaks in their wake. Mitch began laughing like a young boy enjoying a new toy.

A carefree tranquility filled him. He had no worries in the world at this particular moment. He continued moving forward, almost dancing, when a noise came from behind him—from back by the door. Mitch stopped in his tracks. *What was that? Shit, is someone coming again*? Mitch was suddenly consumed with the uneasy feeling that he was again being watched—scrutinized by unseen eyes. Uncertainty replaced pleasure and Mitch quickened his pace.

What was that?

Mitch swore he heard another noise but couldn't be certain. *Someone else is down here!*

He began running, holding his torch in front of him. A sudden coldness engulfed him, and he realized he was starving. He hadn't eaten in almost a day.

Where the hell am I? Shit, another noise! It's getting closer!

Mitch picked up his pace as he heard footsteps echoing through the tunnel behind him. Breaking into a full sprint, he dashed through a narrow opening. As he progressed, the smoke began to subside, and the walls around him became more visible. A small beam of daylight penetrated the tunnel about one hundred feet ahead, marking his escape route. Mitch could hear the footsteps behind him; someone was closing the distance.

He rushed toward the light. The steps were getting closer, and Mitch swore he could hear labored breathing behind him. Racing to flee the unknown entity pursuing him, Mitch clearly saw the opening that emitted the light into the tunnel. Ten more feet to go, Mitch estimated.

But it was too late. He felt something grab his shoulder, attempting to pull him back into the uncertainty of the tunnel.

40

Steve Grabowski's face looked like a Halloween horror mask. The fire had left a permanent red scar across his left cheek, and his nose was crooked. He was not pleasant to look at, and although most people thought he had it coming to him, he blamed Mitch Blais. The only certainties in Steve Grabowski's life were that he was locked up at Sherman Point, and he was going to make Mitch Blais pay.

Grabowski strutted into the cafeteria wearing his Sherman Point-issued uniform and a look of disgust on his face. He was accompanied by a skinny, dirty-looking kid with brown, scraggily hair. The kid followed Grabowski's every move, involuntarily twitching his head and shoulders every few seconds.

"Losers," Grabowski said, loudly enough for everyone to hear.

"Yeah, losers," the skinny kid repeated, indicating that he and Grabowski were thinking the same thing. "Losers, all of them," he said, his head nervously jerking to the left.

"Shut up," Grabowski said. He pushed his way through the lunch line, staring into the eyes of anyone who attempted to question his overbearing presence. He, like Mitch Blais, was bigger and tougher than most of the kids at Sherman Point. The main difference between the two was that Mitch didn't see the necessity to remind everyone constantly of his physical prowess.

Grabowski took his full tray of food and looked around the cafeteria for the one guy he really wanted to find—Mitch Blais. The skinny kid followed compliantly, twitching his head and waiting for Grabowski to make a move. After several seconds of looking, Grabowski found what he considered the next-best thing. Sitting alone in the corner of the cafeteria, face staring straight down at his food, was Mitch Blais's roommate, the kid everyone called Turtle. Sensing the opportunity to get a message to Blais, Grabowski made his way to the almost empty table and plopped his tray across from Turtle. The skinny kid took a seat just a few feet away.

Turtle never looked up, even though a sense of anxiety came over him. He continued eating, hoping not to be bullied by the goons now seated next to him.

"Hey, you're that kid, Turtle, that rooms with Blais," Grabowski said, looking down at Turtle.

"Turtle?" the skinny kid repeated with a silly laugh while he squirmed in his seat. "What a stupid name."

No response.

"Hey, kid, I'm talking to you," Grabowski said, raising his voice in an effort to illicit a response. "What's a matter? Are you stupid or something?"

Turtle just continued eating. He did not look at Grabowski. He remembered what some of the counselors had taught him: Sometimes if you ignore mean people, they will go away.

"Now you listen to me, shithead," Grabowski said, grabbing Turtle's arm and pulling him across the table. "You tell that son of a bitch roommate of yours that he's dead! Got it?"

The skinny kid's excitement became evident. He was twitching and jumping out of his seat. "Dead, dead, dead!" he kept repeating.

Turtle looked up at Grabowski in fear but still did not reply. He trembled slightly, again hoping Grabowski was done with him and he would go away. Grabowski's reddened face and bent nose made him look even tougher than he was. Turtle swallowed hard.

Sensing the fear, Grabowski pointed at Turtle with his free hand. "Oh, what's the matter? Is Turtle a little scared right now?" Grabowski said, realizing he had his present victim right where he wanted him. "Well, I'm gonna make sure you don't forget to tell Blais that I'm looking for him. Do me another favor, give him this for me," Grabowski said as he closed his fist and cocked his arm back, about to send a punch squarely into Turtle's face.

"Here comes the boom," the skinny kid said, snickering.

Turtle was paralyzed by fear, but then something happened. He was tired of being a victim, tired of the world happening to him, and tired of not having any control over it. He had a lot to offer, as Mitch had pointed out to him when they talked about his knowledge of Sherman Point and the girls who'd disappeared. Turtle felt a surge of adrenaline pulse through his body. No longer would he allow people to push him around, and he certainly wasn't going to sit by and be bullied by the likes of Steve Grabowski—a guy to whom he had never done anything. This time he was going to do something!

With full force, Grabowski shot his fist forward straight at Turtle's nose. Surprising him, Turtle moved inches to the right. Grabowski's fist flew past without even grazing Turtle. Grabowski was stunned just long enough for Turtle to flip his tray of food up into Grabowski's badly mangled face, catapulting all of its contents onto him. Grabowski scrambled to his feet, wiping spaghetti and sauce from his distorted face, clearing his vision just enough to see everyone around him laughing hysterically at his expense.

The skinny kid sat trembling in a silent disbelief, unsure of what to do.

Grabowski staggered forward, moving in the direction of Turtle, who was now pelting Grabowski with dinner rolls, one hitting him in the head and the other striking his right eye.

Grabowski's anger intensified in direct correlation to the volume of the laughter around him. He bolted forward, ready to pummel Turtle, but his sneaker slipped on the spaghetti-covered floor; and he fell backward, his momentum stopping when his head smashed into the linoleum. A star-studded blackness filled Grabowski's head. He rolled over, grunting his disapproval as guards swarmed the area, restraining him in an effort to thwart any further retaliation.

The skinny kid jumped up. He looked left and then right, twitched several times, and began to run. But the guards quickly squelched his escape effort.

Turtle sat down and took a sip of his milk. Everyone in the cafeteria shot looks of astonished amazement in his direction. This quiet kid who usually went unnoticed would forever be known as the guy who took on the biggest bully at Sherman Point and won.

The chant started from a back table and quickly spread through the cafeteria. There was no mistaking the name being repeated as the sound became clearer. The kids in the cafeteria were chanting in unison, "Turtle, Turtle, Turtle!"

Turtle smiled and casually took another sip from his carton of milk.

41

The grip on Mitch's shoulder impeded his forward progress toward the opening that was revealed by the daylight. He put all his energy into wiggling away from the constricting force behind him. Five feet from the opening, he exerted one last burst of energy and broke free of the constraint. He was free!

Mitch burst from the tunnel opening, the sunlight momentarily blinding him. He looked back, prepared to defend himself, but no one was there. Confused and somewhat disoriented, Mitch found himself standing at the edge of an enormous field of onions. The yellow onions were all partially visible, protruding from the ground, their green tops extending upward, toward the sun. There were thousands of them.

Collecting his thoughts and surveying his surroundings, Mitch noticed that he was below the cliffs that supported Sherman Point. The brick-and-mortar edifice that was Sherman Point peered down at all that was beneath it. It looked odd. Different, but Mitch was unsure how.

His stomach began to grumble, protesting the lack of food. He was tired and excessively hungry. It wasn't his first choice of a meal, but he gladly ripped an onion out of the ground to eat it. Any food would satisfy his gnawing hunger.

Mitch peeled the first layer of onion and examined it with moderate skepticism. It looked fully grown and the strong smell reminded him of the onions that Grandma Jackie grew in her garden. Once convinced of their edibility, Mitch began devouring the onions, attempting to satisfy his hunger. He ripped apart layer after layer, examining each fragment and then shoving it into his mouth. Mitch ate onion after onion until he couldn't possibly consume another morsel of food. He had satiated himself to the point that he felt sick. All he could smell and taste was onion. He sat contentedly in the shade of an old oak tree, looking up at the ominous Sherman Point. He felt tired and the meager attempts he made to keep his eyes open were in vain. He quickly and placidly fell into a deep, satisfying sleep.

Without warning, Mitch was snapped out of his slumber. He had no idea how long he had been asleep, but the sun was still out. A strange clomping noise filled the air. It was getting louder. Mitch scrambled off the dirt path that ran adjacent to the onion field and scurried behind the oak tree. He poked his head out to get a glimpse of the source of the noise.

He recognized the road as the one that twisted and turned on its way up to Sherman Point, but it seemed different. It was dirt. There was no pavement. Mitch concealed himself as best he could behind the tree and peered cautiously through the bushes. He could hear a group of people coming up the path. Mitch got his first glimpse of the people as they came around a bend in the road. Confusion and disbelief filled Mitch's head. *It can't be!* What Mitch saw in front of him couldn't possibly be real, yet there it was, no more than ten feet away!

42

The hand was surprised when it reached down and picked up the cell phone vibrating on the table. The hand slid the phone open, revealing the screen and a text message.

We have a special order and must send a package out ASAP.

The hand waited more than a minute, and then it typed out the words:

Seems like a risk at this point with all the eyes that are on the project right now.

The hand hit "send," and waited impatiently, tapping the table.

The rewards are greater than any before so it is worth the risk. It is for our mutual friend with very deep pockets.

The hand paused, and then replied.

Still seems risky with everything that is happening as of late.

Almost immediately, a response came.

If you hadn't screwed up with the Lambert girl this wouldn't be the case. So you will do it or suffer the consequences.

Again, the hand paused. Then it responded.

Understood.

It hit the "send" key.

And another thing, this will be the last package as it is costing our friend much money.

The hand shook nervously as it put down the phone. Then, trembling, it reached into the bag one last time and pulled out a black ski mask. In a hushed tone, a voice said, "Perhaps we can be done with this business now."

43

Mitch stared in amazed disbelief as two beautiful, black horses galloped up the dirt path, a black carriage in tow. A driver sat in front of the topless wooden carriage, and four passengers sat in the back, two to a seat, facing one another. As the carriage approached, Mitch could see that there were two women and two men being chauffeured. Their clothing was very strange, and Mitch thought they must be headed for a Halloween party. The women wore strange, large-brimmed hats and dresses that bulged on the shoulders. The men were sporting black top hats and long, black coats. Mitch watched as they rolled by. His curiosity piqued, he decided to follow the carriage from the safety of the woods.

Mitch kept pace with the carriage, soon finding himself outside the main building of Sherman Point. Astonished, he saw many similar horses and carriages in a row, waiting to be parked by a valet in a designated area. People walked about the main entrance, talking and laughing, all seemingly waiting for something to happen. Everyone wore clothing similar to that of the people in the carriage, and Mitch decided that it must be some sort of costume party. He waited in the woods, keeping an eye on the festivities. Then a woman called out in excitement, "Here they come!"

The main door of Sherman Point swung open and the spectators gazed with intense anticipation. First, several men came out, wearing white pants and white tops that resembled lab coats. Some came out alone, and others were pulling people who wore white jackets, with their hands crossed and restrained in front of them, and what looked like leashes attached to their backs. The faces of those in the restraints were filled with a horrified uncertainty as they were dragged off to a designated area on the side of the building. Gasps radiated from the crowd as several men resisted, violently kicking and screaming. This certain sign of noncompliance seemed to amuse the audience.

A long line of people emerged from the building, most wearing white, hospital attire that seemed old to Mitch. Uncertainty continued to rattle around Mitch's head. He wasn't sure what he was watching. Clearly, these people were inmates and workers at Sherman Point, but he hadn't seen any of them before. What were all the people doing here? And why were they dressed so oddly? Mitch continued to watch as he attempted to process the spectacle in front of him.

The crowd of dirty-looking inmates on the side of the building grew. Some walked about talking to themselves, while others just sat on the ground, rocking. Several fights almost broke out between those being placed on display. The hospital workers became violent, hitting several men in the head with clubs—a primitive yet effective way of keeping order. All the while, the well-dressed visitors from the carriages walked around, chatting and laughing, and pointing out various oddities. Some yelled at the patients and others threw bread in their direction, as if they hoped for a show.

Mitch continued watching the people being led to the viewing area, and then, to his astonishment, he saw her. Therese Harriet Coleman walked to the viewing area on her own accord and sat on a bench away from the other inmates. Several onlookers came over and stood in front of the bench, waiting for something to happen.

"Gather 'round, all thee interested in seeing the girl who talks to ghosts!" a man in an elaborate black suit and sporting a long beard yelled as he motioned with his arm.

Therese sat on the bench as people stared at her, and chaos unfolded around her. She stared blankly into the distance until Mitch sensed that she was looking right at him. He poked his head out from behind a tree, and to his surprise, he heard Therese yell, "Mitchell, it's OK! Come on out! They can't see you!"

The spectators cheered and laughed as the young girl continued to yell in the direction of the tree line, "Come on, Mitchell, it's OK. This is why I brought you here!"

Mitch exited the woods and walked down to where the crowd had formed. To his surprise, not a single person looked in his direction. He negotiated his way through the laughing and cheering crowd and was now five feet from the bench that Therese occupied.

"Over here, Mitchell, have a seat," Therese said, motioning with her hand for him to sit next to her. The crowd laughed and jeered with delight.

"What is this?" Mitch asked, looking at all the inmates wandering about aimlessly, making undecipherable noises.

"It's Sunday, Mitchell. The day Sherman Point allows the public in for a small fee to see all the crazy people," Therese explained, as she pointed toward those unwittingly putting on a show. "They come to see me—the girl that talks to imaginary people from the future."

"Crazy people? People from the future?" Mitch said, still trying to comprehend what was in front of him. "Why is everyone dressed so weird and riding in carriages?"

"They're dressed appropriately for the time period, Mitchell. After all, it is 1868."

Mitch tried to digest what Therese was saying. *How could it be 1868? I must be having some wild dream*, Mitch convinced himself. "What the hell, I'll bite," Mitch said, still uncertain. "Why am I here?"

"You're here because you are the one who can end the cycle of abuse that has taken place at Sherman Point for well over 100 years."

"What?"

"That's right, Mitchell. For well over 100 years, I have waited for you while my soul has wandered the halls of Sherman Point, and now you are here to put an end to the evil forever and set me free."

Mitch didn't accept what he was hearing. The spectators gawked at the girl having a conversation with no one about souls and being set free. It was the best entertainment that money could buy.

"Why me?" Mitch asked.

"Because you, Mitchell, are a protector and purest of hearts than all who have come before you," Therese continued, a smile forming on her face. "You don't realize it yet because you've just begun to open up your heart. But to do that, you have to accept the pain that fills it."

Mitch listened to Therese, knowing the pain of which she spoke. He tried to think of words but couldn't.

"Do you remember what I told you before? You must open your heart, Mitchell, and the goodness within will be seen by all. You carry great power to help and change people, power you do not understand you possess because you are still living with the past sins of others," Therese said, seeing the confusion on Mitch's face.

"What? I don't understand," was all Mitch could manage.

"No one does, Mitchell, until they realize their potential and awaken to who they are and not who others have made them. In a moment of clarity, you will awaken from the darkness that has filled your soul, and your new life will begin. Your past experiences will become lessons to learn from and not an indicator of who you are. Free your heart, Mitchell, and everyone will benefit from your rebirth. They will see the real Mitchell and understand that you aren't a harbinger of resentment or hatred, and they certainly will know that you never killed anyone—nor would you ever."

Mitch sat speechless, absorbing what Therese had said to him. Images flashed through his head of his dad and of war, and of his mother holding him as a toddler. Then Cassandra filled all of his thoughts.

"Open your heart, Mitchell, and not only will you free my soul, but you will prove your innocence and put an end to man's wickedness and hatred. You will save Cassandra."

"Save Cassandra? What do you mean? Save Cassandra from what?" Mitch asked, but before he could get a response, the man in the black jacket and long beard made his way over to Therese. Mitch did a double take. The likeness to Dr. Brady was uncanny. Mitch thought the man could be an ancestor of Dr. Brady. He was accompanied by another man wearing equally impressive clothing and sporting a top hat and cane.

"Is this the young lady you told me about, Doctor?" the man asked as he made his way around the bench, stroking Therese's hair and rubbing her shoulders. "She seems young, but you have promised that she can perform quite adequately, yes?" The man rounded the bench, stood in front of Therese, and used his cane to pull her shirt open, exposing her breasts.

"Yes, that is correct, sir," the doctor assured him. "You can have her for one hour for the specified price, or you can have her for the whole afternoon if you'd like to indulge a little further."

Mitch jumped up in protest, realizing that the doctor was selling Therese to the man in the top hat for sexual favors. "Get out of here!" Mitch yelled to the men.

Neither of them flinched.

"Mitchell, they can't hear you," Therese said. The man looked at her curiously, as she seemed to speak to the air. "Do not worry about *me,* Mitchell. I have died already and haven't a chance for a new beginning, like you."

Mitch looked around desperately, trying to devise a plan to save Therese, only to see the men escort her by the arm toward the building. Mitch walked beside her in a hopeless rage. "I'm sorry, Therese. I'm sorry I can't stop this."

"You can't stop this, but you can stop others from being hurt. Remember what I said. Open your heart, Mitchell, and not only will you free my soul, but you will prove your innocence and put an end to man's wickedness and hatred. You will save Cassandra," she said. A tear made it down to the passive smile on her face. "Go back, Mitchell. Go back and be you."

With that, the men entered the building with Therese and closed the door. Mitch stood in bewilderment on the stairs of Sherman Point, pain in his head and sickness in his heart.

"Free Cassandra?" he said in an uncertain tone as he tried to make sense of what Therese had told him. He staggered from the stairs and went back to the side of the building, where the strange spectacle continued. Stumbling into the fray, Mitch tripped on a rock and found himself on the ground. Dizziness filled his head, and he looked up from the ground to see a man with long, wild hair screaming while the properly attired audience raved in amusement at the afternoon entertainment. Then the clouds spun furiously around, and the brilliance of the sun caused Mitch to snap his eyes shut. With that, all became dark. The darkness pervaded Mitch's mind as he slipped into an uneasy unconsciousness, after which he would never be the same.

44

Cassandra stretched her legs on the brick wall, preparing to go for her jog. The wind blew with more intensity than usual indicating that a storm may be developing. Cassandra would have to deal with a strong crosswind, but it wasn't enough to stop her from going for a run. She breathed in the cool morning air, appreciative of the fact that she had enough credits and trust from the staff to walk or run on the grounds unsupervised. She enjoyed the brief stints of freedom and the resulting exercise to which her appropriate behavior had given her access.

Cassandra ran down the cement walkway, saying hello to the various inmates and guards she encountered. Everyone knew of the privileges she had earned as a model inmate, so instead of being stopped and questioned, she was smiled at and greeted. It almost made her feel as if she were free. But freedom would have to wait another six months. Then, her tenure at Sherman Point would end and her new life would begin.

She continued to run, picking up the pace as the muscles in her legs began to loosen up. She loved to run and loved the "runner's high" it gave her as endorphins were released in her brain. It provided a sense of relaxation and stress relief that she couldn't get from any other activity.

A euphoric glow filled her mind as she passed the one-mile mark and headed for the back of the buildings that ran along the cliff overlooking the ocean. She enjoyed this section of her run mostly because she could look at the ocean from afar and not feel the overwhelming anxiety that she associated with water. She would never swim in the ocean but she appreciated its vastness and the motion of the waves as they crashed on the rocks below. The impending storm caused more intense waves that pounded the coast with a forceful relentlessness. Cassandra found it surprisingly relaxing.

Her thoughts began to wander as she reached the two-mile mark of her run. She found herself thinking of this unexpected relationship with Mitch. Mitch—the guy who's accused of murder. He said he didn't do it, and she believed him. She wanted to believe him. She knew that deep down inside, he was a good man who had endured a hard life, just as she had. He had changed since arriving at Sherman Point, and she saw deep into the layers of his makeup. She knew that the deeper she went, the more pure and beautiful he would become to her. She wanted to believe that she could trust again, but her heart held with deep conviction past betrayals that made it difficult. Normalcy in a relationship with a man is what she hoped for someday, and she was beginning to think that she would take that chance with Mitch.

She came to the small, wooded path that stretched for about five hundred feet before opening onto the common area of the campus. Cassandra enjoyed this portion of the run, as it marked the last third. She always quickened her pace for a strong finish.

Cassandra increased her stride and quickly reached the narrow path that carved its way through the trees. She regulated her breathing while she observed with appreciation the red, yellow, and orange shades of the autumn leaves. The thickness of the colored canopy above emitted only small rays of daylight, creating a dimly lit outdoor room decorated by nature. She knew that, like her, the leaves would be leaving Sherman Point soon.

The shapes along the wooded path began to meld together, and Cassandra's brain delved deeper into the euphoric state provided by the runner's high. She looked ahead and could see the opening to the common area. She alternated her gaze between it and the ground as she checked her footing.

When she glanced back up, an odd shape blocked the path. At first, it seemed like an animal, but as she moved closer, the figure came into focus. Cassandra focused more intently on the form, allowing her brain to register what she was seeing.

Her eyes widened as a terrifying realization filled her mind. At the end of the path stood a large man wearing black clothing and a black ski mask. Cassandra abruptly stopped. Simultaneously, the figure darted toward her in a full sprint. Before the scream could leave her mouth, the figure was upon her, tackling her to the ground.

A hand holding a cloth covered Cassandra's mouth, stifling her attempt to cry for help. She squirmed and kicked in an effort to release herself. Her lungs burned from a chemical on the cloth. Before she knew what happened, Cassandra lay limp on a bed of fallen autumn leaves. Unconscious and motionless, the fight within her that had helped her to persevere all these years was gone. The man in the black ski mask hoisted her over his shoulder, taking her to an unknown future.

45

Mitch made his way into the rec room tired, disoriented, and confused. He had spent three days in the Chamber, and he couldn't get his dream out of his mind. The nurse had just looked him over, as was customary upon release from the Chamber. She gave him a clean bill of health, but Mitch knew something was different. He remembered what Therese Harriet Coleman had said about saving Cassandra, but from what? A fog filled his head, and he tried to sort through flashing images of Therese and what he had seen. Everything around him felt surreal as he walked to a table at the far end of the rec room. A strange, overwhelming taste of onions lingered in his mouth.

"Free your heart and you will prove your innocence," Mitch mumbled under his breath while he looked around the room. He saw many familiar faces, although he couldn't put names to most of them. Most of the faces were young, but devoid of the innocence that should accompany such ages. Pain and despair filled the room. Mitch looked at the hopelessness evident in most people's expressions. He began to think that most of these kids, these teenagers, were far too young to have given up on life. He found himself sitting in the middle of a cauldron of despair.

Turtle approached the table. "You OK, Mitch?" he asked with genuine concern.

"Yeah. How's everything?" Mitch said.

Turtle smiled and began to recap his battle with Grabowski while Mitch was in the Chamber. Mitch could hardly believe what he was hearing from Turtle, who enthusiastically left no detail untold.

"Then he slipped on spaghetti and hit his head. You should have seen it. His little, skinny friend tried to run, but the guards got him too," Turtle said, laughing from deep within his belly.

"Holy shit, Turtle, that's unbelievable. Like I told you, you shouldn't let people push you around. I'm proud of you."

"Thanks, Mitch," Turtle said.

A cute girl with black hair and thick glasses passed the table, shooting Turtle a quick smile. "Hi, Turtle," she said in an unmistakably flirtatious tone.

"Oh, yeah, hey. I mean, hi Vicki," Turtle replied, his face taking on a red hue.

"Look at you, you old dog, you!" Mitch said.

"Hey, what can I say, Mitch? When you've got it, you've got it."

Mitch chuckled, happy for Turtle's newfound notoriety and confidence. Quickly, his thoughts went back to his dream. What did the dream mean? He thought back to the words Therese had said, "Open your heart, Mitchell, and not only will you free my soul, but you will prove your innocence and put an end to man's wickedness and hatred. You will save Cassandra."

"Save Cassandra from what?" Mitch asked under his breath.

The boys' attention was diverted to the TV screen mounted in the corner as red letters spelling out BREAKING NEWS ALERT flashed across it. The news anchor appeared on the screen. She was wearing rain gear and was being pelted by rain that seemed to be falling sideways from the sky. "This is breaking news live from the southern tip of New Jersey. Hurricane Mario continues to pound the shoreline of New Jersey, bringing flooding, heavy precipitation, and winds reaching upward of eighty miles per hour. Residents along the Eastern Seaboard are being advised to track Hurricane Mario, which is projected to head out to sea; however, some forecasts show it moving back toward land, possibly making landfall in northern Massachusetts or on the southern shoreline of Maine. If this is the case, Mario will produce unusually high surf and storm surges, and it will bring saltwater flooding far inland. Regardless, all residents of these coastal areas are encouraged to pay close attention to Mario's path and to heed any warning to evacuate," the newscaster said, shielding herself as best she could from the punishing rain. "Now, back to your locally televised programming," she said. The TV switched back to the *Dr. Bob Show*, sending the rec room into a frenzied chant of "Dr. Bob! Dr. Bob!"

Mitch looked out the rec room window, noticing that the skies had blackened and the wind had picked up considerably. "Hope we don't get hit here."

"I'm with you," Turtle agreed.

Before their conversation about the weather could progress any further, Sameer came running through the doors of the rec room. Out of breath, he said to Mitch and Turtle, "Holy shit, did you guys hear the news?"

"About Turtle, here, showing up Grabowski. Yeah, we—"

"No, man, about Cassandra."

"Cassandra?" Mitch's heart dropped.

"She bolted this morning on her run. They're scrambling everywhere looking for her. She's got about a six-hour head start on them, but she escaped," Sameer said, looking at Mitch, "I'm sorry, man, to have to be the one to tell you. I know you guys had something going."

Mitch was speechless. Cassandra escaped? He knew that wasn't the case. She had too much to look forward to and was scheduled to leave in six months. The words came back to Mitch now. Therese Harriet Coleman's message. "Open your heart, Mitchell, and not only will you free my soul, but you will prove your innocence and put an end to man's wickedness and hatred. You will save Cassandra."

Her words repeated themselves in his head over and over again. *You will save Cassandra. You will save Cassandra.* Mitch knew at that instant that Cassandra had not run away. None of the girls had. He wasn't sure what had happened to them, but he knew that Cassandra was in trouble, and he had to save her. He no longer cared about his own well-being or about proving he didn't kill anyone. The only thing Mitch could think about was Cassandra and saving her. He cared more for Cassandra than he did for himself. He loved her, and nothing was going to stop him from finding her and saving her. "Guys, I've got to act quickly. Cassandra's in trouble, and I need to think of a plan!"

"Trouble?" Sameer said confused. "She had enough and took off, man. I know this is hard—"

"I can't explain now," Mitch said, springing to his feet. "You just have to trust me. Something's going on here at Sherman Point, and I'm gonna prove it! Are you in or not?"

"I'm in," Turtle said.

Sameer nodded. "Yeah, sure—"

"Well, well, well. Looky here," Steve Grabowski boomed, coming up behind them. "I've got some unfinished business that I plan on taking care of right now." Grabowski pounded his fist into the palm of his other hand. The dirty, skinny kid stood beside him, a maniacal smile plastered on his face. He twitched almost uncontrollably with nervous excitement.

"Not now, Grabowski," Mitch said, brushing him aside, thinking of nothing but Cassandra.

"Not now for you, Blais, maybe. But it *is* time for that little shithead, Turtle," Grabowski said, anger evident in his voice. Grabowski lunged forward at Turtle, his fist flying through the air. Mitch instinctively jumped in front of the punch, taking it square in the jaw. Mitch fell backward, crashing into several chairs and knocking them over. He rolled over once on the ground, pushed himself up with his hands, and stood up. He put his fists up in front of his face just in time to defend himself.

All activity in the rec room stopped, and everyone's attention was diverted to the fight. People came rushing from every direction, forming a circle around the two combatants as they fought for an advantage.

Grabowski rushed Mitch, throwing a big, roundhouse right to his head. Mitch saw the telegraphed punch coming, and instead of ducking or backing off from it, he stepped directly toward his attacker so that his body was almost touching Grabowski's. Their proximity caused Grabowski's punch to fly past the back of Mitch's head, missing him entirely. Using the momentum Grabowski had created, Mitch grabbed his arm and stepped to his left, hanging onto Grabowski's wrist. With nothing to stop his momentum, Grabowski flew forward, spinning down into the ground.

Grabowski lay on the ground, defenseless; Mitch stood over him, twisting his wrist into an unnatural position while simultaneously stepping down on his shoulder. The pain radiated through Grabowski, and he let out a yell of distress that surprised even him.

The skinny kid watched in disbelief. How could Grabowski be losing? He twitched several times, jerking violently to his left. He'd do anything to win the approval of a tough guy like Steve Grabowski, and he would prove his loyalty now. He reached around to the small of his back and from the waistband of his shorts, he extracted a crude but sharp shank that he had fashioned from the handle of his toothbrush. He had worked for hours on it at night when the guards weren't looking. He had filed down the bottom of the handle on the cement until it was as pointy as it could possibly be. He had wrapped tape around the bristles repeatedly until it morphed into an acceptable handle. He was proud of his work and ready to use it.

Without warning, the skinny kid raised the shank above his head to create as much force as possible to penetrate the skin, muscle, and if need be, bone of Mitch's back, which was now fully exposed, making a large, vulnerable target. He was ready to kill and accept the consequences. He looked forward to earning what he perceived as the "street credibility" that came with killing. The decision was made.

Mitch never saw the skinny kid coming. He continued to restrain Grabowski, waiting to hand him over to the guards or, if he had to, torque his wrist in a circular motion until he heard a crack and the subsequent scream.

The first indication of trouble came from Turtle, who yelled, "Watch out!"

The warning wasn't in time. The skinny kid was just inches away from Mitch and his arm had already started its downward trajectory toward Mitch's back, the shank ready to penetrate exactly where the lungs were located. Mitch never even had time to turn around to see his attacker.

The shank was about to make contact with Mitch when suddenly the skinny kid's arm was intercepted. Sameer had pushed out of the crowd and used his left arm to block the shank. The weapon struck his forearm, just missing the bone and penetrating deep into the muscle. Sameer winced in pain, but continued his assault against the skinny, would-be killer. With his uninjured right arm, Sameer smashed his fist straight into the skinny kid's nose, shattering the bone, and unleashing a stream of blood. The skinny kid's eyes watered terribly as the pain from his broken nose made him see red, and he got sick to his stomach. He fell to the floor, holding his face and screaming. Any desire he had to make a name for himself instantly disappeared as he writhed in a pool of his own blood.

The guards made it to the scene and took control of everyone. A code blue was sounded and more guards rushed into the rec room like a swarm of bees. Sameer and Mitch both stood now, their arms restrained by the guards. They looked at the mayhem around them, not satisfied with what they had done, but happy that they'd come out on top. Mitch saw the shank in Sameer's arm and what was left of the skinny kid on the ground. In a moment of recognition, Mitch realized what had just happened. Sameer had saved his life. If it weren't for Sameer, Mitch would be dead on the ground. He looked up at Sameer, catching his eye. With great humility and a sense of shame for how he had treated Sameer in the past, he said, "Thank you, brother."

46

Cassandra could see the sun setting on the horizon. She was young and innocent. Playful enthusiasm filled her thoughts. The field was flooded with dandelions that brushed against her ankles as she ran about, simulating the actions of an airplane. Free of any concerns or fear, she simply existed in the moment, peaceful and full of happiness.

She dropped and lay in the field, looking up at the clouds moving across the sky and imagining them to be creatures that revealed their true identities only to her. She was young, innocent, and naïve to the complexities of life. She was a child.

The clouds continued their show, while the afternoon sun struggled through them and warmed Cassandra's face. She shut her eyes and saw its reddish glow through her eyelids. She heard the sound of a stream meandering in the distance, across the field. The tranquil sound relaxed her, and her breathing slowed as the sun warmed her body.

Cassandra thought she could stay in this place forever as she felt a flash of harmony engulf her being. She continued to focus on the sound of running water. Its intensity increased and it seemed to be getting closer. She had never liked the water, but found solace in listening to a stream or viewing the ocean tides on a hot day. The sun felt hotter and more intense on her eyes, causing her to squeeze her eyelids tighter. A sheen of sweat formed on her brow, and she realized that the sound of the water was becoming louder. It seemed as though the stream was right under her. The brightness of the sun was becoming uncomfortable.

Uneasiness began to creep into her mind. The sun seemed to be right on top of her face, beaming down oppressively on her nose and eyes. The sound of rushing water filled her ears.

Fear overtook Cassandra as she began to think of her foster dad and the awful nights of abuse. She felt a hand on her chest, pushing her into the water that now began to encircle her. Her heart pumped more quickly and heightened all of her senses. She knew something was wrong.

Panic began to envelop her. She tried to get up and move away from the water and the burning sun. But she couldn't move. The fear of helplessness paralyzed her. *Why can't I move?* Cassandra thought, panicking. The sweat flowed down her cheeks as she attempted to move her limbs to no avail. She gathered her thoughts and realized she needed to escape from the sound of flowing water. She focused all her attention and in one exasperated explosion of effort, she snapped her eyes open.

Suddenly, terror replaced the placid calmness that had filled her dreams. Cassandra let out a long, desperate scream.

No one heard it but Cassandra.

47

Night fell upon Sherman Point. The winds had picked up considerably over the last several hours, and the rain continued to fall at a steady pace. The outer rim of Hurricane Mario had reached the Maine coastline. The news of the big fight in the rec room sent a buzz through the night air. After several witnesses, including two guards, came forward, it was determined that Mitch and Sameer had been acting in self-defense and would not be disciplined. On the other hand, Grabowski and the skinny kid were being transferred out of Sherman Point, and the talk was that the state was pursuing attempted murder charges against the two.

Mitch's thoughts fluctuated between Cassandra and what had just happened in the rec room. Sameer had saved his life. Under the weight of a conflicted heart, Mitch thought back to the lesson his father had taught him when he was just an impressionable young boy—*Never trust a Muslim, son. Never turn your back one of them. They'll stick a knife in your back when all you're doing is trying to help them.* Mitch replayed the words over and over in his mind, but he knew that his experiences were telling him something entirely different. Not only wasn't he stabbed by a Muslim, but Sameer took a shank in his arm, saving Mitch's life. Mitch respected what Sameer had done and knew he owed his friend big time.

Thoughts of Cassandra flooded back into Mitch's mind. He couldn't believe she was gone, and knew something bad had happened. Helplessness consumed Mitch as he paced around his room anxiously. Turtle watched with a concerned gaze. Mitch knew someone at Sherman Point was responsible for what had happened to Cassandra, and he was willing to bet it was Dr. Brady.

"I need more information, Turtle. I know there's a connection between the other three girls going missing and Cassandra," Mitch said, running the other girls' names through his mind. "What's the common link, Turtle? Cassandra, Christie Lambert, Kathy Hurley, and Tanya Gomes. What do they have in common?"

"I'm not sure," Turtle said.

"I've got to see their files," Mitch said.

"Files?"

"Yeah, in Dr. Brady's office," Mitch said, thinking back to when Brady told him that he had a file on every kid, going back ten years. "But how can I possibly get into his office without anyone knowing?"

"I can get you in there," Turtle said as casually as if he were saying that he could get a piece of cake for Mitch.

"What?"

"I know how."

Mitch initially was skeptical, but he quickly realized that if anyone knew how to do it, it would be Turtle. "How?"

"Through the old drainage system and tunnels. It's easy."

"Drainage system? Tunnels?"

"There's an old drainage system that leads to tunnels in the cliffs below Sherman Point," Turtle explained. "Back in the 1800s, the system was used to drain sewage out of Sherman Point and into the ocean. There are old drainage tunnels all over the campus and right underneath us. Most people don't know about them anymore, but—"

"But you're a genius, Turtle," Mitch said, jumping up as a glimmer of hope rejuvenated him. "Can you show me?"

"Oh no, I can't get in trouble," Turtle said.

"Please, Turtle, you won't get in trouble. Cassandra needs me."

"I can't go with you, but I can show you," Turtle said as he took out a piece of construction paper. "I can't give you the map of all the tunnels because Felix took it when he searched our room. That would take some time. But I'll draw you an exact map of how to get into Brady's office using several tunnels and a couple of heating vents."

Mitch watched in utter amazement while his friend, Turtle, worked diligently to reproduce a map from nothing but his memory. No one knew of Turtle's brilliance simply because no one ever took the time to get to know him. People just assumed that he was a kid with autism who was painfully shy and had nothing to offer. This couldn't have been further from the truth. Turtle was a great guy with more talents than most, and now that Mitch had gotten to know him better, he considered him a good friend.

"Done," Turtle announced, "twenty-six minutes and twenty-one seconds. A better time than I predicted." Turtle held the map out to Mitch, proud of his efforts.

Mitch looked the drawing. It was a remarkable rendition of the entire campus with buildings, boundary markers, measurements, ventilation systems, and several out-of-date tunnels that had once served as a sewage system. Mitch could hardly believe what he was seeing.

"You're a genius," Mitch said, shifting his gaze from the map to Turtle and then back. "A genius!"

"Well, that's not the entire tunnel system. Like I said, they took that map."

"How do you know where all this stuff is on the campus?"

"Don't forget about that photographic memory thing," Turtle said with a smirk. "I just look at things like maps and diagrams and if I see it once, I have a picture of it in my head forever. We went to the public library to work on our history term papers, and I found some really old books about Sherman Point. Nobody said anything, so I studied them."

"Just like that," Mitch said, never taking his eyes off the drawing.

"Just like that," Turtle said, a confident smile crossing his face.

"Turtle, you are brilliant!"

48

Cassandra looked around and realized that her head was all that she could move. She wore nothing except her underwear and sports bra. A bright light shone oppressively in her eyes, blinding her and thwarting her efforts to look upward. Ropes were secured tightly around her hands, wrists, and feet. One thick rope scraped against her bare midsection, restricting any movement of her core.

"Help me!" she screamed at the top of her lungs, only to hear echoes of her voice. She convulsed violently in a futile attempt to free herself, screaming all the time, hoping that someone was near. Then she quieted herself and listened for anyone or anything that could help. She heard nothing except a steady stream of water entering the cavernous womb from an unknown source.

Cassandra's breaths came rapidly and uncontrollably. She felt her heart pounding. She tried to slow her breathing and listen more intently.

Nothing.

Nothing but the sound of flowing water filled her ears.

The fog in her head began to subside as she realized she was being held against her will. To her left she could see an old wooden desk with a small battery pack that probably powered the light shining down on her.

"Help me! Somebody help me!" Cassandra's pleas went unanswered. "Oh God, please, somebody!" Tears filled her eyes and rolled down her face. She felt sick. She felt helpless—like a child with no mother to comfort her.

Cassandra lifted her head slightly and looked straight ahead, seeing the ropes wrapped around her waist and her ankles. She realized that she was being restrained on a metal table. The water sounded as if it were coming out of a faucet. Straining her neck to look down, she could see where the dirt floor and the rocky walls met. That was the source! Cassandra saw water gushing in, covering the floor. In an instant, terror overwhelmed her.

"Help me! Oh God, please help me!" Cassandra screamed. The hurricane surge was forcing ocean water into the cavern. Cassandra realized that her worst nightmare was becoming reality. Terror competed with helplessness in Cassandra's mind as it became evident to her that she was going to drown.

"Help me!" she screamed again in desperation.

No one answered.

49

The wind slapped branches against the side of the building, creating a constant reminder of the violent storm that was coming straight at them. Time was running out, and Mitch had to work quickly. He knew he had to save Cassandra and he was undeterred by the thought of any consequence or harm that he might suffer. He loved her and would do anything to get her back.

Tonight was the night, and there was no turning back. The third-shift staff would be guarding them and that meant a relaxation in security. Almost all the kids on the floor were given some sort of medication to help them sleep, and this usually guaranteed a quiet, uneventful night for the guards. Little did they know that Mitch had been gagging up his meds nightly since arriving at Sherman Point.

Mitch waited in bed, patiently listening to the weather outside his window increase in intensity. The wind howled and the rain created a steady pitter-patter rhythm. It didn't sound like Hurricane Mario was deciding to blow out to sea.

The third-shift guards made their way onto the floor, and the nightly change-of-shift formalities commenced. Mitch knew that it would be about an hour before they left their posts to do their rounds. That's when he would make his move.

He had the names committed to memory—Kathy Hurley, Tanya Gomes, and Christie Lambert—all girls who had disappeared from Sherman Point. There had to be a connection between these three girls going missing and Cassandra, and Mitch knew that if he could find that connection, he could probably find Cassandra.

Impatience grew inside of Mitch as he waited for the overnight staff to let their guard down. Under his blankets, Mitch studied the drawing Turtle had given him, illuminating it with a small penlight, also provided by Turtle. The sketch of Sherman Point was so well drawn that it looked like an architect had done it. Every building was outlined, with doors, guard posts, and distances marked. At the top of the sketch was the main building of Sherman Point, sitting atop the cliff. Mitch was amazed at the accuracy of the measurements on the map. Turtle even provided a scale that read, "one inch equals one hundred feet."

This kid was a genius and no one knew it. As the guards had talked and laughed in the public library, Turtle had quietly collected more information on the inner workings of Sherman Point than anyone in history had ever compiled. This unassuming guy had provided Mitch with all the information he needed to move around Sherman Point and get information that might help him to save Cassandra.

And what about what Therese Harriet Coleman had told Mitch? He still had a hard time accepting that she was real, but he couldn't worry about that now. *Open your heart, Mitchell, and not only will you free my soul, but you will prove your innocence and put an end to man's wickedness and hatred. You will save Cassandra.*

Saving Cassandra.

It was the singular thought that filled his mind. He wasn't sure what he was looking for, but if the information was anywhere it would be in Dr. Brady's file cabinets.

Finally, Mitch heard the hallway guard moving away from his post to make his rounds. Mitch slid out of bed and slipped into his sneakers. Propping his pillows and a jacket under his blanket, he created the illusion of a person sleeping in his bed. Mitch looked out the door and saw that the coast was clear. He was about to begin his adventure when he heard Turtle.

"Mitch."

Mitch turned around, putting a finger to his mouth.

Turtle lowered his voice slightly. "Remember, back by seven before the shift change."

Mitch gave Turtle the thumbs-up as he exited the door, pulling a hoodie over his head. He gingerly walked by the unmanned guard station to the stairwell and climbed up to the roof, as Turtle had directed him to do. There was no way Mitch would make it past all of the guards on the lower floors. Even if he did, the main doors were locked and wired to an alarm system. His only option, according to Turtle, was to get to the roof and make his way down on the outside of the building. No one expected a kid to try to escape from the top of the building.

Mitch stood on the roof, a renewed sense of freedom satisfying him. The wind blew intensely, creating a resistance against which Mitch had to work. He accepted the fact that he was going to get wet. It didn't matter. Only Cassandra mattered.

From the rooftop, Mitch could see the Atlantic Ocean stretching for miles under the light of the moon. The waves crashed into the cliffs below with a rhythm orchestrated by nature. The smell of saltwater filled the air and Mitch took a deep, appreciative breath. *Freedom,* he thought. He hadn't killed anyone, but he would gladly give up his freedom to have Cassandra back. Mitch paused for a moment and realized that he obviously cared more for Cassandra than he did for himself. He had opened up his heart to her, and for the first time in his life, he felt the unconditional love of people who were meant to be together. Nothing would stop him from finding her.

The intensity of his feelings made his adrenaline pump more vigorously. But the intensity was different this time. It wasn't driving him to act without thinking. Quite the contrary, this adrenaline was fueled by a motivation and had a purpose—finding Cassandra. The electrifying nature of this feeling inspired Mitch, but now he felt as though he could control his impulses. He still loved the intoxicating excitement that filled every part of him, but now he understood it better and believed he could channel it to achieve more meaningful goals.

Mitch looked over the side of the building, realizing that the drop would surely result in death. Is this what the greasy-haired kid thought before he was pushed to his death? Mitch wasn't waiting to find out. He looked at Turtle's map and located the spot where a downspout was marked. He made his way over to the spout and without hesitation, he flung his legs over the side, grabbed the spout, and began shimmying his way down six floors to the ground.

The rain made the downspout slippery beneath his hands. The thin-walled, metal pipe was not designed to support Mitch's muscular frame, and suddenly he felt his body move backward as a screw pulled away from the building. Mitch's heart raced as he realized that the downspout was giving way, and he might in fact plummet to the ground. He froze. He was more than halfway to the ground. Maybe his luck would hold. He began to shimmy down the pipe again, and then it happened. The screws above him let go, releasing the downspout from the building with a loud cracking sound. Mitch's weight was no longer being supported. He hung on as long as he could. Then, from twenty feet up, he came crashing down, the impact of his body on the pavement creating a thunderous thump.

Mitch lay on the ground, momentarily stunned. He shook his head to clear the cobwebs. He looked up, trying to make sense of the world around him, and spotted the beam from a guard's flashlight at the corner of the building. Footsteps raced his way and a voice yelled out, "You check over there. I'm going to look in the back!"

50

Mitch lay on the ground, his head pounding, the sound of footsteps growing louder. Lights seemed to be coming from the front of the building, but he wasn't quite sure what was happening; he wasn't registering the full extent of his reality.

Instinctively, Mitch switched into survival mode and knew he had to hide. He pushed himself up off the ground and darted for the bushes. In full stride, he hurled himself over the top of a shrub and scurried as far under it as he could. Just then, the guard turned the corner, shining his light in all directions as he searched for the source of the noise.

The wind continued to rip across the bushes, and Mitch peered through a small opening at their base. The guard was no more than twenty feet from where he hid.

Mitch sat paralyzed, watching the feet of the guard walk right up to the bushes where he camouflaged himself. The light flashed over the bushes and into the woods, the guard continuing to search for anything out of the ordinary. He was so close that Mitch could reach out and touch his shoe, but he remained frozen in silence.

A clanging sound came from behind the guard, causing him to swing around, sending the beam of his light along the exterior of the building.

Nothing.

He turned back and took another step forward, pressing into the bush under which Mitch hid. Mitch saw the light track along the ground ten feet from his body. It was heading in his direction. He made the brash decision that if the light got another two feet closer, he would burst from the bushes and make a run for it. By the time the guard understood what had happened, Mitch would have a big lead on him. He would have a chance.

The light continued in his direction, and Mitch felt the intensity building in him. Under his breath he began to count, "Three, two—"

"Hey! Over here!" a gravelly voice suddenly called.

The light stopped and the guard swung around, responding to the hoarse shout.

Mitch sat silently, his nerves calming slightly. The guard turned and began walking toward the building. A second guard approached, pointing his light upward.

"Look. Up there. The downspout let loose."

"Probably from the wind. Should we fix it?"

"Hell no, man, I'm not going up there. We can fill out a report for maintenance. Let those guys earn their money when they come in tomorrow."

"All right, let's get out of here, man. We're behind on our rounds."

Relieved, wet, and anxious to find Cassandra, Mitch took out the map Turtle had made and again he studied it with the assistance of the small flashlight. He sheltered the map, preventing the rain from drenching it. He found the next spot he had to reach: a drainage cover thirty feet from the back of the building, just inside the woods. Assuring himself that no one was around, Mitch maneuvered deeper into the woods.

After several minutes of searching, Mitch found an old, rusted drain cover. Grabbing the cover, he lifted it up, surprised at how little effort it took to extract it from the ground. He flashed his small beam of light down into the hole, and once he was convinced that he could fit, he eased himself into the drain and pulled the cover back into its resting place.

Mitch was in the inner workings of Sherman Point. The walls sweated with moisture, but the tunnel provided a reprieve from the relentless rain. Only three feet by three feet in diameter, the tunnel was snug. The aging artery provided just enough room for water, and in this case, for Mitch to pass through on his stomach. The opening was old; tree roots had caused a solid buildup of earth. Mitch worked slowly, unclogging the obstructions created by years of neglect. It seemed to take an hour before he reached another grate. He peered through the grate, amazed to find that he was exactly where Turtle indicated he would be—in the heart of Sherman Point.

The main maintenance and control room of Sherman Point emitted a constant hum as machines and valves worked without interruption, sending power and heat to all of the building's appendages. All of the vital parts of campus relied on this room. Pipes crisscrossed the ceiling and penetrated various walls, carrying the water needed to support life in the buildings. It was a massive room and Mitch was amazed at its intricate complexity.

Mitch began kicking at the grate that separated him from the maintenance room. It took several tries before the screws gave in to his efforts. Once the first corner was free, Mitch easily bent the grate, creating space to slip through. He landed in a small pool of water created by the constant drip from the artery he had just exited. It ran downward into another, smaller drainage system that excreted the liquid outside of the building. Mitch took some time to wash the mud off his face and hands with the water.

Two nineteenth-century, arched windows marked the far end of the room. They were pelted with rain and debris carried by the swirling winds. He again removed Turtle's map from his pocket and got himself oriented. He had to find the air duct that breathed heat into the building during the winter months. The map indicated that once Mitch found the natural gas furnace tanks housed in this area, he would find the ducts. It wasn't difficult, as the three furnaces that formed the respiration system for Sherman Point were clearly visible on the other side of the control room.

Mitch quickly made his way across the room to the three, enormous, natural-gas furnaces. He noticed three individual pipes that ran from the furnaces and through the wall to the outside of the building, and concluded that this was how the tanks inhaled the gas from the pipeline that delivered it. He went behind the tanks to find the ducts that carried the heat from the furnaces throughout the buildings. It was through one of these vents that Mitch would venture to Dr. Wes Brady's office. He looked from the map to the various ducts, trying to figure out which one was correct. A familiar, intimidating noise suddenly made Mitch freeze.

He spun around, "Oh shit," he said aloud.

Staring up at Mitch from fifty feet away, teeth showing and saliva dripping from their mouths, were Damian and Deuce. The dogs growled viciously and snapped their jaws in unison at their prey.

Fear gripped Mitch. He took a half step back, only to find that the dogs responded and moved more quickly in his direction, clearly intending to take a bite out of him. He took another step back, causing Damian and Deuce to explode toward him, barking savagely, their evil intentions undeniable.

51

Mitch wasted little time putting his plan into motion. Damian and Deuce flashed toward Mitch, each intimidating bark echoing off cement and metal. Mitch had prepared himself in case he ran into the dogs, but now that he was about to be mauled by them, it seemed like it was all happening too fast.

His pulse racing, he quickly pulled two dinner rolls out of his pocket. Holding the rolls in his left hand, he shoved his index finger into each one, creating a hole in the middle. Hastily, he glanced toward Damian and Deuce. The dogs were unfettered and they were locked on their victim. Mitch swallowed hard, knowing his window of opportunity was closing and soon he would be at the receiving end of a brutal attack from two highly trained guard dogs. Mitch shoved his hand into his right pocket, retrieving a handful of the red pills he had been gagging up every night since his arrival a Sherman Point. Now, he was hoping that the pills designed to slow him down would do the same to Damian and Deuce.

Looking up one last time, the sight of the dogs just feet away heightened Mitch's nervousness. He shoved as many pills into the dinner rolls as possible, spilling some on the ground. Mitch could feel the dogs' intensity. They were almost on top of him. He tossed the dinner rolls onto the ground and jumped backward, buying himself as much distance as he could. Then he closed his eyes and let fate take over.

A second passed, and Mitch felt the absence of teeth penetrating his skin. Instead, he heard the tongues of Damian and Deuce slobbering up the treat he had just presented to them. The two dogs feasted on the stale snack with the crunchy center as their primal instincts prevailed. They valued food over violence.

Mitch breathed a slight sigh of relief. "Good boys," he said in a playful tone as he slowly began sidestepping to the left, without taking his eyes off the dogs.

Damian and Deuce finished the rolls, unaware that they had just ingested many milligrams of a sedative. In an undisciplined moment of weakness, they began sniffing about in hopes of finding more snacks to devour. Their paces quickened as they searched the area, but to no avail. Once realizing that no more treats were coming, they again turned their attention to Mitch—the original object of their desire.

Fear crept further into Mitch when he realized that he was again in the dogs' cross hairs. Damian took a vicious snap at Mitch's arm, sending him backward.

"AHH!"

Deuce took a step forward, baring his teeth. And then something strange happened. Both dogs began randomly sniffing all around, turning their heads in different directions. Their movements became less militant and more erratic. Damian involuntarily plopped to the ground, followed by Deuce. Suddenly, the two Doberman Pinschers looked hopelessly up toward Mitch, their eyes glazing over. Relief replaced Mitch's fear as he watched the two dogs roll over, fighting to keep their eyes open. Finally, the drugs took their full effect. The dogs were no longer a threat to anyone.

It reminded Mitch of when Dr. Brady had injected him with a drug, and he became defenseless. He suddenly felt a deep sense of empathy for Damian and Deuce, and he knelt and stroked their brownish coats. *Two peaceful puppies*, he thought. If they had gotten into someone else's hands, they very well could have been nice pets. Mitch didn't hate them for trying to hurt him. He knew that this is what they'd been taught. Someone had trained them to be the dogs that they were today. They weren't born vicious, and with some love and tenderness, Mitch was sure they could be good puppies.

"Thanks for not eating me, boys," Mitch said, jumping up and grabbing Turtle's map. He quickly found the vent that Turtle had marked with a big X. Mitch knew that this vent led right into Brady's office and to the information that might lead to Cassandra. His heart began pumping with motivation again, and he began unscrewing the screws from the vent cover by placing a dime in the grooves and turning it to the left.

Mitch removed the vent cover and looked back toward Damian and Deuce, who lolled in a drug-induced complacency.

"I'll be back boys," he said, hoisting himself into the shaft. The metal groaned in disapproval as he slid inside and began crawling forward on his belly. He looked at his watch. It was 4:15 a.m. He'd have to move quickly to make it back to his unit prior to the shift change. He picked up his pace.

Mitch passed several vent grates and looked down on deserted rooms. The duct occasionally moaned as Mitch shifted his weight, sending a metallic popping sound down the shaft. Aside from the night guards, the building was all but empty, and Mitch was certain that if the noises were heard at all, they'd just be attributed to the storm thrashing outside the building. He kept up his pace until he came to the grate over Dr. Wes Brady's office. Mitch stopped to watch and listen.

Once he was convinced that the office was vacant, Mitch quickly went to work on the vent cover. Prepared to kick it in, he was surprised to find that these interior covers simply snapped on and off to allow easy access for cleaning. He jiggled the grate several times, popping it off and revealing an easily accessible opening into Dr. Brady's office. Mitch lowered himself down and leaned the grate cover against a bookcase.

"Turtle, you're a freaking genius," Mitch said to no one as a smile flashed across his face. He now stood in the central nervous system of Sherman Point, where all the vital information was housed, all because a kid with autism had drawn a map from memory. Again, Mitch allowed a smile to fill his face in honor of his friend, Turtle.

With the small flashlight in his mouth, Mitch went over to the file cabinets. Three names—Kathy Hurley, Tanya Gomes, and Christie Lambert. He didn't know what he was looking for exactly, but he knew a few things. First, he knew that all three girls had disappeared from Sherman Point. One ended up dead in a hospital gown, hit by a car; and the other two were never heard from again. *What about the greasy-haired kid*? Mitch thought. The kid was terrified, and then he ended up dead. He had overheard Brady saying something to Rooney, and then Rooney ended up dead. One thing was clear to Mitch: the greasy-haired kid was right when he said things were getting dangerous, and Mitch was in the middle of it.

Check the names, he had told Mitch. Check the names. Now Mitch had the names, and their files were just feet away. He wasn't sure what to look for, but he was sure he was going to save Cassandra, no matter what price he had to pay.

Mitch read each label on the file cabinets until he got to "G" for Gomes. Reaching up he grabbed the handle and yanked forward.

Locked.

Mitch attempted to open several more cabinets to find the same result. He looked around the room and decided to search Dr. Brady's desk. He pulled out the top drawer and began sorting through a mess of office supplies and papers. Then, in the back right corner of the desk, he found a small set of keys that were clearly marked "file cabinet." Without wasting time, he crossed the room to the cabinets and placed the first key into the lock, turning it quickly to the right.

Nothing.

Mitch repeated this routine with the other keys until finally, the cabinets opened, liberating all the information stored within them. Mitch left the key in the keyhole while he worked his way through the files, looking for the name Gomes, then Hurley, and then Lambert.

Moving swiftly, Mitch removed the three files from the drawers and placed them side by side on the conference table. He scanned the intake pages of the file marked Hurley, Kathy, taking note of the intake date and reason for incarceration. Then he went through the files on Tanya Gomes and Christie Lambert. Shifting his attention back and forth between the files, Mitch searched for anything that would connect them and give him a clue about Cassandra's disappearance. *What do these girls have in common and why did the greasy-haired kid tell me to check the names?* He read feverishly, trying to make connections, and then something jumped out at Mitch on all three intake sheets.

There wasn't just one similarity; these girls all had several things in common. All three were seventeen years old—just young enough to be kept out of the adult criminal justice system. They were athletes in their schools and from their intake pictures, Mitch could clearly see that they were all attractive. Dr. Brady was the intake physician for each of the girls. Each girl lived in a foster home when she was sent to Sherman Point.

To Mitch's surprise, it was the first offense for all three girls, and they were sentenced to over a year—a long time, considering their so-called crimes. Christie Lambert and Tanya Gomes were both arrested for disturbing the peace when they had fights with their foster parents and tried to run away. Kathy Hurley ran away from her foster home, alleging abuse, and when she was caught, she was charged with being a wayward child.

Mitch thought back to what Cassandra had told the group. Like the other girls, she was placed in a foster home after her mom died. She was seventeen and ran track at school, and like the others, she had Dr. Brady as her main psychiatrist. She was sentenced to eighteen months for running away from her foster parents. After what she told the group about the abuse she had suffered at the hand of her foster father, it only made sense that she would take off.

It was starting to add up, but there had to be more, Mitch thought. He dug deeper into the files, and then it hit him. Like himself, Cassandra had been sentenced by Judge Jeremiah Butler. He looked into each file, and sure enough, under the heading of presiding judge was the name Jeremiah Butler. Mitch wasn't sure exactly what was going on, but he knew that Dr. Brady and Judge Jeremiah Butler had something to do with it.

Suddenly, a familiar voice resonated from the hallway just feet from where Mitch stood. He froze. *Holy shit*, Mitch said to himself.

"Good morning, Roger," Dr. Brady said from just outside the office door, "just getting in a little early to prepare for a meeting." He fumbled through his pockets, looking for his office keys.

Mitch looked to his left at the grate from the vent leaning against the bookshelf, and then back to the open file cabinets, the keys dangling from the lock. He moved impulsively while the conversation continued outside. He knew that it would mean big trouble if Brady found him. Mitch didn't care what happened to him, but if he became Brady's next victim, he wouldn't be able to save Cassandra. He quickened his pace.

"Can't find your keys?" Roger, the security guard, asked. "No problem, Doc. Here, let me help you."

Mitch grabbed the grate, stood on a chair, and put it back in place. In one fluid motion, he leaped off the chair and grabbed the files. He looked back at the file cabinet. The keys were still hanging in the lock. He wanted to get the files back to their respective places and remove the keys, but time was running out. He had to make a decision.

It was too late. The lock on Brady's office door clicked, indicating it was no longer secure. The door swung open, and Dr. Brady walked into his office, snapping on the lights.

52

Unaware that she was several hundred feet deep in the cliffs below Sherman Point, Cassandra was cold as she lay on a metal table, restrained and terrified. Hurricane Mario's surge was pushing ocean water into the cavern. By looking to her left, she could see that the water was about knee deep. Now in a more hushed tone than before Cassandra cried, "Help me, somebody." She sobbed, helpless in the womb of Sherman Point. Death by drowning seemed inevitable.

She began to wish that she could make time stand still, but the sounds of rushing water reminded her of her mortality. She was going to die today and no one would ever know what happened to her. She would be another girl who "escaped" from the facility, never to be seen or heard from again. Why was she here? She wondered. Who put her here? Hope slowly faded as she began to let go of her dreams of the future.

The water kept rising. She wondered about her mother and what would have happened if she hadn't died—if drugs hadn't taken her. She'd never had a real family, and now the promise she had made to herself to have children someday and to be a good, selfless mother was no more than a fantasy that would never come to fruition.

She wished she could be reborn and have a new life, a second chance, knowing what she knew now. She would do more on her own and not rely on the adults in her life—the protectors and opinion leaders that she had blindly followed and obeyed. Where had their lessons led her? She lay in a reality of terror where the outcome would not be life, but death. No more tomorrows would reveal themselves.

Anger rose in Cassandra as she recalled the betrayal and pain of her foster father and the blind eye turned toward her by those from whom she sought solace. And what of her mother? Now the thoughts of her mother came not with anger and hatred, but with pity and sorrow. Cassandra knew nothing of her grandparents, and wondered if they had mistreated her mother. She wished she could have reached out and helped her mom and led her away from the world she had chosen. But she was gone. Despite all the pain Cassandra had endured, she still felt love in her heart for the woman who chose drugs over her daughter, causing Cassandra to end up with a foster family that hurt her—a foster family that squelched any trust Cassandra had for people and replaced it with an angry skepticism that formed an emotional wall around her.

But Cassandra did eventually learn to trust again. She trusted the group—Sameer, Turtle, and Tina. She considered them friends. She trusted Dr. Cav, the man who said he would always be there for her—the father figure she never had. And as far as Mitch was concerned, she loved him. She had let him in and she wanted him here now to hold her, to tell her it will be OK. But she was alone, awaiting death by her greatest fear—drowning.

Cassandra went limp physically and emotionally when she again realized that she was alone in the world and she was going to die alone. None of it mattered. Her friends, the newly found trust she had in people, the love in her heart for Mitch. None of it mattered because she was going to die alone in a cold cavern where the only sounds were those of her sobs accompanied by the unmistakable flow of water. Cassandra prepared herself for death.

The lights in Dr. Brady's office clicked on, illuminating the room. Mitch sat in complete silence, trying to devise a plan if Dr. Brady did in fact go to the far end of his office, thus exposing Mitch hiding behind the couch. It was not the best hiding spot, but considering how quickly Mitch had to act, it was his only option. Mitch took deep, slow breaths as he tried to bring his adrenaline down. The thought again occurred to Mitch that if Dr. Brady did in fact find him hiding in his office with the missing girls' files in his hand, he might never be heard from again.

He would make a run for it if he had to, but clearly, Dr. Brady and the guards would know who he was. He could jump Dr. Brady, but that would only get him in more trouble. Mitch sat anxiously, waiting to react to what Dr. Brady would do next.

Mitch looked from behind the couch and could see the side of Dr. Brady's head and face while the man sat his desk. He appeared to be reading something. He was stroking his beard nervously, removing his glasses from his nose and then putting them back. He continued to review the papers in front of him, exhaling heavily from time to time.

Mitch watched as Dr. Brady got up and moved to the front of his desk. Papers in hand, he paced back and forth, talking to himself in a barely audible voice. Then Mitch heard the man say, "Shit, what a mess," as he slammed the papers onto the top of his desk.

Dr. Brady continued to pace, running his hand over his bald head and through the hair of his elongated beard. He mumbled under his breath. Suddenly, he stopped in his tracks and said, "What the hell?"

Following Dr. Brady's eyes, it was clear what he was seeing. Dangling from the file cabinet hung the keys, exposed for everyone to see. Dr. Brady slowly made his way over to the cabinets. "Who left those there?" he said.

Mitch felt his muscles tightening. He watched as Dr. Brady walked to the file cabinets, looking around his office with inquisitiveness. He turned the key to secure the files, and then removed the keys from the lock and placed them on top of the file cabinet.

Mitch's heart raced as Brady began walking around the office humming, and then saying in a low voice, "Now, how did those keys end up in that file cabinet, I wonder?"

Mitch held his breath and didn't move. Dr. Brady's footsteps came closer and closer to the couch. He stopped right in front of the couch. Mitch's adrenaline raced, and he planned to explode from behind the couch, knock over Brady, and make for the door. He saw the couch shift slightly as Dr. Brady's hand touched it. Brady began to lean forward to look over the top of the couch, and Mitch resigned himself to making a move. Mitch stared at the top edge of the couch, as Brady's fingers wrapped around it.

Now, Mitch told himself.

54

Mitch was about to explode from behind the couch and knock Dr. Brady over when a cell phone rang. Startled by the ringing, Dr. Brady released his grip on the couch and stood upright, swinging around to look for the phone. He raced to his desk and grabbed the cell phone, bringing it to his ear. "Yes, this is Dr. Wes Brady."

Mitch could again see Dr. Brady from his vantage point. The man was nervous about something as he spoke into the phone.

"Yes, I know the information is rather hard to believe, but you must," Dr. Brady said, his hand shaking as it held the phone to his ear. "We haven't time to waste and we must act now if we want to be successful." Desperation was evident in his tone. He started to pace again.

Mitch continued to listen as Dr. Brady pleaded with the caller. "You must listen to what I'm saying," Dr. Brady continued, walking to the other side of the room parallel to the couch. "I empathize with your position, but we must act without delay or we may miss our chance," Dr. Brady said. He stopped walking and deliberately peered in the direction of the couch. Squinting, Dr. Brady looked more closely toward the couch, and a nervous flash filled Mitch. He was sure Dr. Brady was looking right at him. The intensity in Dr. Brady's voice increased.

"What? That is completely unacceptable. We haven't the time," Dr. Brady said, spinning around and heading to his desk. He began rifling through his drawers, looking for something. "I cannot make that promise," Dr. Brady said to the caller, his hand shaking. "Understood. Consider it done," was the last thing Dr. Brady said before he slid the cell phone shut. He threw it on his desk.

Dr. Brady moved quickly to the closet in his office and swung the door open. Mitch could see Dr. Brady, but he could not see the contents of the closet. He heard rustling followed by a loud grunt. Mitch peered from behind the couch in time to see Dr. Brady pulling a large, green bag from his closet. He was exerting a considerable amount of energy dragging the bag across the floor. The green, canvas bag was large enough to store a body, Mitch thought. Then a sickening thought flashed in Mitch's mind. *What if it was a body? What if it was Cassandra's body?*

Mitch's impulses told him to jump out and pounce on Dr. Brady. He took a second and contemplated his options. He would wait. He had to wait if he was going to do this right and save Cassandra. *Just wait.*

Dr. Brady hurriedly placed the bag over his shoulder. He headed toward the office door, then he stopped and looked curiously back at the couch. Without hesitation, he placed the bag on the floor and crossed the office toward the couch. Dr. Brady again wrapped his hands around the top edge of the couch and leaned over to check behind it.

Looking downward, he saw nothing but dust on the hardwood floor. "That's it, these things must stop before I completely lose my grip on reality," he said. He retrieved the bag and left his office.

55

Robin Clarkson slammed down the receiver of her aging desk phone. She'd received a report of yet another girl who'd gone missing at Sherman Point, and the story simply didn't add up. Her investigative skills were keen, and although she'd been unsure at first, she now had a pretty good grip on what was happening at Sherman Point. With the help of some information from a very unlikely ally, Clarkson had surmised who was responsible for the murder of Myles Harwich and for the disappearance of the girls. She just needed to get in front of him and rattle him a little. She knew he would crack.

Time was a valuable commodity at this point, with Hurricane Mario bearing down on the coast. Soon, it would be too late and the chances of finding the girl, Cassandra, would be gone. The governor had ordered a mandatory evacuation of the coastal towns, but a girl needed her, and Robin Clarkson would never turn her back on the duties she'd sworn to do.

Her thoughts turned to Mitch Blais and the probation officer, Dan Rooney, whom he was accused of killing. This, she knew, was not the case. Mitch Blais was no killer. Rooney was dead because of what he had discovered. He was going to blow the whistle on the wrongdoings at Sherman Point and certain very influential people could not let that happen. Rooney was dead because he was going to do the right thing, and Mitch Blais simply had been in the wrong place at the wrong time.

Clarkson got her facts straight in her head and then checked her weapon and replaced it in her holster. She didn't want to use her gun, but with what she knew now, she was afraid that it might come down to that. She made for the door, Sherman Point Rehabilitation Center her destination.

Dr. Brady's office fell silent. There was no trace of Mitch except for the toes of his sneakers sticking out slightly at the bottom of the window drape behind which he had repositioned himself when Dr. Brady's back was turned. Mitch made a quick check of his nerves and the time. It was 5:45 a.m. He continued to stand motionless behind the curtain and waited until he was sure it was safe to come out.

He had what he came to get: information—and revealing information, at that. But what was in the bag? He wasn't sure what it all meant, but he wasn't going to give up on Cassandra. Not now, not ever. The greasy-haired kid said that he had overheard Dr. Brady tell Rooney to be careful making such allegations, and then he ended up dead. He knew that somehow, Dr. Brady and Judge Jeremiah Butler were involved in the girls' disappearances, and he would have to find out how if he was going to save Cassandra. Mitch knew he had to get to Cassandra before it was too late—if it wasn't too late already.

A further sense of responsibility came over Mitch now that he had some leads to follow. All four girls were in foster homes, and all four had tried to run away. They were charged with crimes and ended up in front of Judge Jeremiah Butler, who had sentenced them to Sherman Point. None of the sentences seemed fair, as none of the girls had prior records. Mitch continued to think frantically, trying to put the pieces together. The girls were athletic and beautiful, and they all disappeared. They all had Rooney for a probation officer, and he was dead. It wasn't making complete sense, but Mitch knew that if he was going to find more answers, there was only one thing he could do: get to Judge Jeremiah Butler.

The trip back through the air duct went quickly. Mitch eased himself down into the maintenance room and screwed the grate back into place with his dime. The constant humming of the inner workings of Sherman Point filled the air. Damian and Deuce lay ten feet away, placid looks on their faces as the drugs kept them in a state of restful harmony. Mitch again took several seconds to give the dogs some much-needed affection. "Good boys," he said.

Damian and Deuce both looked contently into Mitch's eyes, appreciating the compassion. Mustering just enough control over their bodies, they began to lick Mitch's hands. They were harmless and peaceful.

The drainage pipe was much easier to crawl through now that he had cleared the roots and dirt away in his initial trip. Mitch made good time and soon was extracting himself from the manhole cover just inside the tree line. The wind blew Mitch's hair to the side, and the rain remained a relentless deluge.

Getting back up to the roof wasn't going to be quite as easy. The plan was to climb up one of the undamaged downspouts the entire six stories. To his surprise, a delivery truck sat outside the building. The driver sat in the cab, reading a delivery form. Mitch checked the time. It was 6:50 a.m. He had to move fast.

Waiting for the driver to exit the vehicle and enter the building was torture. Mitch had until 7:00 a.m. before the guards for the next shift would arrive. He checked the time again—6:53 a.m. Time became an enemy to Mitch.

Finally, the driver jumped out of the vehicle and collected some boxes from the back of the truck. Using a dolly, he rolled the cartons though the back door, vanishing from sight. It was now or never—6:56 a.m.

Wasting no time, Mitch bolted to the truck and climbed up to the roof of the trailer. He grabbed an undamaged downspout and began his trek upward. After several near falls due to the wind and rain, he was on the roof, standing outside the door and window of the stairwell.

Sliding through the window was easy, and Mitch found himself in the stairwell, one floor above his unit. He would simply walk down the stairs and slip past the guards when they went to do their final rounds.

Mitch walked down the flight of stairs, the rainwater dripping from his body, and his sneakers squeaking slightly on the concrete floor. He made it to the door of his floor. Stretching his neck, he peeked through the window. Mitch's heart sank when he saw the scene in front of him.

It was too late. The daytime guard stood in the hall, talking to his third-shift counterpart. Mitch stood motionless, his heart racing as he wondered what to do. He listened as the two conversed.

"Any problems last night, Jackson?" the guard asked, taking a sip from his coffee.

"No, everyone slept peacefully."

"I'm sure everyone did," the guard said, taking another haul from his cup. "Let me put my stuff in the office and I'll do your last bed check for you."

"Suit yourself," Jackson said, yawning and stretching his arms. He began gathering up his things from around his chair and shoving them into a backpack.

***

Turtle sat up in bed, his clock reading 6:59 a.m. Where was Mitch? This wasn't good, and Turtle wasn't sure what he would say when the guards discovered that Mitch was missing. He rolled out of bed, put on his slippers, and walked to the door. Looking left down the hall, he saw the guard, Jackson, gathering up his stuff. Turtle quickly turned his head to the right and saw Mitch's face in the window of the door. Mitch put his hands up in the air, silently pleading with Turtle to help him.

"Can I help you, Turtle?" Jackson asked, knowing he probably needed to use the bathroom at this hour of the morning.

"Bathroom, please," Turtle said in a quiet voice.

"Sure."

Turtle walked into the hallway, when another voice rang out from down the hall. It was the second guard returning to his post. "Turtle, what are you doing up at this hour? Go back to bed. It's Saturday. I've got to read the paper."

"Bathroom," was all Turtle said, passing the guard as he continued down the hall toward the bathroom. His mind was racing. What was he going to do? Then, in a flash, he knew. Without warning, Turtle dropped to the floor, clutching his side. He began screaming, "My stomach! Oh God, it hurts!"

Both guards rushed to Turtle's side as his screams filled the hallway. "Calm down, Turtle, we'll get you help. What hurts?"

"My stomach," Turtle said again in a high-pitched yell.

Both guards were down on the floor when Jackson said, "Call the nurse." The second guard bounced up and headed to the guard post to make the call.

When Mitch realized that Turtle was distracting the guards, he quickly opened the door a crack, slid through, and headed for his room. He rushed into his living quarters and immediately removed his wet clothes, kicking them under his bed. The sounds of Turtle's moans still filled the air, giving Mitch just seconds more to complete the deception. He rushed to the closet, retrieving his bathrobe and towel from the hook. He wrapped himself in his robe and threw the towel over his head, concealing his wet hair. Casually, he strolled to the threshold of his door and watched the chaos in front of him.

"Is he all right?" Mitch asked, feigning genuine concern.

"He'll be OK," Jackson said, partially diverting his attention from Turtle. "What do you need, Blais?"

"Just wanted to take a shower."

"Not now. Get back into your room."

"OK."

The hallway door swung open and a nursing triage team entered with a stretcher. "Clear the way," the nurse ordered, making her way to Turtle.

Mitch, like the rest of the curious onlookers, watched from his door as the nurses and guards attended to Turtle. Turtle let out a loud scream as they lifted him onto the stretcher. Clearing a path, the nurses rolled the stretcher down the hall, Turtle moaning the whole way. As the stretcher approached the doorway to his room, Turtle turned his head to see Mitch standing there, looking at him. Turtle let out a long moan as he passed Mitch. Their eyes met and Turtle flashed a quick wink in Mitch's direction.

It took everything for Mitch not to laugh at the incompetence of the guards and the brilliance of his friend, Turtle. The brilliant autistic kid with the photographic memory had just fooled everyone. Mitch could hardly believe it. No one would ever think that Turtle could or would pull off such stunt, but Mitch knew better. He knew Turtle was so much smarter than anyone had ever given him credit for, and in this case, he was able to save Mitch from big trouble. More importantly, Mitch could continue on his quest to save Cassandra. He knew he had to get to Judge Jeremiah Butler. He just didn't know how yet.

57

Turtle was still in the infirmary, the medical staff scrambling to diagnose a condition that didn't exist. Mitch continued to marvel at Turtle's quick thinking and resourcefulness. He truly appreciated the bond he had developed with his new friend.

It was late in the afternoon and the majority of the kids at Sherman Point were in the rec room, engaged in their ritualistic activities. Kids huddled around the window to marvel at the force of the storm. Rain continued to fall and trees gyrated in the intense wind, bending into abnormal positions and then violently snapping back in the other direction. Those uninterested in storms sat in front of the TV to watch *The Dr. Bob Show*, but not Mitch. He sat at a table with Sameer and Tina. Sameer's arm was wrapped in heavy gauze, concealing the twelve stitches required to close his wound. It was a reminder to Mitch of the sacrifice his friend had made while saving his life.

Mitch revealed to his friends everything he knew about Cassandra and the other three missing girls. He told them about his wild dreams and about Therese Harriet Coleman. He told them about Dr. Brady and Judge Jeremiah Butler.

"I've got to find her," Mitch said, looking at Sameer and Tina. "I know Judge Butler knows something, but how can I get to him?"

"I'm not sure, Mitch," Sameer said, "but I'll do whatever I can to help."

"Hell, yeah. Me too, Mitch," Tina said, curling up in her chair. "Cassandra's my girl."

"You guys have already done so much to help me," Mitch said appreciatively to his friends. "I can't ask you to get in any deeper. I'll figure out what to do."

But do what? Judge Jeremiah Butler was somewhere out there and Mitch was incarcerated at Sherman Point. He needed a plan and he needed one soon. Desperation began to mount, and the seconds were ticking away.

A sudden, collective moan of disappointment filled the room when the words, "SPECIAL NEWS REPORT," flashed across the TV screen in red, interrupting the *Dr. Bob Show.* Felix and his entourage of guards made their way over to the TV, clearly interested in an update on Hurricane Mario.

"Shut up," Felix ordered. He pushed his way through the group of kids using his oversized belly as a battering ram. "I said shut up—or else. What don't you pissants understand?"

A quiet came over the room, and everyone's attention became fixed on the meteorologist standing in front of a computerized weather screen. A map of the East Coast was visible, and a massive, red, circular image representing Hurricane Mario sat out in the middle of the Atlantic Ocean.

"We have a very serious condition forming with Hurricane Mario that residents on the coastlines of northern Massachusetts, parts of New Hampshire, and southern Maine should pay close attention to at this time," the weather man said in an incredulous tone. "The East Coast has not seen a storm of this magnitude in many years. Some are calling it a super storm. What we have," he continued, pointing to the map, "is an anomaly. Usually, a hurricane is pushed eastward out to sea by the jet streams of the prevailing winds, and this is what we initially saw with Mario. However, another weather system has formed across the Eastern Seaboard, resulting in the upper-level trough, or upper-level winds, bending or diverting the path of Mario back toward the East Coast."

All eyes in the rec room were now glued to the weather report. Hurricane Mario might be headed straight for Sherman Point.

"This is an extremely serious condition, especially because now that Mario is heading west, it will push the ocean water into the coastline, creating massive coastal flooding, flash floods, and possible power outages," he continued, emphasizing that Mario's projected path was on a direct collision course with the coast. "This is a category three hurricane with an 800-mile-wide span and winds that could reach upward of 120 miles per hour. The worst part of this storm will be the flooding, and we can expect a storm surge of up to twelve feet. If you are on the coast, you are encouraged to heed any mandatory evacuations orders from your local emergency management people, as we are probably going to see flooding of this magnitude only once in our lifetimes. So please be safe and follow the advice of local officials. Now, back to regular programming."

The TV immediately switched to a brawl on the stage of the *Dr. Bob Show*.

"Oooh, baby!" Tina said, squirming in her seat, apparently electrified by the inevitable arrival of a natural disaster. "This isn't going to help you get to the judge, Mitch."

"I don't know, Mitch. You got any ideas?" Sameer said.

A desperate, empty feeling came over Mitch. He didn't have any ideas, and he wasn't sure how he would get out of Sherman Point to find the judge. Cassandra occupied his thoughts. His love for her was real, and he didn't care what it took to save her. He didn't care if it meant his life. The only thing he knew was that he had to think. Think…but nothing came. Mitch hadn't felt hopelessness and despair like this since the day he heard that his father was dead. Without Cassandra, he had nothing left to live for and he certainly didn't care about a hurricane bearing down on him. He welcomed the destruction.

Without warning, sirens began to blare on the grounds of Sherman Point. Felix began barking orders. "We are in code-blue status and everyone will line up in an orderly fashion." Kids began popping up, following Felix's directions in fear of retribution for noncompliance. "We will be going back to the dormitories and preparing for a mandatory evacuation ordered by the governor. You will follow each and every direction. Until further notice, all privileges and level statuses are suspended," Felix said, peering over the crowd, looking for anyone who dared to challenge his authority. Damian and Deuce were now positioned at his feet, growling. "Basically, we own your dumb asses right now. Please give me a reason to kick them. Now, line up and prepare for evacuation procedures."

"That's it," Mitch said, jumping into line, his demeanor changing from gloom to excitement.

"What's it?" Sameer asked.

"The evacuation," Mitch said. "I'm getting out of here during this evacuation!"

58

The inmates of Sherman Point collected two days' worth of clothing in preparation for the evacuation ahead of the full brunt of Hurricane Mario. Turtle reported back from the infirmary, feeling much better despite an ailment that really didn't exist. Mitch again thanked him for his quick thinking and obvious intelligence. Mitch, excited at the opportunity to escape and get closer to finding Cassandra, paced the room with increased vigor. He was talking to himself.

"What's that?" Turtle inquired in response to Mitch's incoherent mumbling.

"What? Oh nothing," Mitch replied, still walking the length of the room. "I need to find Judge Butler. He's got something to do with this."

"He's the one that sentenced me here too," Turtle said, watching Mitch do laps around the room.

"Well, he sent the four girls who disappeared here, and that isn't the only coincidence. I plan to get some answers from him. I know he's involved. I just don't know how to get to him."

"Go to his house."

"I would if I could. I don't know where he lives."

"I do."

Mitch spun around and looked at Turtle, stunned but not completely surprised, at this point, by all the information Turtle housed in his brain. "What?"

"That's right. I did a lot of research at the library on those field trips," Turtle admitted, a smile forming as he contributed to Mitch's quest to save Cassandra.

"Turtle, Turtle, Turtle," Mitch said, going over and wrapping his arms around his undersized roommate. "Without you, kid, I'd be done. You saved me, my friend!"

Turtle was happy and proud to receive such praise from Mitch. He felt like part of a team for the first time in his life. Quickly, he wrote the judge's address on a small piece of paper and handed it to Mitch.

Without notice, Felix appeared in the doorway, clipboard in hand and self-importance in his tone. "Let's go, ladies. Everyone is headed back to the rec room for evacuation. That means you, sweethearts. Line up."

Mitch and Turtle fell in line behind the rest of the evacuees. They made their way down the stairs to the main exit and waited until Felix gave the order to the other guard to release the lock on the door. The kids filed outside, bracing themselves against the strengthening winds and heavy rain of Hurricane Mario.

"Double time," Felix snapped, sending the entire group into a slight jog to the rec room. It was a futile attempt to outrun the rain. Turtle began to fall behind, and before he knew what hit him, Felix shoved him in the back, sending him skidding on the wet cement.

"What the hell," Mitch said, stopping to help his friend up.

Turtle grabbed Mitch's arm and pulled himself up.

"I told you chumps to hurry up. Let's go!" Felix said, laughing slightly.

Mitch whispered in Turtle's ear, "Don't worry, Turtle, he's gonna get what's coming to him."

The inmates began to file into the rec room. Felix was on one side of the door, and another guard was on the opposite side, taking inventory of each inmate who entered. They counted them off by twos, based on who roomed with whom. Felix stood on the stairs under an awning, shielding himself from the rain. He looked down his nose at those in his charge. The wind and rain continued to pummel them, and Felix took pleasure in their obvious discomfort.

The line progressed at a brisk pace, each inmate being checked off and accounted for before entering the rec room. Turtle was next in line. He approached Felix and the other guard, aware of the surprise that they were about to encounter.

"Turtle," Felix said to the other guard, indicating his presence. The other guard made the appropriate check next his name. "And…" Felix began looking around frantically. He jumped off his perch and began scrambling through the line of adolescents. The rain now soaked his uniform and head as he went from the end of the line back up to the front, and approached Turtle. "Where is he?"

"Where's who?"

The red in Felix's face brightened, his anger reaching its pinnacle. "You know who, shithead. That wiseass roommate of yours. Blais."

Turtle spun around, looking in all directions, clearly mocking Felix. "Oh my, he vanished," Turtle said, smiling up at Felix, enjoying the fact the guard had been duped.

"Shut up!" Felix snarled. He looked at the other guard, who put his hands up in the air indicating that he didn't see anything. Felix ran his fingers through his thinning, rain-soaked hair, wondering how he would explain to his superiors that he lost an inmate. "Find him!" Felix commanded.

***

Mitch made his way around the maintenance building. He looked through the large, old, nineteenth-century windows at the gas furnaces and vents he had manipulated the night before to sneak into Brady's office. Continuing around to the back of the building, he found several aging utility vehicles. He chose the oldest pickup truck he could find, knowing that it would be the easiest to hotwire.

Once convinced he was alone, Mitch opened the door of a 1986 Ford pickup truck that looked as if it was on its last legs. He pushed the seat forward, finding several tools in a utility belt. With the help of a screwdriver, he pried off the ignition cover. Moving quickly, he dug the wires out from inside and touched them together. The truck coughed in protest several times, and then jolted to life.

Mitch's sudden anticipation of freedom was quickly suppressed when he picked his head up and looked over the dashboard. To his dismay, he saw Damian and Deuce racing in the direction of the truck. Their now familiar growls and barks were clearly audible above the sound of the punishing winds.

Mitch slammed the door shut just as Damian and Deuce made it to the truck. The two jumped up to the window that shielded Mitch from the onslaught. They barked and growled incessantly for several seconds, and then they abruptly stopped when they recognized Mitch as the guy who had petted them in the maintenance room the night before. A comfortable familiarity came over Damian and Deuce, and they began lightheartedly licking the window, covering it with saliva.

Mitch tapped on the window in a playful manner and said, "See boys, I knew you were good boys." Damian and Deuce jumped down, allowing Mitch to put the truck into drive and pull away. Mitch could now refocus his attention on saving Cassandra.

59

Usually, the absence of guards at the main entrance of Sherman Point would be a cause for concern. Today, however, was different. All available personnel had been summoned to the rec room to assist with the evacuation and the disappearance of one of the inmates. They weren't expecting any arrivals due to Hurricane Mario, and no one would have predicted that the missing kid would simply drive off the point. But that's what Mitch was doing.

He looked down the main road at the vacant guard post, noticing that the wooden guardrail was down to stop traffic. Mitch got excited as he revved the engine, slamming the truck into drive. The wheels took several seconds to gain traction on the wet pavement, but when they did, the truck shot forward toward the gate. Mitch braced himself as the truck smashed into the gate, snapping it in half, and leaving a splintered mess behind.

A surge of impulsive adrenaline steamed through Mitch's body as he looked at the main entrance of Sherman Point in the rearview mirror. A momentary flash of freedom filled him when he realized that he had just emancipated himself from his captors. The elation subsided rapidly, and Mitch refocused his attention on saving Cassandra—if it wasn't too late.

Judge Butler lived in a large house, secluded in the woods, about twenty miles from Sherman Point. Mitch still wasn't sure what he would do when it came time to confront Butler, but he did know he was going to do whatever it took to find Cassandra.

The roads were deserted. Most people apparently had taken the advice to evacuate the area. This worked in Mitch's favor, allowing him to drive at a high rate of speed. He held the wheel tightly, battling the crosswinds that threatened to blow him off the road. The windshield wipers went back and forth vigorously, displacing rain and battling the occasional branch that landed on the windshield. Mitch punched the gas pedal.

A long stone wall about eight feet high surrounded the property of Judge Jeremiah Butler. Mitch passed the main, iron, security gate and continued to drive down to the end of the road. His plan was to scale the wall and make his way to the house through the woods. Maybe Cassandra was in the house.

Mitch looked through the glove box of the truck for anything that might help him. He found a flashlight, but not much more. Exiting the truck, he made his way to the stone wall and muscled his way up to look over the top. He could see the house, but it was pitch black. Mitch figured that the storm had knocked the power out, and maybe this meant that any security system fortifying the house would be rendered useless. Invigorated by the thought, Mitch scaled the wall, dropping down into the woods with a thud.

The rain was relentless, and the wind howled through the trees. Mitch made a beeline for the house, protecting his face from the erratic swaying of tree branches. In a short time, he found himself in the driveway, huddled behind an SUV. Waiting and listening, he determined it was safe, so he scurried to the backyard looking for a more concealed entrance.

A massive, red-cedar deck protruded off the back of the judge's house. At the back of the deck, a sliding-glass door allowed entrance into what appeared to be a dining area and a kitchen. Mitch covertly made his way to the sliding door and stood to the side of it. He looked through the window until he was sure it was safe to try the door. Grabbing the handle, he was surprised to find that the door slid open freely. Mitch slipped into the house, sliding the door shut quietly behind him.

The house was silent and pitch black except for the beam of light from Mitch's flashlight. Taking deliberate steps, he made his way through the kitchen and into the living area, unsure of what he would find. The judge didn't appear to be home, leading Mitch to believe he would have time to search the place for clues. *Maybe an office would hold some answers,* he thought. He decided he would search the house looking for the judge's study.

Mitch moved slowly, but with enough purpose that he was being efficient. He made his way down the hall, shining his light into bathrooms and storage areas. It wasn't until he reached the end of the hall that he found the study. Mitch flashed the light into the room, revealing bookshelves lined with law volumes and periodicals. He slithered into the study, his light leading the way.

Mitch followed the line of books until his light panned across a large mahogany desk. While passing the desk, the light briefly illuminated something that didn't immediately register in Mitch's mind. Something was behind the desk. Mitch stopped the path of the light and quickly flashed it back to the chair.

Time froze. It took several seconds for his brain to process what his eyes were fixed upon. A surreal confusion paralyzed him as he stared straight ahead, speechless and motionless. The form was in the spotlight, and there was no mistaking what it was. Mitch was ten feet away from the lifeless body of Judge Jeremiah Butler, his throat slit from ear to ear.

The blood began to pump back to Mitch's extremities and instinctively he knew that he shouldn't stay in the judge's house any longer. His senses heightened immediately, and a thought came to him. *What if the killer is still in the house?*

Mitch knew it was time to hightail it out of there before he became the next victim or was wrongly accused of killing yet another person. Without further thought, Mitch spun around to exit through the door through which he had just entered.

Several quick steps toward the door revealed that the escape route was obstructed by the shadowy outline of a man. Startled, Mitch stood a mere twelve inches from the figure, the beam of light from the flashlight exposing who shared the room with him. Before Mitch had time to react, a hand came down on him, covering his nose and mouth with a rag drenched in chloroform. He grabbed the shoulders of his assailant, but it was too late. The chloroform had successfully depressed the functions of Mitch's central nervous system, rendering him unconscious at the feet of Dr. Wes Brady.

60

Time stood still, and Cassandra gave up all hope that she would ever be found alive. The sound of water continued to rush into her cavernous tomb, and she lay helpless, restrained on a table—a sacrifice awaiting slaughter. The light powered by the small battery burned into her eyes, creating a reddish glow all around her.

A noise from behind Cassandra sent an optimistic surge of energy through her body. "Help me! Is someone there?" Cassandra yelled, hearing the unmistakable sound of a door creaking open, followed by feet descending a stone staircase, and then sloshing through knee-deep water. "Help me! Who is it? Help me!"

She strained her neck to the left and caught a glimpse of a man making his way toward the bench on which the battery sat. A black ski mask concealed his identity.

The man stood at the bench, checking the battery and reading through some papers he removed from his pocket. Cassandra could see that the water was well above the man's knees, extending to the midpoint of his thigh. Terror engulfed her. "Please, mister! You have to get me out of here!"

Again, no reply.

"Please!" Cassandra continued to beg for help while her thoughts involuntarily went back to her childhood. In her mind, she could see a loving mother, back at a time before drugs had stolen her natural, maternal instincts—a time when Cassandra felt safe and secure like a young child should. Then in a flash, she was at her mother's funeral, alone in the world, a motherless child vulnerable to the wickedness and evil that the world could bestow upon the innocent. She was helpless—as she felt now.

Why did her mother choose drugs over her? The answer to this question went to the grave with her mother long ago. And what of her mother's selfishness that resulted in Cassandra being placed with a foster family that didn't care? She had been left at the mercy of her foster father, Ronnie, who was more interested in satisfying his perverted lust for young girls than serving as a protective father figure, as the state hired him to do. Then it hit Cassandra: maybe the man across the room was Ronnie, back to finish his sadistic business. Cassandra felt like a young girl again, desperate to be saved.

"Ronnie, please don't," the words left Cassandra's mouth before she knew what she was saying. "I won't tell, Ronnie. I promise."

Initially confused, the man in the black ski mask turned to look at Cassandra. He raised his finger to his mouth, indicating that Cassandra should be quiet. Slowly, he walked toward her.

The abuse in the bathtub consumed Cassandra's mind as she struggled in vain to free herself from her constraints. "Please don't put me under the water, Ronnie. I promise I'll be good."

The figure stood directly above Cassandra, his eyes piercing her soul through the slits of the black ski mask. The man reached down, putting his hands around Cassandra's neck, and in a singsong fashion, he said the words that had terrorized Cassandra in the past. "It's time to wash away our sins."

Cassandra trembled uncontrollably. How did Ronnie ever find her? It didn't make sense. Was he responsible for all the girls going missing? Cassandra felt the grip tighten around her neck as she looked intently into the eyes of her captor, attempting to understand the reprehensible depths of such a monster. The eyeholes of the black ski mask outlined a pair of degenerate eyes and provided an unforeseen clarity. Their green hue reflected off the light. Disbelief overwhelmed Cassandra, and in an instant, she suddenly realized who was holding her against her will. "Oh God, no! Not you!"

61

Mitch felt his head swaying back and forth involuntarily as he slowly returned from unconsciousness. He struggled to open his eyes and decipher the images in front of them. Debris flew freely about in a spotlight straight ahead, and through the grogginess, Mitch realized he was looking out of the windshield of a vehicle. His head continued to sway in response to the van's reaction to the strong wind.

With a quick glance to his left, Mitch made out the image of Dr. Brady driving the van at the highest rate of speed allowable under hurricane conditions. Mitch said nothing; he was still trying to make sense of his current situation. He looked down to his right, only to find handcuffs locking his right hand to the door handle.

Dr. Brady was the first to speak. "Good. You're awake," Brady said, momentarily taking his eyes off the road to make a quick analysis of Mitch's level of consciousness.

"What…where are you taking me?"

"I'm sorry I had to resort to such drastic measure, but you—"

"What have you done with Cassandra?" Mitch said, his thoughts beginning to clear. "Where is she, you bastard!" Mitch surveyed the rest of the van, taking note of the large, green canvas bag that he'd seen in Brady's office. It looked like it housed a body.

"Mr. Blais, you need to calm down if we're going to save Cassandra."

"Save Cassandra?"

"Yes, Mr. Blais, save Cassandra," Brady said, turning the van down another street, the tires slipping on the rain-covered asphalt. "I think I know where she is, but we're running out of time."

Mitch was confused. Images of the dead judge rattled in his thoughts. He began thrashing his confined hand around in an attempt to jar the handcuffs loose.

"Oh yes, those. I'm sorry about the handcuffs and having to drug you, but I had no other choice," Brady said as he quickly swerved the van to the right to avoid a fallen tree limb. Mitch's head slammed off the passenger window. "I had no time to spare and I couldn't take the chance that you would be uncooperative."

Mitch looked toward the bag in the back.

"Oh that," Brady said, acknowledging that Mitch was looking back toward the green, canvas bag. "That's my survival gear and the maps we confiscated from your roommate."

Mitch recalled the detailed maps of Sherman Point that Turtle said he had reproduced by hand. He wondered why Brady had them.

"It wasn't until I saw those maps that it all came together," Brady said, not taking his eyes off the carnage that mother nature was inflicting. "Those maps are nothing short of incredible. That kid Turtle is quite talented, and if it wasn't for what I saw on those maps, it would never have come together."

Mitch already knew of Turtle's brilliance, and he was surprised that such a well-credentialed psychiatrist like Dr. Brady was just figuring it out. "What about Rooney and what the greasy-haired kid heard you guys talking about?"

"Greasy-haired kid? Oh, you mean Myles Harwich. Yes, Myles overheard something Rooney had said about an underground cavern system below Sherman Point. It didn't make much sense until I saw Turtle's map. Rooney figured out that girls were being kidnapped and held in the largest cavern, deep below Sherman Point. He came to me because he was about to blow the whistle when he, well, you know what happened to both of them. The judge, well, someone got to him also, but I know he was in on it too."

"What's happened to the girls? Is Cassandra OK?"

"Why the girls were kidnapped remains a mystery to me, but they were kidnapped. And Cassandra? That we are going to find out shortly, Mr. Blais," Brady said, flashing an empathetic look toward Mitch. "On a positive note, Mr. Blais, it's clear now that you never killed your probation officer, and I think I can prove who did."

Mitch absorbed the words Brady had just said. In his quest to save Cassandra, he had forgotten all about his own pending issues. He had one singular focus and purpose: Cassandra. He had opened up his heart to her and nothing else mattered. It still didn't. He had to get to Cassandra, and Brady seemed to know where she was. "Is she below Sherman Point?"

"I think so, and that's where we're headed," Brady explained. "And as soon as we get there, I will free you if I think I can trust you. Can I trust you, Mr. Blais?"

"Yes," Mitch said, if for no other reason than to be liberated so he could find Cassandra. "One last thing. If you didn't kidnap the girls and kill Rooney and Myles Harwich, who did?"

"Mr. Blais," Brady said with soberness in his voice, "you wouldn't believe me if I told you!"

62

A disheartened vulnerability filled Cassandra, the totality of the betrayal before her becoming evident. Her hope for the goodness and righteousness of people left her in an instant as her reality became clear. The man standing above Cassandra reached his hand to the bottom of the black ski mask and slowly pulled it up over his face, confirming for Cassandra what she had already figured out. In a melancholy voice of defeat, Cassandra looked up and simply said, “Why, Dr. Cav?”

“Why Cassandra?” Cavanaugh said with an aggressiveness in his voice that was previously foreign to him. “Because of money. I’m talking lots of money.”

“Money?”

“That’s right. Money, Cassandra,” Cavanaugh said, running his hand up Cassandra’s bare thigh and over her underwear to her exposed midsection, stopping when he met the rope that was wrapped around her waist. “Do you have any idea how much a young, beautiful, and athletic girl like yourself fetches in the sex-slave industry?”

Cassandra felt nauseated as she realized she was going to be sold into sexual slavery, no doubt like the other girls who had disappeared from Sherman Point. A defiant rage surfaced from deep within her and the words flew out. “Fuck you!”

“Oh now, now, Cassandra. Don’t get ahead of yourself. We have a lot to overcome before we get to that,” Cavanaugh said, spreading his arms and looking at the ocean water rising beneath them. “Oh, I almost forgot. You’re not too keen on water, are you?”

A mixture of anger and desperation boiled in Cassandra. Dr. Cav’s betrayal was now clearly evident. “You told me I could trust you. You said that you would always be there for me.”

“Oh yes, that,” Cavanaugh said with a degree of sarcasm in his voice. “You see, Cassandra, I have very expensive tastes in cars, houses, and women. My meager salary simply wasn’t cutting it, so when Judge Jeremiah Butler came to me with this great idea, I jumped at it. I had to keep up appearances with all that ‘I’m here for you, you can trust me and we’ve got such a strong community’ bullshit. But now, honey, here’s your real lesson: life ain’t fair.”

“Judge Butler?” Cassandra said, now further confused.

“Oh yes, old Jerry Butler. It was perfect. He’d find beautiful, young girls like you,” Cavanaugh said with a smile, assuming that

Cassandra would appreciate the compliment, "who lived in foster homes and didn't have any real families that might end up asking lots of questions. Nobody would care because all of you girls had histories of running from your foster families. You were runaways. It only made sense that you would 'run away' from Sherman Point. And what could we do with our lax security caused by budget cuts? Eventually, you would all fade into distant memories, and I'd get rich."

Cassandra stared at Cavanaugh with raw contempt, instantly hating the man she once looked up to as a paternal figure.

"Do you know how we make our money? We sell you girls to the Russian mob here in the states. It's perfect," Cavanaugh boasted, clearly proud of his nefarious enterprise. "They simply bring a boat to an opening in the cliffs beneath Sherman Point that's only accessible at high tide, and we load you on from this cave. Bye-bye, young ladies; hello payday. Did you know, Cassandra, that there are twenty-seven million slaves in the sex business throughout the world? No one will miss a girl like you. No one's looking for you. Everyone at Sherman Point has already evacuated. It's just us left here, and *trust* me, I'm not telling anyone."

"Trust me." Cassandra had heard those words before from Cavanaugh, and they were meaningless. She despised the man more than she despised anyone in the world. She looked at him with disdain in her eyes. "If I ever get out of here, I'll find you and kill you."

Cavanaugh looked down at Cassandra with pity. He didn't take her threat at all seriously. "OK then. Well, we had several issues to contend with before we could move forward. First was that gluttonous pig, Judge Jeremiah Butler and his 70 percent cut of the profits. Now he doesn't get a cut at all, except the one across his neck." Cavanaugh paused with a macabre smile on his face as if reliving his execution of the judge in his head. "Now there's this nasty Hurricane Mario. Who saw this coming?" Cavanaugh said, playfully splashing water on Cassandra's face.

Cassandra gagged, spitting the salty water out of her mouth.

"Well, I must bid you farewell for the time being," Cavanaugh said, heading back to the oak door. "I'll be back after the storm to see if there's anything left of you for the Russians."

"Dr. Cav, wait. We can work something out," Cassandra said in desperation.

"There is nothing to work out, Cassandra. More than likely, you will die an agonizing death by drowning," Cavanaugh said, absent of any emotion. "And believe me; with what the Russians are going to do with you, well, dying is really your best option."

"Dr. Cavanaugh!" Mitch said with an equal amount of disbelief and anger. "No way! He—"

"I'm sorry, Mr. Blais," Dr. Brady said, his eyes fixed on the road, "but it's true. The data doesn't lie and it all points to Dr. Paul Cavanaugh."

Mitch couldn't believe the words he was hearing, and frankly, he wasn't sure if Brady was just saying them to divert attention from his own guilt. He again looked at the handcuffs and the green, canvas bag in the back. None of it made sense, but Brady said he was going to save Cassandra, so the best option Mitch had was to try to trust the man.

Mitch silently processed everything he'd just been told, thinking about the cave system that Dr. Brady mentioned. He thought back to his dream and the tunnels into which Therese Harriet Coleman had led him. Maybe she had done it for a reason. Maybe Dr. Brady was telling the truth, and Cassandra was deep below Sherman Point in a cavern of some sort that was only accessible through the tunnels. Mitch eyed the green, canvas bag again, knowing that if Turtle's maps were in there, then they were perfect and probably the only thing he could trust for sure.

Dr. Brady gripped the wheel tightly, making every effort to stay on the road despite the fury mother nature was unleashing on the coastline. He clicked on the radio. The announcer's voice was difficult to hear above the crackling of poor reception.

"Again, a mandatory evacuation has been ordered by the governor for those on the coastline of southern Maine. If you have not yet headed inland, you should do so immediately, as Hurricane Mario is producing winds in excess of 115 miles per hour, and widespread flooding is already evident along the coastline. Again, please heed the advice of emergency management experts and head west, away from the shore."

Dr. Brady and Mitch were not going to conform. The two looked out the windshield of the van and saw the danger produced by Mario. The van proceeded toward Sherman Point.

"Sherman Point has been completely evacuated, so our efforts should be unimpeded," Dr. Brady said, breaking the silence. "We'll get everything from the bag we need. According to Turtle's map, there's an old entrance to the tunnels on the west side of the building, off in the woods. Once we find that, we should be safe underground from the storm," Brady said, slowing the van down to turn onto the road leading to Sherman Point. Punching the gas pedal, Dr. Brady accelerated the van down the long, narrow road toward the guard booth. Without stopping, he passed the unmanned booth, noticing that the wooden guardrail had been smashed. Mitch didn't offer any explanation.

The van continued down the serpentine route, Dr. Brady swerving to avoid falling branches. The tires of the van were barely able to stay tight to the road due to the rain. Mitch grabbed the dashboard with his free hand, steadying himself in an effort to avoid smashing his head against the window again. In a split-second flash of realization, Mitch screamed, "Look out!"

A giant oak tree had already given in to the winds and was bent askew, its bulbous root structure that had supported it for hundreds of years was violently ripped from the ground. With a cracking groan of disapproval, the tree now plummeted to the ground, stretching across the main drive of Sherman Point.

Dr. Brady slammed both feet against the brake, sending the van into a wild skid, the back end fishtailing out of control. Mitch braced himself in preparation for an impact. The tree got closer and closer, the van's tires unable to grip the road sufficiently. In a violent collision, the tree abruptly terminated the van's forward momentum. Inertia took over, catapulting the van's occupants forward. Mitch's body made contact with the dashboard immediately, knocking the wind from his lungs. Dr. Brady's head smashed full force into the windshield, shattering the glass on contact. He shot backward then slumped forward over the steering wheel. The two lay motionless, all sounds ceasing accept those created just outside the van by Hurricane Mario.

64

Robin Clarkson gripped the wheel of the unmarked cruiser, trying to keep the wind from blowing her off the road. The rain pelted the windshield, making it almost impossible to see, but she was determined to get to Sherman Point before it was too late. Reaching over, she turned the volume on the radio up so she could hear the latest weather report. The announcer's voice remained calm as he issued an evacuation warning for all those living in the coastal areas.

Robin Clarkson turned the radio off and muttered, "Bullshit," under her breath. Usually, the report of a girl missing from the adolescent unit of a local rehabilitation center would have been routine, but not this time. This time, the rehabilitation center was Sherman Point and Robin Clarkson knew that there was more to this story than met the eye.

Another missing girl had been reported as a runaway, but Robin Clarkson knew better. She had gotten the call that the girl disappeared after her morning jog. This was the fourth girl to vanish from Sherman Point recently, and none of it added up. Why would a girl take off with a hurricane bearing down on the coast? And what about Myles Harwich? The fibers under his fingers matched the black fibers she had found on the roof. Were they fibers from a black ski mask? Had Myles Harwich managed to grab it as he was pushed? Robin Clarkson wasn't sure, but she was getting the same, intuitive feeling in the pit of her stomach that she used to get when she was sent out on patrol with her unit in the Middle East. Something wasn't right, and she was going to find out what it was.

The police cruiser slid on the wet pavement as it turned onto the road leading to Sherman Point. Clarkson raced down the road, surprised to find the guard booth vacant and the wooden rail destroyed. It was hard to tell whether the wind had broken the rail or if a car had smashed through it. Regardless, she needed to get some answers and didn't have time to investigate the matter further.

Robin Clarkson came upon the scene quickly. It was evident that a large tree had come down in the storm, and a van had crashed into it. Someone stood in the back of the van, something oddly shaped on his head. The person heaved a large bag onto his back and jostled it to center its weight. Immediately, Robin Clarkson activated the lights of the unmarked cruiser, prepared to help the victims of the crash.

The chirp of the siren and the bright spotlight surprised the man with the bag and the strange headgear. Robin Clarkson could see him turn. She brought her cruiser to a complete stop and exited the vehicle. "Are you OK?" she asked, pointing her flashlight in the man's direction. Clarkson saw a vague familiarity in the man's features.

He never completely turned around, but instead, without saying a word, he bolted into the woods, not checking to see if he was being pursued.

Robin Clarkson stood there for a moment, surprised to see the man run off during a hurricane. "Stop! Police!" she shouted, but to no avail. The man disappeared into the dark, thick woods of Sherman Point.

65

Mitch struggled to catch his breath. The impact of the crash had sent him forward and knocked the wind out of him, but it was clear that Dr. Brady got the worst of it. Blood gushed out of his forehead and covered his face and shirt. Mitch could not tell if Dr. Brady was breathing or not. He went to reach over with his right hand, only to be reminded that it was handcuffed.

The keys had to be somewhere in the van, Mitch thought. He opened the glove box, but without luck. Mitch then realized that they must be on Dr. Brady. He looked over at the bloody mess that was now Dr. Brady, and with his left hand, he began moving Brady's body into a position to check his pockets. The easiest pocket to access was Dr. Brady's shirt pocket, so without hesitation, Mitch reached into the blood-soaked shirt pocket, and to his surprise and satisfaction, his hand felt a small key ring with two keys on it.

Mitch didn't waste time unlocking the handcuffs and setting himself free. He could now get back to the task at hand—saving Cassandra. The passenger door didn't open on Mitch's first several attempts, so he leaned back against Brady's body and kicked it with both feet. After several attempts, the door opened a few inches—enough that Mitch could force it the rest of the way.

Mitch scurried to the back of the van and opened the back door. Unzipping the green, canvas bag, he was surprised to find a full set of survival gear. He rummaged through the array of ropes, picks, knives, and several tubular cases housing Turtle's maps. The wind violently slammed the van door into Mitch's shoulder twice, so he repositioned himself, placing his body weight up against the door. He still struggled to keep it open.

Mitch spread out the map of Sherman Point and its underground labyrinth of tunnels and caverns inside the van, protecting it from the elements. With a flashlight he removed from the bag, he illuminated the map. It was simply unbelievable. Turtle had reproduced the entire map from memory using nothing more than a pencil and a ruler. Dr. Brady was right about one thing. It was remarkable. Mitch quickly found the opening in the woods and traced his finger down a tunnel into what looked like a belly in the middle of a body. A series of tunnels led into the same opening, represented by a circle on the map, and then from there, more tunnels led out of the cliff system into the ocean. One distinct tunnel went upward, leading directly under Sherman Point. Mitch quickly folded the map up and placed it back into its cylinder. Placing it back in the bag,

Mitch retrieved a head lamp similar to those worn by coal miners. He positioned it on his head and zipped the bag up, preparing for his trek into the woods.

Mitch saw the headlights shining on the trees before he heard the siren of the unmarked police cruiser. He positioned the green, canvas bag on his back and waited a second, his heart racing. The police probably thought he killed the judge, and he surely would be blamed somehow for Dr. Brady's condition. Mitch briefly turned his head toward the vehicle and saw only one occupant.

The car door opened. "Are you OK?" a familiar female voice asked. She shone a bright light on Mitch. He didn't reply. Acting strictly on impulse, Mitch shot off to his right, leaping over a boulder and disappearing deep into the woods.

He could hear the woman shout, "Stop! Police!" but he never stopped running until her light was no longer visible.

Robin Clarkson stood on the edge of the road watching the figure disappear deeper into the darkness of the woods. She knew she had to secure the crash scene and check for any victims. She let out a long sigh while still looking into the black, swirling forest. She braced herself against the wind, rain dripping off the hood that covered her head. "Mitchell Blais," she said with grave concern in her voice.

66

The water came at a steadier pace than before. Cassandra could move her head to the left to see that the water had covered the bottom of the narrow, stone staircase that descended into the cavern. The rhythmic lap of water against the steps sounded like a clock ticking away the minutes left in her life. Desperation now turned to an uncomfortable acceptance of her fate. She was going to die deep in a cave unknown to most people. No one would know what happened and no one would mourn her passing. For all people knew, she ran away from Sherman Point and was never heard from again.

She had been betrayed. It was the ultimate betrayal by a man she had looked up to as a father figure, by a man who had looked into her eyes and told her that she could trust him, that he would be there for her no matter what. That was what he had told her, but in reality, he was selling her as a sex slave to the highest bidder. She was nothing more than a commodity that Cavanaugh could profit from to feed his own lavish lifestyle. He was a monster, and death now seemed a better alternative than falling into the hands of people who were going to continue with the sexual abuse that had robbed her of her innocence.

Cassandra's faith in humanity had been squelched by the men in her life whom she was supposed to be able to trust. She had little left in her heart for others, but what she did have, she reserved for Mitch. She loved Mitch and believed she could trust him, but that was a delicate dance that two people had to engage in simultaneously. Where was he now when she needed him most? Had he given up on her?

Cassandra lay on the metal table, a bright light flickering in her face. Water was rising all around her, swallowing everything in its path. It wouldn't be long until it covered her, and she would be no more. There was nothing more in her world. There was no hope, there was no salvation, and there was no Mitch. Cassandra resigned herself to the fact that her nightmares were now reality, and the water would take away her body and soul. She began to pray that the water could truly wash away her sins before she left the world forever.

An old graveyard deep in the woods provided access to the tunnels below Sherman Point. Clearly marked on the map provided by Turtle, the graveyard sat approximately a quarter mile away from the main road. Long forgotten, this necropolis had not been used since the nineteenth-century when Sherman Point had buried the souls of the unwanted and alone there. According to the map, the entrance to the tunnels was inside an old crypt created by a natural rock formation that served as a mass burial center.

Mitch struggled against the elements. The rain now began to fall sideways, as if it were being shot out of an unseen hose. Lowering his head, he pushed forward, the wind blowing the lamp off his head several times, and knocking him to the ground. The graveyard was well marked on the map; the difficulty getting to it was due to the elements, not to the work of his friend, Turtle.

Mitch finally reached the spot where the graveyard should be. Looking around, he noticed several worn and faded stones that no doubt served to mark the final resting places of the departed and forgotten. Behind the stones stood a unique land formation that looked almost like a shed created by nature. It was rounded and stood about seven feet in height. Years of overgrowth had concealed any entrance that might exist, but this is where Turtle's map said it would be, and Mitch had complete faith in Turtle's abilities.

Mitch threw the canvas bag to the ground and rifled through its contents. Deep from within the bag, he pulled out a small pickax. He made his way over to the face of the hill-like structure, and began impaling the pick into the sod. The earth and gravel had been softened by the rain and the digging was easy. He worked diligently, plowing through the earth until it felt like the pick had penetrated rotted wood and was unobstructed on the other side. Reaching his hand into the newly created hole, he easily pulled away the rotted wood. Within minutes, he had created a large hole, and grabbing the green bag, he squeezed himself through it.

The crypt provided relief from the ravishing wind and rain unleashed by Hurricane Mario. Mitch shook off as much wetness as possible and repositioned the head lamp. The crypt was old and covered in cobwebs. On the floor, lying flat, were faded stones bearing the names of the dead. The stones were placed side by side, taking up every spot available. Mitch determined that this was how the bodies were buried—one on top of the other until the lack of space prohibited anymore dumping of bodies. Taking a water bottle from the bag, he began washing away years of dirt and grime that concealed most of the names on the stones. He quickly realized that each stone had a heading based on the year of burial. On a hunch, he worked his way down the stones until he reached the year 1868. Pouring the water over the surface, Mitch made visible all the names that had been carved into the stone. After reading the names sequentially, Mitch found what he was looking for. There, etched in the stone for all eternity, was the name he sought, Therese Harriet Coleman. Again, Therese Harriet Coleman was speaking to Mitch from beyond the grave and getting him closer to saving Cassandra.

Careful examination of the burial chamber and the stones housed within it led to no immediate answers about an entrance to a tunnel system. Sweat dripped off Mitch as he investigated every corner of the crypt, searching for access. Frustration quickly set in, and Mitch found himself desperately clawing and digging at the ground and walls in search of an entrance. He plopped himself on the ground next to the gravestone with Therese Harriet Coleman's name on it.

"What now, Therese?" Mitch yelled at the top of his voice. "You led me all the way here for nothing? Can't you hear me?" Anger now drove Mitch's emotions. He looked down at the stone and began pounding it with his fists. "Save Cassandra, save Cassandra! That's what you told me. Now what?"

Mitch's fury continued to build. Time was running out, and he had come this far. Cassandra needed him, but what could he do? Blood began to drip from his knuckles. He turned 360 degrees, looking for any hint of an answer.

"Cassandra!" Mitch howled, still pounding the stone with his fists. In a fit of resentment toward the world, Mitch summoned all his strength, picked up the aged stone labeled 1868, and raised it above his head. Turning toward a natural earthen wall, Mitch threw the grave marker, watching it make contact with the wall and fracture into pieces.

Time stood still for Mitch. He derived a certain degree of pleasure from releasing his rage, but the real satisfaction came when he looked down to the ground where the grave marker had rested. To his amazement, a small hole in the ground was now visible. Concealed for years by a memorial to the dead, the hole was no bigger than two feet by two feet. Mitch directed his head toward the opening, shining the light of the head lamp deep into it. Clearly visible about eight feet down was a dirt floor. With a new, rejuvenating rush of adrenaline, Mitch quickly assessed his situation. The hole was far too small for Mitch to drag the entire green, canvas bag through, so taking a quick inventory of his needs, Mitch took a long knife with a slender wooden handle attached to a belt. He quickly wrapped the belt around his waist and adjusted his head lamp.

Moving quickly, Mitch unrolled Turtle's map for the last time. He studied the tunnel system for several seconds, and then he took one long, last sip of water from a bottle in the bag. Without hesitation, Mitch slithered his way through the hole.

The light from the head lamp revealed a small tunnel about six feet high and three feet wide. It was just wide enough for Mitch to walk through unencumbered. He moved as quickly as the narrow, stone channel would allow. He trekked forward for what seemed like an eternity, the walls and dirt floor remaining unchanged with each passing foot.

Mitch began to wonder how long he would need to press forward before finding something, anything. The passageway seemed to be getting smaller and closing in on him, squeezing each breath out of him. He had to keep moving forward for Cassandra.

It felt like an hour had passed. Mitch kept moving, the light illuminating five feet in front of him. He began to wonder if he was going in the right direction, and even worse, if he was going to ever find the cave or Cassandra.

Suddenly, Mitch stopped. Exhausted from his efforts, he gasped for each breath. He allowed his heart rate to come down and his breathing to regulate so he could listen for what he thought was a sound. There it was. Mitch could hear the sound of water. The sound of a steady flow emanated from somewhere up ahead in the tunnel. It must be an access to the ocean or to another tunnel. Whatever the case, it was something different, and Mitch shot forward, searching for the source of the noise.

It wasn't more than one hundred feet ahead when Mitch came upon it. The tunnel he followed came to an abrupt end, and Mitch found himself standing in a large, rounded vestibule. The water was two feet deep. Mitch was suddenly overcome with the sense that he had been here before. His surroundings felt eerily familiar as he looked around, his light revealing several feet of cave at a time. He looked in the water and noticed hundreds of small objects floating around. Then it hit him—rats! Hundreds if not thousands of rats were floating in the water.

Mitch took a deep breath and thought about Cassandra. He thought about the things they had shared emotionally and the plans they'd made. Mitch thought about touching Cassandra and kissing her again. Suddenly, the rats didn't matter. Mitch's love for Cassandra far outweighed his childhood fear of rats. He would do anything to save her, and a bunch of squealing and drowning rodents wouldn't stop him. Nothing would stop him. Mitch stoically began walking through the water. Rats raced to him to take a bite, but Mitch simply pushed them aside. Eyeing the ledge on the other side, Mitch continued until he was able to climb out of the water. Mitch looked back at the rat infested-soup he'd just negotiated and laughed.

The sense of déjà vu persisted, and Mitch knew he was on the right path. It was only minutes before he came across a familiar-looking, fifteen-foot-tall oak door at the base of what looked like a cave within the tunnel system. He raced to the door and applied all the pressure he could against it. It wouldn't budge. He looked down and saw water slowly seeping through the crack under the door. He tried to push the door in, but again his efforts were met with resistance. Mitch began pounding on the door yelling, "Come on, you son of a bitch! Open!"

Then he heard it. A sound. It was the sound of a voice yelling something in return. Mitch began pounding harder on the door. "Hello! Cassandra, are you in there?"

It was barely audible, but clear enough that Mitch could make out the words. He stopped what he was doing and listened intently. The second time he heard it more clearly. It was perfectly decipherable. Cassandra again yelled out, "I'm in here! Please hurry!"

69

All hope had been lost when Cassandra felt the water flowing over the table. The ocean water moistened her bare skin, and she knew it was just a matter of time before she drowned. All her prayers and hopes had gone unanswered, and she prepared for death. Her troubled life, devoid of love and happiness, would end, and the memories of her pain would go with it. A miracle is what she needed, and it now seemed as impossible as the future she'd imagined. She began to sob uncontrollably. Tears streamed down her face, her wails accompanied by the intensified sound of surging water.

The water was rising more quickly now, and Cassandra knew her estimate was off—she would be dying sooner than she'd thought. The water continued to stream over her body, and a banging sound began to echo through the cavern.

A banging sound! Cassandra suddenly thought. It was coming from the door. *Someone or something is banging on the door!* Maybe it was her mind playing tricks on her, but she couldn't chance it. Desperate, she yelled, "I'm in here! Please hurry!"

Mitch immediately recognized the voice as Cassandra's and knew he had little time to waste. He began pounding and pushing at the door, but it wouldn't budge. The water was now flowing around Mitch's knees. He had to think.

"Hurry! The water is coming up! I'm going to drown in here!"

"I'm coming," Mitch yelled back, frantically searching for a solution. Then it came back to him—the rats. He had been here before and the door was the same one he'd seen in his dream. Jumping onto the ground, Mitch urgently searched for a cylindrical hole. He put his hand under the water and ran it across the surface of the ground until he found what he was looking for. Mitch stuck his finger into the rounded depression and knew this was the spot. He reached over, taking the knife out of the sheath, exposing its long, wooden handle. In an act of desperation, Mitch plunged the handle of the knife into the hole as far as it would go.

The results were immediate and far more dramatic then Mitch expected. The cave began to shake, and rocks began plummeting to the ground. Mitch covered his head and scurried under an incline while the violent barrage continued for several minutes. Mitch looked over to the door, but to his dismay, it hadn't budged. The pressure of the water against it prevented it from moving inward. Hope began to wane as Mitch wondered how he would get into the cave.

Another giant vibration violently shook the ground, and with that the trembling stopped. Mitch looked up just in time to see a massive boulder sliding loose from the position it had held for thousands of years. Rolling off a ledge, the boulder succumbed to gravity and smashed through the top of the cave and into the cavern holding Cassandra. The boulder landed just feet from the metal table, making an enormous splash.

Mitch holstered his knife and raced up the slippery incline until he was high enough up to grab hold of the edge of the opening. Pulling his head up, he looked downward through the hole, his head lamp illuminating a shocking sight. Ten feet below, Cassandra lay tied to a table, water just inches from engulfing her nose and mouth.

Cassandra looked up, a joyful yet desperate optimism steeling her emotions as she saw the man she loved—her savior—peering down at her. Suddenly, life seemed worth living. Mitch had never given up on her. She was loved. Her life did have meaning, and she wanted to live. "Oh, thank

God, Mitch! Please hurry!" Cassandra managed, salty water entering her mouth.

"I'm here, Cassandra!" Mitch yelled back in a confident and reassuring tone. "I won't leave you. I promise. You can trust me!"

Before he could say another word, there was a horrific crash as a wall gave way to the water pressure. Water rushed into the cavern, completely submerging Cassandra. In an instant, Mitch could no longer see Cassandra below him.

71

Mitch acted on impulse upon seeing the women he loved swallowed up by the ocean. Instinctively, he dove into the water-filled cavern and swam downward until he was touching Cassandra's arm.

The two made eye contact underwater, and the desperation in Cassandra's eyes was evident. Mitch hastily went to work removing his knife and cutting the ropes around Cassandra's arms. Now, with her hands free, Cassandra began frantically pointing at her mouth, indicating that she was almost out of air. Mitch looked reassuringly into her eyes, and with one finger, pointed up. Using the table for leverage, he pushed himself upward, breaking through the surface of the water. Without wasting time, Mitch took a massive gulp of air and reentered the water, heading for Cassandra.

Reaching Cassandra's face, he could see that desperation had given way to panic and she was about to involuntarily inhale life-ending seawater. Mitch reached out, placed his hand around the back of her neck, and pressed his lips tightly against hers. With a long exhale, Mitch blew enough oxygen into Cassandra's mouth to give her a few more precious seconds of life.

Then he bolted for Cassandra's lower extremities and continued to carve away the ropes, freeing Cassandra's legs from their constraints. Mitch again pointed upward, and they ascended, eager to gulp more oxygen. Cassandra held Mitch's ankle for security and direction.

Mitch was the first to break the surface again, gasping for air. The second his head was above water, he felt Cassandra's hand let go of his ankle. She did not surface. Desperate for an explanation, Mitch dove back under to find Cassandra frantically thrashing at a rope that was still tied around her midsection. A six-foot length of rope ran from Cassandra's waist back down to the table, where it was fastened around a metal leg, preventing her from ascending any further. Mitch quickly grabbed the knife from its casing and cut the restraint right at Cassandra's belly button, freeing her forever.

The pressure of the incoming water pushed the two upward with enough force to accelerate their escape from the womb of Sherman Point. Mitch shot through the hole first, breaking free to the other side of the cave, and gravity instantly rolled him down to the ground. He immediately looked back at the opening to make sure Cassandra was behind him.

Cassandra was liberated from the restraints that had confined her, and was now headed for the opening that would give her a second chance at life. She was reborn with a new beginning. Mitch had come back for her, and now she knew there was someone in the world for her. There was someone who would not give up on her and betray the sacred trust that binds two people for eternity. She was in love with Mitch, and he loved her. It was a fresh start with all the optimism and hope that life initially offers. She wanted to live.

The water pushed Cassandra through the hole as it filled the cavern below her. She too was pushed out of the opening and rolled down into the cave, landing at Mitch's feet. Cassandra breathed in heavily and let out a long, instinctive cry. Mitch wrapped his arms around her.

"Thank you for saving my life," Cassandra said between frantic breaths. "I love you."

"I love you too, but we gotta move," Mitch said, looking up at the hole they had just exited. Water began gushing through it so forcefully that the rim of the hole burst outward, releasing a torrent of water on the two. "Hurry!" Mitch yelled, beginning to run toward the tunnel entrance. He ran as quickly as possible, holding Cassandra's hand behind him. And then, without explanation, he stopped.

"What's the matter?" Cassandra asked, looking back at the water running down the side of the underground cave.

"We can't go this way," Mitch said, surveying his options. "We won't make it. The water's coming too fast. It's gonna fill everything down here."

"Then what?" Cassandra asked, urgently looking back at the rising water.

"I remember on Turtle's map. There's a tunnel with a ladder going up to Sherman Point. It's closer. If we hustle, we can make it."

The two sprinted down a long corridor fashioned by nature. They ran as quickly as possible, Mitch's head lamp lighting the way. "Where is it, Mitch?" Cassandra pleaded in between strides. A sound suddenly filled the passageway. Cassandra and Mitch both stopped and listened intently. "What is that, Mitch?"

Mitch didn't say a word. He continued to listen as the noise became more audible and intense. There was no mistaking what was headed in their direction. The thunderous sound of a wall of water was screaming toward them. "Run!" Mitch yelled.

Mitch grabbed Cassandra's hand and all but dragged her behind him. The water gained on them quickly, moving at a much higher rate of speed than any human could run. Mitch looked back, estimating that the water was about fifty feet behind them now. He knew it would only be a matter of minutes before it would overtake them, crushing them instantly. They kept running.

A slight bend in the earth revealed what they were searching for—a tunnel that ran upward with an old, iron ladder bolted into the stone, just as Turtle's map indicated. No words were exchanged as Mitch stopped below it, took Cassandra by the waist, and lifted her upward. Cassandra grabbed the rusty ladder rung and made her way up several feet to safety. Looking down, she yelled, "Hurry, Mitch! Please hurry!"

Taking one last look behind him, Mitch saw that the rushing ocean water was less than twenty feet away. He jumped up to grab for the first rung, only to have his hand slip, sending him crashing back to the dirt floor. Mitch got up and looked back. The water was upon him.

With all the might he could muster, Mitch again jumped up, his hands grabbing the bottom rung of the ladder.

It was too late. Mitch clung to the ladder, but the lower part of his body still hung down, exposed to the full force of the water. The unrestrained energy of the water hit Mitch directly in the midsection, sending his legs forward and yanking his left hand off the rung.

"Mitch!" Cassandra yelled, working her way back down to him.

Mitch hung on to the ladder with his right hand, his head below the surface of the water. The power of the water was too great, and Mitch could feel his grip slipping. It was over. He wanted to tell Cassandra to run. He wanted to tell her that he loved her, but no words would leave his mouth. He held as long as he could, but he couldn't match the power that mother nature released against him. His hand was slipping, and Mitch could feel himself being sucked into the tunnel.

Almost at the same instant that the powerful current overtook Mitch, he felt something grab his hand. Reaching his second hand up out of the water, he felt it being grabbed also and pulled back onto the ladder rung. With his own strength and the help of the unknown force, Mitch was able to get his head above water, and he pulled himself out safely, wrapping his arms around the third rung. Looking up, he saw the smiling face of Cassandra, who had grabbed his hand just in time to save him. "You didn't think I'd leave you behind, did you?" she said.

The two made their way up the creaking ladder, water rushing below them in an underground river.

The ladder stretched upward for approximately one hundred feet, groaning with each step they took, reminding them that it could give way at any second. Mitch gave Cassandra the head lamp now that she was leading the way. They kept climbing without speaking.

The ladder ended at what looked like an old manhole cover. Cassandra easily pushed it out of the way and exited the tunnel, followed by Mitch. "Where are we, Mitch?" she asked.

Mitch looked around, seeing the wind slamming against rounded, nineteenth-century windows. Hurricane Mario had blown out several panes. He heard a familiar hum behind him and turning, he saw the three large, gas furnaces—the life source of Sherman Point. "We're in the maintenance room," Mitch said, acclimating himself again to the familiar surroundings.

"How do you know?"

Mitch looked at the bent corner of the vent he had manipulated to get to Dr. Brady's office, and with a smile, he said, "It's a long story. I'll explain later."

"Why don't you explain now," a voice hacked from behind Mitch. It was accompanied by the familiar growls of Damian and Deuce.

Mitch and Cassandra spun around to see Felix standing there with Damian and Deuce obediently by his side, their jaws snapping as they barked viciously. "I thought I might see you two coming this way," Felix said, as another window was smashed behind him.

"We all need to get out of here, Felix," Mitch said, looking out the window at the damage being caused by Mario.

"Oh, I plan on getting out of here. But as far as you're concerned, you ain't goin' nowhere."

Mitch made a quick move to his left, only to be halted by the response of Damian and Deuce, who moved in unison with him. "What now, Felix?" Mitch said, eyeing the storm that raged just outside the windows.

"What now, you stupid shit?" Felix said wiping sweat from his forehead. He pointed at Mitch. "You're gonna die, and as for your pretty little girlfriend, I'm gonna make sure she's delivered as planned so I get paid. Did you think I'd let a stupid little punk like you steal my money from me? That bitch is in her prime," Felix said, flashing a sadistic smile in Cassandra's direction. "She's worth top dollar."

It was now clear to Mitch that Cassandra was going to be sold for sex, and that Felix had been in on the abduction of the girls from the beginning. He needed to think of something or Cassandra was in big trouble.

With a grin, Felix again looked at Cassandra. "Maybe we can get acquainted when I'm done here with your boyfriend," Felix said, sticking his tongue out and wiggling it in an obscene hint of things to come. "After all, ain't nobody left here at Sherman Point but us."

"You're not taking her anywhere," Mitch said slowly, using his arm to move Cassandra behind him. "Not without going through me."

"I wouldn't waste my time," Felix said, looking down at Damian and Deuce. Saliva ran from the dogs' mouths. "I let my dogs, here, do my light work." Felix reached down, grabbing Damian and Deuce aggressively by the backs of their necks and pulling them close to his mouth. "It's time, you dumb asses! Kill him!"

Damian and Deuce shot forward, barking viciously. "Mitch!" Cassandra yelled, pulling herself closer to him in an attempt to shield herself from the attack.

Mitch squatted down to one knee and put his hand out. "Good boys, you remember me from the other day," Mitch said calmly, looking at the dogs. Their teeth showed and their barks echoed through the room.

"Oh, it's OK boys. I know you're not bad dogs. This is just what you were taught. Come here, boys."

"Mitch, what are you doing?" Cassandra pleaded.

Again, Mitch used his arm to position Cassandra behind him. "Come on, boys," was the last thing Mitch said before the dogs were upon him.

Oddly, right before pouncing, Damian and Deuce stopped in front of Mitch and began to sniff him, indicating they were familiar with his scent. Remembering him as the guy who had petted them the night before, Damian and Deuce began playfully licking Mitch's face and allowing him to rub their heads affectionately. Cassandra stood motionless behind Mitch, amazed at the events unfolding in front of her.

"What the hell are you doing, you stupid mutts!" Felix yelled, disgusted with the dogs' display. "I said kill him!"

Responding to Felix's voice, Damian and Deuce again began growling and barking. Cassandra tensed up, but Mitch kept talking to the pair. "You're good boys, aren't you?" he said in an amiable voice.

"Kill, you stupid, useless mutts!" Felix barked.

At the command to kill, Damian and Deuce looked at Mitch and then slowly they turned around, setting their sights on Felix. Moving deliberately, Damian and Deuce started toward him.

"What…what are you doing?" Felix stammered.

Damian and Deuce looked at their tormentor and began barking and growling furiously. Years of abuse that was bottled up inside them surfaced, and vengeance filled their intentions. Feeling the tide turning, Felix whirled around and rushed through the exit. But his fate was sealed. Damian and Deuce sprinted forward and pounced on Felix in a vicious display of revenge.

Screams filled the air. Felix's skin was torn and shredded mercilessly as Damian and Deuce turned on their oppressor, freeing themselves from years of torment. The carnage continued until Felix ceased resisting.

Cassandra listened to the ghastly screams of the dying man in disbelief and horror. "Oh my God," she cried.

"Let's go, Cassandra. We need to get out of here," Mitch said, grasping her hand. "I know a place we can hide from the storm."

73

Mitch and Cassandra raced for the side exit directly under the large, arched windows, leaving Damian and Deuce just outside the maintenance room to finish their business. The wind continued to rip at the body of Sherman Point, blowing out more panes of glass and sending a shower of jagged shards down upon the couple. Sherman Point emitted an unfamiliar whimper in response to the damage being afflicted upon her.

Cassandra and Mitch were about to pass through the door when a shocking sight stopped them. Turning the corner just in time to halt their escape was Dr. Cavanaugh, a gun in his hand and hostages in front of him. A bloody and badly cut Dr. Brady stood, barely conscious, next to Robin Clarkson. Her holster was empty; her gun was jammed into her spine.

"Well, kid, you certainly messed things up for me this time," Cavanaugh said with an irate glare at Mitch. "Move," he said, jabbing the gun into Clarkson's back.

The branches of the trees outside banged on the windows incessantly.

"You see, the only ones leaving here today are me and that sweet little lady there," Cavanaugh said, gesturing toward Cassandra. "I can't pass that type of cash up."

"You're not taking her anywhere, Cavanaugh. You'll have to go through me first," Mitch said, shielding Cassandra behind him.

Robin Clarkson looked over her shoulder at Cavanaugh. "Think about this, Cavanaugh, additional units will be looking for us shortly. You don't want murder hanging over your head."

"Oh don't I?" Cavanaugh responded, smashing the butt of the gun into the back of Clarkson's neck, sending pain radiating through her body.

"And for you, Blais," Cavanaugh said, leveling the gun at him, "the end has arrived."

Cavanaugh went to pull the trigger, but before he could squeeze off the shot, a massive oak tree plummeted through the power lines outside and then smashed through the nineteenth-century windows. Instantly, the lights went off. Glass exploded throughout the room as the tree came down full force on the three natural-gas furnaces, crushing them. The gas pipes leading to the outside were severed, sending an evil hissing sound through the room. Just outside the window, the winds of Hurricane Mario whipped the power lines into a spark-filled frenzy. The lines flapped uncontrollably in all directions.

Clarkson, recognizing the natural diversion, spun around with a reverse crescent kick, knocking the gun out of Cavanaugh's hand. The two struggled, Cavanaugh sending her to the ground with a backhand slap across the jaw. From the floor, Clarkson saw Cavanaugh rushing to retrieve the gun. Mitch bolted forward, trying to get to the weapon first.

A large crackling sound filled the air, and sparks intermittingly illuminated the maintenance room. The ruptured power lines danced violently, grazing Cavanaugh and throwing him back on his heels. The three rushed in the same direction, all getting to the gun at the same time. They rolled over one another, grunting and clawing. Then the sound of a single shot filled the air, the flash of the muzzle briefly lighting up the chaotic scene.

Cassandra screamed.

The gas pipes hissed.

The power lines continued their dance, every few seconds sending out sparks that flashed like a nightclub strobe light.

Robin Clarkson lay on the floor next to the battered Dr. Brady, a bullet lodged in her shoulder. Mitch stood just beside her, at the mercy of the gun being pointed at his face.

"You little shit," Cavanaugh said, the sparks illuminating his face every few seconds and revealing his evil intent. "Now I'm going to kill everyone here and I'm taking that bitch with me."

The next flash of light found Dr. Cavanaugh pulling the hammer back on the gun, aiming to discharge a bullet into the skull of Mitch Blais. Just then, a power line whipped downward, landing behind a furnace and igniting a river of gas. Flames swirled violently around the room, whipping by Cavanaugh and sending him onto his backside. Moving upward, the fire hovered near the ceiling of the maintenance room.

"Oh my God Mitch, look!" Cassandra said, pointing to the fireball.

Mitch looked up into the inferno, and in the flames, he saw the image of Therese Harriet Coleman. Her face bore an evil, vengeful glare, which she directed at Cavanaugh. Time seemed to stand still.

"Blais, you're a dead man!" Cavanaugh screamed. He stood up and fired a single shot in the direction of Mitch, missing him by inches.

With that, the fireball circled once in a blistering swirl. Therese Harriet Coleman let out an ear-piercing scream that had been pent up for over a century. The bolt of flame shot down, instantly encircling Cavanaugh and wrapping him in a fiery shackle.

Cavanaugh let out a harrowing screech as the fire devoured him, setting him and his wickedness and hatred ablaze.

Mitch and Cassandra stood frozen, watching the events unfold in front of them.

The glowing rage consumed its captive. Then the flame rose above what had been Cavanaugh's head. The face of Therese Harriet Coleman again appeared. She looked in the direction of Cassandra and Mitch.

"Save her, Mitch. Save Cassandra," the vision said. "You must go now."

Mitch grabbed Cassandra's arm and ran over to Clarkson and Brady. "Can you walk?" Mitch asked Clarkson, who got to her feet and then helped the badly injured Brady up.

The four headed for the door, the intensity of the fire behind them casting a deathly orange glow. Mitch and Cassandra helped Brady and Clarkson forward, moving as quickly as their injuries would permit.

The group was just a few feet outside the building when an explosion in the maintenance room sent all four hurtling twenty feet through the air. Mitch sheltered Cassandra from falling debris and then rolled over to witness the spectacle. A second, larger explosion ripped through the night, sending a massive flame a hundred feet into the sky. In the flame, Mitch could again see the image of Therese Harriet Coleman flickering. For the first time, he could see on her face a serene smile of peace. Mitch heard the words in the wind, but he knew from where they came.

"Thank you, Mitchell Blais. Thank you for freeing my soul." And with that, the flame spiraled up into the night sky, taking with it the soul of Therese Harriet Coleman and the pain and suffering that had plagued Sherman Point for years.

Clarkson moaned and rolled over. "We've got to get out of this storm or we're dead."

"I know where to go," Mitch said, helping Brady up. "Help her, Cassandra," Mitch said, gesturing toward Clarkson. "Follow me, this way."

Mitch led the group over to the dorm building and around back, where the downspout had fallen the previous day. They rushed across the cement driveway and into the woods, to the manhole cover concealing the tunnel Mitch had used to gain access to the maintenance room. He ripped the cover off the hole, and one after the other, they scurried into the safety of the underground bunker as tree limbs crashed down around them.

Mitch entered last, replacing the cover. The four sat huddled together in the underground shelter, riding out the storm. A calming sense of safety came over them. Cassandra pulled herself closer to Mitch. She held him tightly and whispered in his ear, “Thanks for not giving up on me. Thank you for letting me trust you.”

No further words were spoken. Their lips met in a caring kiss. The years of pain were behind them, and they both knew that they would journey through life together now.

74

Hurricane Mario was the worst storm to hit the southern coast of Maine since the mid-1800s. The coastline was devastated, and as far as anyone was concerned, Sherman Point Rehabilitation Center was leveled forever.

With the information provided by Detective Clarkson and Dr. Brady, a full-scale investigation was launched into the sentences imposed by Judge Jeremiah Butler. The investigators found that many kids had been sent to Sherman Point unfairly, and subsequently they were released from state custody. As for the girls who remained missing, the state formed a task force to investigate the Russian Mafia and its role in human trafficking.

The kids who legitimately were in need of assistance were reassigned to facilities that would indeed help them. This was the case for Tina, who would remain committed to the state for treatment. As for Sameer, Turtle, and Cassandra, their sentences were revoked, and they were credited with time served.

After saving the lives of Dr. Brady and Detective Clarkson and based on their recommendations, the state dropped all charges against Mitch Blais. Any questions that lingered regarding his part in the death of Probation Officer Rooney were put to rest. No charges were filed against any of the parties responsible for kidnapping the girls. All those involved with those dastardly crimes were now dead.

***

Mitch and Cassandra stood in the graveyard arm in arm in front of the marble tombstone that read:

Here Lies David M. Blais
1975-2006
Veteran of the Wars in Iraq and Afghanistan
Husband and Father

A lump filled his throat as Mitch thought back to his dad and the love he had for him. He was a good father and a man who put his country and his family first. He would always be Mitch's hero.

The last time Mitch stood in front of this grave, he was a boy filled with confusion and hatred for an enemy that had, in fact, stolen his father's soul and will to live. But his anger and resentment were misplaced. He was a naïve boy seeking revenge against anyone similar to the enemies who had taken his father from him.

Now Mitch stood as his own man with autonomous thoughts and beliefs born of his own experiences and not influenced by previous generations. His father had told him never to trust a Muslim, but he knew now that his father had been wrong. His father's words came from the horrible, unseen battle scars of war, but that didn't make them right. Mitch knew now that his father wasn't infallible, and that made him human. Mitch had no less love in his heart for the man, and would remember his father forever with the same reverence that he had as an innocent child.

"Are you OK?" Cassandra asked.

"I miss him."

"You'll always miss him, but he'll forever be in your heart."

"I was gonna honor him by joining the marines, but now I'm not so sure."

"You can honor him in other ways."

"How's that?"

"You can honor him by carrying with you all the love and positive things he stood for, while deciding what can stay in the grave with him forever."

Mitch pondered the words for a moment and knew that Cassandra was right. Someday Mitch would tell his own kids about their grandfather, the war hero and loving family man. He would let the brightness of his life overshadow any flaws and carry forward to the next generation the lessons that would affirm his life as meaningful and exemplary. He would honor his father's memory by being a good and honest man who could look inward at his own flaws and have the courage to change them.

A horn honked from the driveway. Sameer and Turtle leaned against a car, looking toward Cassandra and Mitch.

"Let's go, lovebirds," Sameer said. "If we don't hurry we'll miss the visiting hours for Tina."

"All right, we're coming," Mitch said as he and Cassandra turned and began walking toward the car, holding hands. "Oh, wait a minute," Mitch said, turning back and looking up a steep incline. Putting his fingers to his lips, he let out a long, piercing whistle.

From over the hill came Damian and Deuce, running playfully side by side, jumping at each other like two kids playing in a park. They headed for the car. Behind them, a figure was making his best effort to keep up with the dogs.

Mitch and Cassandra laughed at the sight of Charlie, who was headed in their direction. In a playful voice, Mitch yelled to his best friend, "Come on, Charlie! You can do it!"

Copyright Notice

ISBN-13: 978-1492775676
ISBN-10: 1492775673
LCCN: 2013917573
donna.harker@comcast.net
Seekonk, MA 02771

Made in the USA
Charleston, SC
03 March 2014